CANDY COLORED SKY

by bestselling author

GINGER SCOTT

Copyright 2021

Ginger Scott, Little Miss Write LLC

No part of this book may be reproduced in any form or by any electronic or mechanical means, including information storage and retrieval systems, without permission in writing from the author. The only exception is by a reviewer, who may quote short excerpts in a review.

This book is a work of fiction. Names, characters, places and incidents either are products of the author's imagination or are used fictitiously. Any resemblance to actual persons, living or dead, or events is entirely coincidental.

Cover Design by Ginger Scott, Little Miss Write LLC

eBook ISBN: 978-1-952778-38-4

print ISBN: 978-1-952778-08-7

For Tim and Carter.
We have chased so many sunsets.

CHAPTER *One*

Apparently, last night was homecoming. I probably heard about it in class. The news just didn't stick in my head and make it to my social calendar, which is as wide open as the Wyoming prairie. The Trombley girls only cover their mint green Volkswagen Beetle in blue and yellow window paint and streamers once a year. That's how I know. Their tiny car serves as my autumnal equinox. It has for five years. The first two when Morgan Trombley, the oldest of the three daughters, still lived in the two-story house that sits as a dusty blue mirror image to our brown one across the street. These past three years of homecoming reminders have all been the courtesy of middle daughter, Eleanor, who's a senior like me. One day, it will be Addy's—the youngest of the Trombley girls—turn to decorate the hand-me-down car and send the young male hermit neighbor—*that's me*—the sign that fall is upon us.

The yard across the street is eerily still, a contrast from the evidence that it wasn't so quiet over there a few hours ago. Someone draped green and yellow streamers through the Trombley trees, and there are red Solo cups sprinkled around the lawn. I must have slept through the party. And I'm guessing from the school spirit scene out my window that the Oak Forest High School Badgers won the football game. I suppose I'm a Badger, too. That whole community spirit thing that others feel with our high school eludes me. I feel more Badger-adjacent than full-fledge Badger.

I turn my attention from the window and glance toward my bed, the blanket neatly folded hotel-style around the pillows. The only evidence that I slept there is the turned-up bottom of the comforter that I must have kicked over my legs to keep them warm. My laptop is still open with my half-finished essay. I fell asleep mid-sentence last night and clearly let it slide off my chest to the corner of my bed. The blinking cursor draws me in, and when I drag the computer closer I notice the battery icon is a glaring red.

Seven percent. *Ha.* A few more minutes and I might have lost all of last night's hard work.

I save the draft and close it, moving my computer to my desk to charge it back to full strength. My grandpa's second coughing fit is happening right now. When he first moved in six months ago, I worried when he had these at five, six, and seven in the morning. He told me if war didn't kill him a nicotine-induced cough "sure as shit wasn't about to." I have my doubts, but for two decades he's proven all of us family worry-warts wrong. Now they've become part of my routine. I don't really need to set alarms anymore. Sixty-four years of smoking has turned Grandpa Hank into my personal wake-up call device.

"You up, Jonah?"

It doesn't hurt that he usually follows his 7 a.m. round

up with a sturdy pound against our shared wall and this question.

I pound back.

Twice.

"Time for coffee?" I shout.

He coughs out a laugh, and even though it sounds godawful, it makes me chuckle. "Don't you know it!"

I flip the corner of my comforter back over my mattress, the easiest bed-making ever, grab my Chicago Tech sweatshirt from the floor, and poke my head through. I'm tangled in the twisted arms by the time I enter the hallway, and Grandpa Hank puffs out a short laugh before helping me sort things out.

"You're the only person I know who can solve a quadratic equation but can't put on a damn shirt," he muses.

"Quadratic equations actually aren't very hard. They're kinda beginner math," I deadpan.

His lip ticks up, lifting his scraggly beard and mustache along with it.

"You're a real smart ass, Jonah."

"I heard *smart* in all of that, so thank you," I joke back, patting his chest with my palm as I pass him to head down the stairs.

Grandpa Hank is my favorite person. He always has been. He was around a lot more than my dad, his son, ever was. Not that my dad was an absent parent or anything, at least not by choice. Randy Wydner was incredibly responsible, albeit not enough to get a life insurance policy. My guess is he did the calculations on his age and health and found it wholly unnecessary. Fitting, then, that the same responsibility might be what killed him. My dad literally worked himself to death, putting in seventy-plus hours a week for a decade straight to help his best friend's tiny start-up company become what it is today—a leader in the future of AI. Not that my dad saw any of the riches from that success. My mom likes to try to sell the both of us on the lie that my dad just passed away before Corbin's company went public last year and broke out huge. And on the surface, that's all factual. But Mom and I are still here, and while Corbin is off yachting on the fruits of my dad's literal labor, his two living dependents are barely staying afloat. If Corbin were a real friend, he would've thrown a few scraps our way. That's how I see it. Grandpa Hank sees it that way, too. He calls him Crooked Corbin in front of Mom. When it's just me and him, he calls him a Real Son-of-a-Bitch. Both are accurate.

"How about you make the coffee and I scramble us some eggs?" Grandpa asks.

I swallow hard, my back to him and my attention on the coffee pot, and utter out a tepid, "Sure." My grandpa's eggs are runny as hell. They're barely edible. I have to eat them fast in order to choke them down. The unfortunate result of that is that my grandpa thinks I gobble them up because I like them so much. I just don't have the heart to break it to him. Every time he stands at that stove, he waxes on about his years as a cook in the army. I bet the soldiers slurped those suckers down out of desperation, too. I remind myself each time that I can use the protein. Runny eggs are as close as I get to working out.

Mom's already gone to work. She started taking on weekend shifts at the garage in Old Town, answering phones and keeping up with the books. I don't think the owners actually need the help; they aren't very busy. It's a charity gig, but it pays the gas and electric bills, so my mom goes dutifully. Thank God for the business of doing taxes. It's all my mom does in both jobs, and she's the last person her company will ever let go, or so she says.

"You hear the big ruckus across the street last night?" My grandpa's question is his way of asking why I don't go to parties. He thinks I need a social life. He's right. He's also caught me staring across the street on more than one occasion. He's polite enough to not bring up the "pretty blonde girl" this early in the morning; he usually waits for his evening whiskey to kick in to needle me.

I do stare, though most of the time I'm too afraid to actually talk to Eleanor. In fact, we've probably only exchanged words a handful of times. All of the Trombley girls are beautiful, but Eleanor, she's special. Eighteen, hair that falls in waves, and a cheerleading uniform that fits as if she was born to wear it, she's literally a dream girl. *My* dream girl.

But it's more than how pretty she is that has me captivated. I can't quite pin what it is exactly, but ever since junior high, I have been smitten with her. Like the way awkward superheroes fall for normal humans with no explanation at all. Sadly, I possess no superhuman skills to wow her with or employ to leap into danger to save her. That doesn't stop my massive crush, though. Maybe it's her confidence, or maybe the smile she wears like a badge of honor, pushing her cheeks into round cherries. I could pick her laugh out of a crowd in a heartbeat. It's as though it was created for me to hear, to recognize, and I don't really know why.

I shake my head, realizing a lot of time has passed.

"I must have really been knocked out," I finally respond. I gently kick a chair leg to make room for my thin frame to slide in while my grandfather coughs out a laugh at my expense. I have a feeling he knows I was daydreaming about Eleanor. I set his coffee by the seat next to me, then cradle my own mug and breathe in the steam coming from the top. I'll need this smell to trick my brain into telling my mouth that these eggs I'm about to get aren't a threat.

Grandpa shuffles in a circle, pan in one hand and one of mom's blue plates in the other. He slides what he likes to call an omelet onto the dish before setting it down in front of me.

"*Mmmm*," I hum through tight, lying lips.

This time, the cheese he sprinkled on top is melted. That's a positive step.

My lips pressed to the rim of my cup, I suck down a hot sip that coats my tongue with the bitterness of pure black coffee, then immediately scoop up a quarter of my eggs. The texture is its usual gag-worthy self, but I've managed to temporarily burn my taste buds enough to get through this first bite.

"Someone has a birthday next week." He's talking about me. The big one-eight. It's not that I've forgotten, I just don't get excited about my birthdays anymore. When I was nine or ten, we had parties. There would be cake and presents, and Dad actually took time off from work. It's hard not to see my birthday as a financial inconvenience now. Especially since my mom insists I don't work part time during the school year. I saved a good amount from cleaning movie theaters all summer to pay for incidentals, but it still doesn't feel like enough.

Grandpa slices a thick pat of butter and swirls it in the hot pan; it crackles as it melts. I wonder how much of what I'm eating is egg and how much is butter.

"You think about what you want?" he asks, turning to meet my gaze. It shakes me out of my head and I shrug.

"Not really." There's a tinge of pity in his eyes while we

stare at one another, both probably realizing how sad that statement is. I'm a boy about to hit a huge milestone and I couldn't care less about the celebration of it all.

I drop my focus back to my plate and immediately shovel another forkful of eggs into my mouth, relieved when I see my grandpa turn his back to me again in my periphery. Sometimes, it's hard to pretend things are normal. I do such a good job of convincing myself that this life is fine when really, it sucks a lot of the time. It's tougher to keep up the act when someone's calling me out on it, even though he doesn't mean anything by it. I know if he could, my grandpa would rewind time and try to change the present for my mom and me. The pessimist in me is pretty certain we'd end up right where we are. I still wouldn't have a clue who my father really was—what made him tick. The things that made him so brilliant also made him closed off.

"Hey," Grandpa barks. I gulp down bite number three and dart my focus toward him with my fake satisfied grin plastered in place. He's uninterested in my culinary opinion, though, and nods toward the window above the sink. "There's a lot of coppers over at that house you're always staring at."

I'm both embarrassed and rushed with intrigue.

"I'm not . . ." I shake my head as I get up and move toward the window, knowing that finishing that statement is pointless. *I am always looking at that house across the street.*

Grandpa Hank slides back toward the stove and cracks more eggs to serve himself, but he leans to the left to stare out the window alongside me. He wasn't exaggerating. There are five squad cars outside the Trombley home, two in the driveway and another three pulled up alongside the curb. There aren't any lights flashing, and we would have heard sirens. Weird that they showed up sometime between me being upstairs and making my way down here.

"I bet that pretty blonde you're always looking at is up to funny business," Grandpa says. He waits for my sideways glance to pretend to pinch a doobie and draw in a hit. He follows it up with a cackling laugh as he elbows me in the ribs.

"Eleanor isn't like that," I defend. I don't know for sure that she *isn't,* but my instincts tell me she plays by the rules —*mostly.* I don't think I've ever seen her stumble into her house after a late Friday or Saturday night. Her older sister did that plenty of times. The only thing Eleanor does is get kissed in the car. Shamelessly, I've watched most of those goodnight kisses. At least the beginnings of them.

Why am I thinking about all of this now? Damn Grandpa Hank! Old fart didn't even wait for the whiskey to start in on me today.

I stare on, partly because there's no way I'm going back to those eggs when they're cold, but mostly because I'm glued to the scene unfolding across the street. Two officers pace around the front of the yard, stopping to squat and look closely at the grass every few feet or so. Another cop walks toward the back of the house with a German shepherd. The dog's nose is fixed in the blades of grass, his head weaving methodically from left to right along the ground.

"Hey." My voice is hushed as I alert my grandpa. I feel as if I'm on a stakeout or something. "Look, there's another."

Dumping his egg mush onto a plate, he abandons the pan in the sink then sidles up next to me, eating while we stand squared with the side-by-side window panes. A woman dressed in a black suit gets out of the new car, and walks up the center path in the Trombley front hard. I catch a glimpse of her gun at her side as she shifts her jacket. She stops to talk with one of the officers who's been fixated on something in the flower bed. I hadn't noticed before, but he's wearing blue gloves.

"I don't think this is good, Jonah." My grandfather's words are dulled, and as I turn to glance his way, his expression is just as void. He finishes his eggs and clears my plate once he's done, not even bothering to ask if I want more. I don't. And for once, it's not because I can't stand the texture passing over my tongue.

No. Right now, I feel strangely sick. My gut is heavy with a sense of doom. And a selfish paranoia. The pretty blonde girl I like to stare at across the street hasn't come outside since I've been looking out this window.

CHAPTER *Two*

Events like this have a way of grabbing everyone's full attention in a matter of hours. Oak Forest isn't a big city. It isn't even that close to Chicago, the city we all *say* we're from when anyone asks. This place is a suburb of a suburb, a clustered grid of streets that look the same at every turn. Giant oaks line wide, uneven sidewalks that have been cracked from years of snow storms and massive root systems. Before today, the biggest news to happen in Oak Forest was the arrival of the *actual* car used in the original *Ghostbusters* movie. Orson Symanski won it in an auction six years ago. He brings that sucker out for every New Year's parade.

Today's news is a little different. The first media truck showed up in front of our house about two hours after the cops arrived across the street. Grandpa Hank isn't afflicted with the same debilitating social anxiety I am, so he ran out to offer the camera guy and reporter lady coffee and got the scoop before the news officially broke on Channel 7 thirty minutes later. Addy Trombley is missing.

Somehow, eight hours have passed since the beginning of all this, or at least the beginning as Grandpa Hank and I know it. For the Trombleys, it's been a harrowing thirteen or more. It's the *more* that is full of mystery. Nobody seems sure exactly how long the nine-year-old has been gone. That's the hook the media is hanging on to for now, and it's playing out in living rooms up and down our street—throughout Chicagoland, really, thanks to the five o'clock news feed.

It's playing out in ours.

"I can't believe nobody saw anything." My mom plops down on the opposite end of the couch and hands me a bowl of warmed-up leftover pasta. She's still wearing her work shirt and her name badge that reads KARA. We've been consumed with the news for the last three hours. Mom came home from her shift early, the owners of the garage deciding to close up out of respect for the heartbreaking news. In reality, they wanted to sit glued to their televisions like the rest of us. Nobody will admit it out loud, but one of humanity's greatest flaws is how excited we become when tragedies happen.

"Jonah didn't even hear the party. Nose in those books of his," Grandpa Hank says, prying the cap from his second beer as he settles into his worn blue easy chair. I shoot him a glare and he coughs out a short laugh.

The police came to interview us about two hours ago, and for all the times I've stared out that window watching the Trombleys with a certain dash of envy, I missed seeing the most important incident of all. I was useless. We all were.

"It's weird watching your own front yard on the news," Mom says, pressing the volume button on the remote to bring up the latest reports.

The glow of our living room window can be seen behind the live shot. I crane my neck and pull the flimsy curtain panel open an inch and squint when my eyes are hit with the harsh spot on the reporter.

"She went to my high school," I mumble.

"That broad?" Grandpa says. I turn back in time to see him gesture toward the television, only to have my mom smack his wrist.

"What was that for?" He rubs his skin, then holds the chilled beer bottle against it as if her small slap actually hurt. She scowls at him, urging him to fess up to his misogyny.

"Fine. *Lady,*" he grumbles. Mom clicks her teeth together and mutters, "Jesus Christ."

"Yeah," I cut in, ending their semi-playful spat. "She spoke at last year's graduation. I guess she's the most famous person to come out of Oak Forest, or something like that."

"Horseshit," Grandpa barks. Mom and I both flash our attention to him. He shrugs. "Your dad's more famous than she is. He's just famous among smart people, and this town is full of real idiots."

My mom softens to him again, reaching over and squeezing the same spot on his arm that she smacked a moment ago. She misses Dad, and she shows it in these little moments of reverence. I only wish I could feel that same awe they do. Instead, I don't really feel anything. Other than Grandpa living here and Mom being a lot more stressed, my life hasn't changed much in the absence of my father. I didn't really know him. That fact does make me sad, though, because now . . . I never will.

I take after my mom physically. She's slender, whereas my dad was always on the stocky side. I get my height from both of them, reaching six feet by my sophomore year. The rest of me, though, is a carbon copy of my mom. Dirty blue eyes, as she calls them, and copper-brown hair that doesn't fall straight or curl. It means when I wake up in the morning, I look like one of those pencil-toppers I used to buy at the book fair in elementary school, wild strands poking in all directions.

I did inherit my father's mind, and that scares me a little now that he's gone. School has always been easy, but I have caught myself more and more obsessing on the work. My dad turned into a man who studied life rather than lived it. As much as I don't want the same fate, it sometimes feels inevitable. My path has been carved.

" . . .When police showed up at the Trombley residence, they weren't sure what to expect. They say it's procedure to investigate missing person reports with a certain sense of skepticism. As an officer, they're not sure what they're walking into. Is this the case of a runaway? Abuse or domestic violence? A teen drug problem? But what law enforcement quickly learned was that none of those shoes fit the Trombley case. The problem is, they've never really seen anything like this before. Addy Trombley is just a little girl, last seen skating in her driveway yesterday afternoon. Seemingly, under everyone's noses, she simply . . . vanished."

"Stupid," my mom mutters at the TV, knocking back the rest of her warm tea and bolting from the other end of the sofa where she'd been sitting near Grandpa. "These news people think they're so clever with those little sayings. *None of those shoes fit the Trombley case.* I mean, my God,

Rick and Patricia are living a nightmare and this, this *broad,* is playing around with nursery rhymes while her network exploits their tragedy. It all makes me sick."

"Oh, so *you* can call her a broad," my Grandpa says, earning an instant glare from Mom.

"I was using it for effect," she shoots back.

"Well, what do you think I was using it for?"

"Chauvinism," she retorts.

Grandpa and I don't crack a smile in her presence, but the moment she leaves the room and is out of ear shot, he leans forward and cups his mouth toward me. "Don't mess with your mother. She's *always* right. And she has a mean left hook," he jokes, rubbing his arm. I expected him to say something else at first, but he's always quick to take up Mom's side beyond their usual jokes and banter.

"Hey." I meet Grandpa's squinty stare and for a few seconds he gnashes his whiskered lips together in thought. It feels as though I'm about to get a lecture.

"I wanna give you your birthday present now." He coughs through his effort to stand up from the chair, and moves toward the side table near the front door, pulling out the small drawer and removing a wrapped package the size of a Bible. I'd think maybe that's what I'm being given if I didn't know what a heathen my Grandpa is. Mom walks in as he's about to hand the gift to me.

"Oh, I didn't think we were doing this until next week-end," she says, a smirk playing at the corner of her mouth. She taps her fingernails against her refilled tea mug and perches on the arm of the couch. I hold her stare for a second, seeing if I can get her to crack. She only shakes her head.

I expect a card with some cash inside and maybe a flat-pan cake with some sprinkles for my birthday, which is definitely at odds with the heavy package now resting in my hands. I can tell it's a book, but it isn't your normal hardback or the latest Brandon Sanderson. The shape is too odd for that.

"Well, go on." Grandpa Hank nods at my hands.

The goofy grin of a child takes over my mouth and I laugh out nervously while I fumble with the paper. It doesn't take long to unwrap the beat-up notebook with well-worn leather binding and an ink stain smudged across the spine. Turning it over in my hands I study it, and after noting his trademark handwriting engraved with pen on the cover, I realize it belonged to my father. He wrote like a typewriter, complete with the little hoods over his lowercase A's and tails at the ends of his D's and T's. I used to look at his notes in his briefcase when he packed up in the morning and always wondered how he wrote so much in such a meticulous way.

"It's Dad's." I glance up just long enough to catch Mom's glossy eyes and half smile. I lift the book and suck in my lips, feeling some reverence for this notebook, but probably not as much as I should.

"Now, I know what you're thinking. 'Great. I turn eighteen and all I get is a crappy old notebook,'" Grandpa says.

I breathe out a laugh at my grandfather's guess at my inner dialogue.

"No, I like it," I say, thumbing through the first few pages.

"Well, you will . . . when you crack that hood of the thing that goes with it," he says.

It takes a few seconds for his comment to sink in, and when my head pops up from reading my father's notes, my sudden realization is quickly confirmed by the glimmer of a gold key dangling from his index finger. I haven't seen that key in years. It used to hang on the small hook by the back door, a nagging reminder of my dad's long-gone teenage years.

"All registered, and insurance is paid up for six months, mostly because it's considered a *hobby car* until you can get it running, but . . ." My mom stops mid-sentence and moves close enough to weave her arm through mine and rest her head on my shoulder while I flip through the pages of notes my father left behind.

"You really think I can get Dad's old Bronco up and running?" I'm being serious because right now, I have major doubts. I'm book smart, sure. I'm great at math and I figured I'd study engineering in college, but the inner workings of an automobile feel a bit impossible, especially a seventy-two Ford that hasn't run, at least not well, since my dad was seventeen.

"I know you can," Grandpa answers. "My gift to you is I will pay for the parts. Whatever you need."

"Yeah, but that's the thing. You guys, this is— I mean, I would *love* to drive the Bronco around, but I have no idea where to begin. And insurance after six months. Mom, we can't afford that unless I work part time, and . . ." My hand finds its way into my hair and I grip at it, feeling overwhelmed.

"Page one."

I stare at my grandfather for a beat, my brows dented as he leans forward and taps on the notebook clutched in my hands.

"That's where you begin. Page one. Your dad kept that diary of everything he ever did to that heap of metal. From the moment he bought it for four hundred bucks to the last time he tinkered on that thing when you were in diapers.

Damn thing's too old to still have a manual so he figured he'd make his own."

On Grandpa's suggestion, I flip to the first page and begin reading. His analytical mind wasn't great at being conversational, but there's a bit of humor to his words.

Step 1: Battery and gas, you idiot!

"He always hoped it would be yours one day. We'll make the insurance work. You worry about the normal things a kid your age is supposed to worry about." Mom squeezes at my arm, and a shiver runs through my body. Maybe it's a tinge of guilt over getting something so big I don't really feel I deserve it, or worse, properly appreciate.

"Happy birthday, kiddo." Grandpa's mustache lifts with his crooked smile.

"Thanks." I lift the book again and take the keys as he hands them over.

"It's in the garage. I had an old buddy give 'er a tow from the storage yard he was keeping it at for your dad as a favor. Go on, spend some time with her." Both he and my mom tilt their heads toward the garage door, urging me forward.

My feet feel like lead, though. I've never been more sure I'm going to fail at something in my life, and this includes that time I decided to try ice skating backward with Lindsey Monahan in junior high. I fell on my ass then, and I'm pretty sure the same fate awaits me now. But I haven't seen my mom look this alive in months. The least I can do is spend some time in here every now and again pretending I know what I'm doing.

I step into the garage and let the door close behind me, feeling along the wall for the light switch. I smell oil in the dark, and when the fluorescents above finally kick on, my eyes fill in the rest of the picture. The yellow paint has held up. For the most part, there's still a decent sheen on the doors and the hood. The seats are ripped to shreds from years of wear, though, and even through my novice eyes I know there are serious pieces missing from the dash. It's as if my dad stopped halfway and left many things in limbo.

Needing fresh air, I hit the button to raise the garage door and lean in through the Bronco's open driver's side window. In my own selfish bubble, I'd forgotten about the chaos happening at the end of my driveway. A reporter and his camera man jet to their feet from the open back of a van. I hold up my hand in apology, sorry I disturbed them. But when they meander up my driveway, the nicely dressed one with a microphone in his hand, I regret being open and friendly. They took this as an invitation.

"Hey, there!" The guy's wearing jeans and a sweater vest over a shirt and tie. In two words, I detect a slight accent—Texas, Oklahoma maybe. He's not local, that's for sure.

"Hi," I stammer out, gripping my dad's notebook while my arms rest along the open window. My eyes dart to the circus forming in our street. The last thing I want is for more people to see me, to approach me, to want to talk about the family across the street, a girl I barely know.

"Would you mind if we asked you a few—"

When the garage door begins to shut between us, I jerk my head back to see my Grandpa standing behind me, his thumb poised over the button on the remote. He waves at the two-man media crew, then switches to giving them the bird when the door blocks their view.

"Sorry. I forgot they were out there," I say, my own words echoing in my head. *How could I forget?*

"I figured when I heard the door open."

My grandpa has a bit of a limp. It's at its worst in the evening and early morning. He ambles to the front of

Dad's Bronco and slides his hand along the crevices in the grill, feeling for the latch. He nods at me to join him as he lifts the heavy metal. I jump in, knowing enough to at least find the support bar to hold the hood in place.

"She's a beauty under the hood," Grandpa muses.

"*Mmm.*" I nod in agreement but honestly, I don't have a clue what I'm looking at. The book in my hand may as well be written in Pig Latin and deciphered using a cereal box decoder ring.

"You *can* do this." My grandfather's heavy hand lands on the center of my back. He must sense my reservations. I'm sure they are vibrating off my skin.

I clutch my dad's book to my chest, my thumbs nervously running along the corners of the pages that are no longer sharp. Maybe this is why Dad and I never really bonded. He could look under this hood and understand the workings of the engine so easily; all I see is a lot of dirty wires haphazardly taped together and strung around random filthy motor parts that do important jobs, I'm sure, but all look the same.

"Want a tour?" Grandpa leans his head under the hood and quirks a brow.

I shrug and set Dad's book on the fender, leaning over for a better view. Holding on to the sides of the cavity, I breathe in deep. "Gotta start somewhere, I suppose."

"Battery. You start here." His hand hovers over the one thing in this mess that looks new. I'm guessing it is.

"Right." I chuckle.

For the next twenty minutes, Grandpa walks me through the path that starts with a key in the ignition and ends up at a series of belts that run the motor. It's one giant loop, and it's overwhelming. I manage to sport a convincing smile by the time we close up and head inside.

To truly pull this off, I'm going to have to obsess like my old man did. I know Mom and Grandpa have visions of me piling my friends in this thing and racing off for the weekend in the woods, but all I can see is the need for perfection, the frustration when things don't work as they should, and the spiral until I basically live in this garage. All of this, of course, assuming I have any automotive inclination at all.

Mom is still curled up on the couch in front of the TV when Grandpa Hank and I come in. Having just been approached by the media zombies lurking on our sidewalk, I'm less drawn to watching them on screen. I kiss my mom on top of her head and lean over to hug her from behind the sofa.

"Happy early birthday, Jonah. I promise there will still be cake on the actual day." A sleepy smile barely stretches between her cheeks. She'll fall asleep down here, probably along with Grandpa.

I tell them both good night and drag my own tired legs up the stairs. I don't know why I feel so listless. I haven't done a thing all day except talk with officers and flip around local news channels. I don't think my muscles have relaxed since we found out Addy is missing. My shoulders hunched up to my ears and have yet to fully drop.

In the shelter of my room, I close the door and toss Dad's book next to my laptop where my essay still needs an ending. There's no way my mind can focus on comparing protagonists in *Lolita* and *Crime and Punishment*. It's hard to contemplate two fictional hero-villains while something possibly equally horrific to their deeds is unfolding for real outside my window.

My light on dim, I poke open the shutter slats and stare at the scene that is somehow growing in size despite the late hour. It doesn't take long for my gaze to wander up the driveway to the Trombley front door. Any evidence of yesterday's homecoming festivities has been swept away, replaced with markers on the lawn and police tape closing off places still to be dissected by the investigators. The bright orange and yellow wreath on their red front door seems so out of place.

I'm not sure how long Eleanor's curtains have been open. Perhaps she just flicked on the light, and that's what caught my attention. Regardless, it's obvious she's looking at my window, and I'm temporarily pinned in place with my heart pounding at getting caught staring at her personal nightmare. I'm sure the neighbors are staring at her house through their windows too. Our entire street is probably spying on the Trombley house in some way or another. Hell, I bet the retired guy who lives three houses down and does nothing but yell at people who let their dogs poop on his lawn is on his roof with binoculars. Still, it feels as though I should know better. *I* should respect their—*her*—privacy at a time like this.

I rock back on my heels and am about to give in to the temptation to slowly back away and turn off my lights when Eleanor lifts her arm and presses her palm against the glass. The thunder in my chest skips; sharp tingles run down my spine. I open my slats wider when my feet finally unglue from their spot on the floor, and even though my insecurities scream at me to run and hide, my arm operates independent from my brain and I manage to hold up my hand in response. I keep it raised for several seconds, waiting for her to drop her palm from the glass. When her head falls to the side against her window, I open my shutters completely, folding them to the side, and sit on the edge of my desk so I can do the same. Something about this feels utterly necessary. Maybe the voice in my head is crazy, but it's telling me that Eleanor needs me to be here, like this, for just a little while.

I pull my knees up and cross my ankles so I can hug my legs. My desk is kinda small, and this position is not very comfortable, but I hold it while the two of us stare down below. The bright lights of yet another news crew lights up the front walk and damp flower beds in Eleanor's front yard. The newswoman standing in the spotlight isn't anyone I've ever seen on TV, but the sophistication of their operation makes me believe that this news team is bigger than Chicagoland.

My attention shifts from the newscast after the woman begins talking, and while Eleanor's gaze remains fixed on the strangers in her lawn, mine is locked on her. So many times I've glanced over there—okay, *stared*—and she has been laughing, pacing while she talks on the phone with her friends, or posing as she snaps photos that I later find on her social media. This version of Eleanor Trombley is a shell. The laughter is gone, and there is no sign of it returning in the unblinking eyes and sagging shoulders a hundred feet away.

The bright lights below glow for fifteen minutes, maybe twenty, and when they shut off my eyes find it hard to adjust. The front of the Trombley house suddenly appears dark, buried under the heavy shadows of their enormous tree. I blink for several seconds to regain my focus on the wreath, waiting for the orange and yellow to return. By the time I can make out the door, Eleanor's window is dark and her curtains drawn. The ghost of a girl has gone. To bed, I hope, though I doubt anyone in that house is sleeping tonight. For whatever reason, I don't immediately abandon the uncomfortable perch of my desk. Something compels me to stay, to stare at the unmoving curtains a little while longer. I tell myself I'm merely watching over my friend, but that's not true. We aren't friends. We're people who live on the same street who recognize each other. I'm being nosy. Also, a small part of me hopes Eleanor comes back and waves to me again, and just how selfish is that?

CHAPTER *Three*

The media circus tripled overnight. I awoke to the sound of trucks beeping while backing up to jockey for position in the makeshift parking lot police set up in our street. There's a small path roped off with yellow tape and cones allowing the five houses closest to the Trombleys' access to back in and out of driveways. Traffic is temporarily one-way only. I have nowhere to be, but Jake should be here in twenty minutes for geometry tutoring and, given what I know of his skills at navigating shapes, he's bound to mess this up. This is his second go at this class, trying to earn something better than a D.

I pause halfway down the stairs to finish firing off my text to him with directions to enter from the south instead of the north, but by the time I get to the last step I realize my message isn't necessary at all.

"Dude. You think I wasn't showing up early to see the shit show outside?" Jake is a six-foot-four basketball star at our high school. He's the most popular guy on campus, and the fact he's my only friend makes zero sense. We've known each other since kindergarten, though, and for whatever reason, when it became clear he was destined for the jock route in life and I was more on track for the debate team, he still stuck by me. I have literally manhandled him through passing fifty percent of his classes, which is probably part of the reasoning.

"Did you see the body?"

Jake is also an idiot.

Grandpa Hank grumbles and refolds his newspaper, blocking my friend from his view, but he shoots me a pointed glance over his reading glasses to let me know he's biting his tongue.

"God, Jake. There is no body. Addy is missing."

"Oh." Jake's mouth hangs in this awestruck open form for a few seconds, his brow pulled in. "I thought, you know, because on Twitter it said—"

"What did I tell you about Twitter?" I interrupt.

"Twitter does not make it fact," my friend recites, as if it's a tenet he had to memorize to earn a badge.

I've had to drill a lot of life skills like this into Jake's head. Of course, he's the one who goes to parties on Friday and Saturday nights while I stay in and read or get ahead on my college essays.

I guide my friend to the kitchen table and he pulls out his last test for us to review. He's getting better. When we started working on geometry, he could barely pull off a D on his exams. The last two have been solid C's, including this one.

"Not bad," I praise, holding up a palm. We high five.

We spend the first several minutes retracing what he did wrong on the problems he missed. I write up a few samples for him to try on his own, and after working together for about forty minutes, I feel good that he'll get at least two more right on his next try. Must be nice to be an athlete and get a second shot at basically everything academic.

"You tell dumbass here about your birthday present?" Grandpa doesn't mince words with Jake, and it's a weird line where I can never tell whether he likes my friend or can't stand him. Jake finds the trash talk endearing, so I guess that's all that matters.

"Bruh, I missed your birthday?" Jake pulls his oversized flat-brimmed ball cap from his head and runs his hand through his curly shoulder-length hair, wearing genuine regret on his face.

"My birthday is still on November third. Like it always is." I wait for Jake's reaction with my crooked smile, but he just nods, as if relieved.

"It's in the garage," Grandpa urges. I think he's a little excited to show it off. All it does for me is twist my stomach in knots. Telling Jake about the Bronco makes it this real project I'm going to have to tackle. I finally fell asleep last night with the comfortable idea that I could string the project along through senior year and manage to leave for college without actually taking apart anything.

"You got a car!" Jake's jacked, and he speeds out of the kitchen to the garage before I can get out of my seat.

"You better get in there with him before he starts touching shit. That kid is bound to break things," Grandpa says, motioning in Jake's direction with his coffee mug.

He's not wrong. Taking in a deep breath, I get to my feet and leave the books on the table, following my friend into the garage. Jake is already behind the wheel when I get to him, and I have to stop him from pressing the horn.

"There are still a dozen news outlets on the other side of the garage. Please don't make them all rush over here," I say, reaching in through the driver's side window and covering the center of the wheel to stop him from doing any damage.

"Right. My bad. Seriously, though, Jonah, this is a sweet ride! Can we take it out?"

I grab at the back of my neck and wince.

"That's the thing. It doesn't exactly run. *Yet.*"

Jake's shoulders drop and his hands slide from the wheel.

"Yeah, it was my dad's. It was always his project car, but he did most of the work on it before I was old enough to remember. It ran great for a while, but that was years ago. My mom and Grandpa Hank registered it for me and my grandpa said he'll pay for the parts. I just have to figure out where to start." I slide my palm along the seam where the hood meets the side panel. I'm not even sure I could get the hood open again on my own.

"Sweet. I'll help," Jake offers, cranking open the door and skipping to the front to stand by me.

"You know cars?" I'm suspicious because we just spent ten minutes on how to prove something is a triangle.

Jake shrugs.

"A little. I mean, I can change the oil in my dad's car, and I've replaced the battery in the Jeep, and I've changed tires a bunch of times. It's all logical stuff. We can figure it out."

I can't help the laugh that gurgles out of my mouth in response.

"What?" He's a bit offended. I can tell by the crease between his brows.

"No, sorry. I'm just surprised. You don't strike me as a mechanic. That's all," I say.

"Yeah, well, you don't strike me as a math geek but, well . . ." He paints his hand in the air, circling my frame.

"I look exactly like a math geek," I laugh out.

He sighs with a tinge of sarcasm.

"You do. But that's not a bad thing," he says.

While he moves toward the garage door, I remain in place as I kick around the words he just said. I can't help but feel that looking like a math geek might be a little bit of a bad thing. It might have something to do with my very slim dating history. I've kissed three girls—ever. And I don't think I did it well.

When Jake drags the step stool from the corner and parks it against the garage door, I snap out of my fog. He's standing on it a second later, rubbing dirt from one of the window panes with his sweatshirt sleeve.

"What are you doing?"

He glances over his shoulder at me and shrugs.

"Being nosy and shit."

I'm struck with a battle of conscience, straddling this line of not wanting to join the gawking neighbors pretending to be out for walks, and wanting to see what's happening right this minute because such is human nature. The Trombley house has been quiet today, for the most part. Nobody coming or going, not that there's anywhere for them to go. My mom said someone showed up with food this morning and left it at their front door as she was leaving for work. They must feel so trapped. All of them. I saw the small red SUV in the driveway after my mom left. That's how I know Morgan must be home from college. I keep having these fleeting thoughts about everything as it unravels. Like, I wonder if Morgan secretly wanted to stay away. Did she really *need* to be here? What kind of child would I be? That I entertain the notion of staying away makes me question my morals and family loyalty. I may be more emotionally broken than I thought.

"It looks pretty chill out there. I think we can open the garage." He looks back at me for approval, but all I feel is the same panic that seared down my spine last night when a reporter wanted to talk to me.

Before I can get a real answer to come out of my mouth, Jake blows me off completely, hopping from the stool and slapping his palm on the garage door button. My legs lock instinctually and my eyes scan our driveway as it comes into view, but Jake seems to be right. Two media trucks are parked about twelve feet off the end of our driveway in such a way that the view of our garage is pretty well blocked from the others. It's also lunch hour on a Sunday. I breathe out in relief.

"I've got all afternoon. What do you say we open this baby up and see what we're dealing with?" Sudden tension crawls back into my chest at my friend's offer.

"I don't know. It's Sunday, and I've got an essay to finish, and—"

"Don't pussy out on me. You know you finished that essay already. You're just afraid."

He's right. I don't like things that I don't automatically know how to do. I shirk off trying anything new. I won't even stray on the menu at Tommy's, sticking strictly to hot dogs and never once trying the Italian beef.

"Fine, we can look under the hood or whatever," I mutter like a petulant child, dragging my body forward to join my friend at the front of the Bronco—*my* Bronco. A gift from my dad's grave, from my mom and grandfather's hearts. All I can think about is how I wish it wasn't mine.

"You're gonna need this." My grandfather joins us in the

garage, heading right toward me. He stops to press my dad's notebook against my bicep.

"Thanks," I say, taking it in my palm.

He winks at me when I glance up to meet his gaze.

"Your dad was always meticulous about his tools, so I imagine everything you need is in those cabinets." He nods toward the far wall of the garage, to the dusty metal doors that haven't been opened in a year, *at least*.

Jake walks over to crack the doors open, and I wonder if he somehow knows I can't bring myself to do it. Those tools are one more part of my dad that I never got to know. He used them years before I was in the picture, and the times he broke them out while I was alive were few and far between, and usually to repair broken things around the house.

"Wow. Talk about a labeling freak," my friend says.

Grandpa chuckles, seeming to know what Jake is referring to. Curious, I walk over and peer over his shoulder to find the familiar handwriting on strips of white tape lined across peg boards and various drawers of hardware. I'd bet that every size is exactly where it should be.

"Yo, this reminds me of your chemistry labs. Nerds don't fall far from the tree." My friend gently pokes me with his elbow into my gut. I rub the spot and breathe out a laugh. He's right. I did get my dad's penchant for *over*-organization.

I'm not sure what makes me turn—perhaps it's my grandfather's lack of response to Jake's needling—but when I do, I see what has him tongue-tied.

Eleanor looks like a ghost, her skin pale and eyes sunk deep in their wells. She reminds me of my mom in the days after my dad died, spent from crying and void of light. Eleanor leans against the frame of the garage entry like a lost dog desperate for food and shelter but terrified to trust any hand willing to feed it. My eyes blink wildly as I scan the scene behind her, expecting to see flashes from cameras and reporters scrambling to fire up their mics to get a sound bite from one of the Trombleys. Nobody seems to have seen her cross the street. Perhaps they don't care, or are biding their time to make sure any interview they get with her really counts.

"H- Uhm, hi." I gulp. I'd probably react this way under any circumstance that brought Eleanor Trombley into my garage, but the experience over the last thirty-six hours has my grandfather temporarily lost for words too.

"Hey." Her voice is weak and raspy, that of a girl who probably hasn't slept since she was up all night partying after homecoming two days ago.

"Hi." I repeat my initial response, a little clearer. It sounds as lame as it did the first time. I'm not sure whether I should smile or wear a somber expression. Should I give her condolences? Apologize, or offer to help out? Those are things people say in circumstances like this. *Should I—*

"How are you doing, Elle?"

Of course, Jake knows her better than I do. I sink back on my heels and dip my hands into the pockets of my jeans.

She lifts the shoulder that isn't leaning against the wall in a response to my friend as he steps closer, opening his arms to give her a hug. She moves from her sheltered space and wraps her arms around him in slow motion, as if her limbs are too heavy to lift. Her dead eyes lock on mine as they hug.

Grandpa clears his throat, and I'm not sure whether it's to jar me out of my trance or hide his own insecurities over not knowing what to do.

"We're all really sorry for your family," Grandpa finally

utters, managing to pull himself together. "You . . . you wanna come in, sweetheart?"

His words are endearing, without the chauvinist tinge my mom always scolds him about. They're flavored by his age and a sincere worry that weighs down his eyes. He pulls a folding chair from the stack we keep against the wall for his card games he sets up in the garage on Thursdays so him and his old army buddies can smoke without my mom losing her mind.

"Oh, uhm . . ." Eleanor glances behind her toward her still house and the quiet media trucks. Some of the police tape has come loose from the cones the officers set up earlier today and it twists in the wind. She and I both stare at it for a few quiet seconds. I break first, moving my gaze to her. I'm suddenly overcome with a deep understanding of exactly how she feels.

Out of place. Lost, and unsure.

Like me, most of the time.

"I got a car. Well, a truck. A Bronco. I'm not sure what you classify it as. A sport utility? It was my dad's, and it doesn't run yet. It used to. Sort of, but . . . well." I nervously vomit out words.

Both my friend's and my grandpa's eyes are on me, probably oozing pity while they mentally shout at me to shut the hell up. I keep my focus on Eleanor, though, her attention jerked from the chaos behind her the moment I speak. Her pouty lips hold open as she stares at me, and it's hard to tell whether they want to smile or quiver with a bottled-up cry.

This is the most I have ever said to her at once, and nothing about it was eloquent. Eleanor is not the kind of girl who makes fun of people on the fringes of high school social circles, though. And even if she were, now would not be the time. I'm a distraction. I have a job to do.

"It was a birthday gift," I continue. I glance to my left and am hit with my grandpa's now encouraging eyes. He nods for me to go on while stepping closer to Eleanor, his palm outstretched to guide her to the green metal chair he set up against the wall.

I look back to Eleanor and her head tilts to one side.

"Is today . . . your birthday?" Her eyes wrinkle, as if my birthday is something she's supposed to know, a date circled on her calendar.

Her arm stretched out toward Grandpa Hank, she lets him play the part of gentleman and take her to her seat. The sight of it tickles me for some reason, and my mouth smiles on one side.

"Happy birthday," she says, and I realize I never answered her.

"Oh, thanks. I mean, it's next weekend, but that counts, I guess."

"*Pshhh*, dumbass," Jake mumbles, flicking the back of my head as he crosses the space behind me and moves to pop the hood. It's not as if my friend and I sit around and talk about crushes, but it's impossible to live where I do and not let my attraction to Eleanor Trombley slip out a time or two over the years. At one point during freshman year, Jake offered to make an introduction at a bonfire after a big football game. Instead of going to the party though, I decided to stay home and get ahead on my advanced English reading for the semester.

My cheeks flame in embarrassment after Jake's teasing, but when I glance back to Eleanor, she's laughing at my expense, and I don't really mind. It isn't the kind of laugh that comes with sound, but her shoulders shake and her eyes slit with the fullness of her cheeks. It's a brief reprieve from the ghost that showed up wearing her skin.

Eleanor is bundled in black sweatpants several sizes too big for her frame and a Sherpa-lined camouflage coat that looks ready to head out for a seasonal hunting trip, probably borrowed from her father's closet. Somehow, she still glows like an angel. The cold air has kissed her cheeks and brought pink to her freckled skin. Her eyes are a dull green that sometimes looks more brown in the dark. I've stared at them from across lab tables and in the cafeteria for four years. Under the bright fluorescents of my garage, they shine like emeralds. And the blonde hair, usually pulled high in a ponytail or curled into these perfect waves around her shoulders, is twisted into two knots at the base of her neck.

"The boys were just getting started for the day. Young Jacob here has offered to help. You're welcome to stay." Thank God Grandpa Hank is able to find his way back to acting like a human.

"Yeah, Jonah doesn't know shit about cars." Jake snarks out a jab at my expense.

I wince, squeezing my eyes shut. This time, Eleanor's laughter produces an airy sound. It makes his insult sting less.

"And young Jacob here doesn't know shit about spelling or math, so that's why he hangs around all the time," Grandpa Hank says, coming to my rescue. I ratchet my shoulders up to my ears and grit my teeth, but Eleanor simply laughs harder. Jake, thankfully, isn't offended one bit, barking out a quick admission and saying it's totally true.

For a moment, the green eyes from my dreams seem to find solace in my dusty blue ones. If only for a breath, the madness of reality dissolves on the other side of the garage, and Eleanor can simply be a beautiful girl faced with three very different guys all trying to win her attention. Right this minute, all is incredibly normal, at least for her. And it makes the aching discomfort in my chest from my social anxiety worth every single second.

CHAPTER Four

Eleanor didn't say much after those first few minutes in my garage. She sat in that chair next to my grandpa for maybe an hour, and any time her attention wandered from Jake and me toward her house, Grandpa pulled her back in with one of his army tales or some story about my dad when he was young. I enjoyed those accounts as much as she did.

Some of them were stories I've never heard before, like the time Grandpa caught my dad sneaking home drunk when he was sixteen. My dad was typically a quiet man, even in his youth, but for whatever reason, he managed to walk home from a party my uncles had dragged him to seven miles away and could not shut up about it after slipping undetected through the front door. He woke my grandparents to describe all the things he'd seen during his walk.

"A regular tour guide, straight from Anheuser-Busch," my grandpa joked.

When Eleanor left, the stories stopped. Jake and I poked

around under the hood for another hour or so, then called it a day. We pulled out the battery and the alternator, and I made sure to label wires as we went along, like my dad wrote in his book. It drove Jake nuts, but the activity left me feeling a few percentage points smarter about how a seventy-two Bronco works.

I brought my dad's notebook to school with me today, and it's given me something to do during lunch besides eavesdrop on the various rumor-pods doling out the latest news about Addy and the Trombleys.

Eleanor was just named homecoming queen at Friday's game. For some, seeing her fall from grace so quickly feeds an addiction for gossip. They must separate themselves from the reality of it all in order to be so entertained. Why else would a missing nine-year-old spawn so many cruel conspiracy theories followed by cackling laughter? Girls who, just last week, fought over a spot at Eleanor's lunch table now cast shade and question whether the princess of Oak Forest High had something to do with her baby sister's disappearance.

"We're heading off-campus for Tommy's. You coming?" Jake throws an arm around me while I shuffle my way toward the cafeteria. I shake my head and hold up my notebook, touching it to my head.

"Studying. Thanks, though," I reply.

He grimaces.

"The Bronco is supposed to be fun. I swear to God, you're the only person I know who can turn such a kick-ass present into homework. You sure you don't wanna come along?" My friend leans his elbow into my arm, urging me, but any temptation I may have felt fades the second two of his basketball buddies pile into our conversation, peppering me with maybe a dozen questions on what I know about the Trombley case.

What's crazier is I'm pretty sure they were at the Trombley party that night, and Addy was last seen the afternoon before the game. I wonder if they've been interviewed by police. Jake was. He has yet to stop bragging to me about his alibi—spending the night at Charlotte Hickman's house while her parents were out of town.

I make up an excuse to duck into a restroom when his circle of friends closes in expecting answers I don't have. When I'm sure they've gone and the rest of the lunch rush is either in line for food or settled at a table, I find a window nook in the hallway and make myself completely unapproachable, sort of par for my course. I pull a brown bag from my backpack and unwrap my peanut butter sandwich, crossing my legs out in front of me and balancing my dad's notebook open on my thigh.

An old photo slips from the pages, and I manage to catch it before it drops to the floor. The image is folded, flattened from years of being used as a page marker. I straighten the crease and study the young couple standing in formal clothes in front of the familiar Bronco's front end. There are hints of the people I recognize as my parents in these faces, but they're so young. The divot from worry that's become a permanent scar between my mom's eyes is gone, replaced by smooth skin and a wave of light brown hair that my dad is about to sweep away from her eyes. Her chin tilted toward him, she's gazing up at him like a teenager in love, which I suppose is exactly what she was. Mom's always adored my father, that's something I've never doubted. But there's something about seeing the beginning of their affection for each other that has me caught. Even more than the way she's looking up at him is the way he's taking her in, completely. How did this man become so obsessed with his work that he quit pausing to look at her like this?

A tiny flower is tied around my mom's wrist. It's purple, like her dress, I think. The color in the photo has faded some, everything a little yellow. This looks like a prom photo. They don't quite look old enough to be seniors; they're maybe seventeen in the shot.

Seventeen, just like me.

Curious, I flip the picture over, hoping for a date or some other clue, but the only thing written on the back is a line from a poem or something, written in my dad's perfect typewriter-like handwriting.

Candy Colored Sky

I ponder those words, flipping the photo around my fingers for a few seconds before tucking it back into the book's pages and finishing my pathetic brown-bag lunch.

I think about the photo for most of the day, but don't pull it out again until my walk home from school. I'm busy studying it as I trip over a new line of tape closing off a bigger section of my street. I stumble but catch myself before completely falling to my knees and taking out one of the traffic barricades with me. The number of people outside the Trombleys' has doubled from when I left this morning.

I punch in the code to open our garage, continuously checking over my shoulder to make sure I'm not being followed or watched. My paranoia skyrocketed after the first night when the reporter asked me to talk. Most of the cameras are clustered around an officer talking from the center of the street. They've blocked the view of the Trombleys' house from reporter cameras with a huge crime scene truck, and there's a little more clearance in front of my driveway.

"My dad says by tonight they'll have most of the media staged near the corner."

"Jesus!" I grip my chest and leap backward several feet at the sound of Eleanor's voice. I was so wrapped up in the press conference behind me that I wasn't paying attention to the garage door rising in front of me—or the girl occupying the same green folding chair she was in last night.

"Sorry." Eleanor's pale pink lips stretch to one side and curve into an apologetic smile that only lasts a second.

Under my sternum, my heart pulses with enough force to crack the bone. I flatten my palm over the flannel button-down in an attempt to calm the thunder underneath.

"It's fine. Yeah, I just . . . How?" I stammer through several thoughts in a few nonsensical words, then end up pointing at the chair she's folded herself up in. She looks down at the ground around her, almost as though she's floating on a life raft being circled by sharks.

"I saw your grandpa out getting the mail. I asked if I could sit in here a little while, away from the noise, ya know?" Her eyes lift briefly then drift away from mine, her attention again lost to the cold garage space around her.

"You wanted to be in here, with the lights off?" *I'm an idiot. Of all things to utter, this is what I say.*

"They were off?" She lifts her chin and squints at the now glowing bulbs at the end of the garage opener mounted on the ceiling. She isn't being sarcastic. I can tell; my sarcasm meter is well-honed.

"They come on with the door . . . but they weren't . . ." I

realize the inner-workings of our garage door wiring isn't important and move to the button to close the door again, switching on the real lights so we don't end up in the dark —*again.* Maybe that's what she wants though, to hide in the dark.

Eleanor is close to my height, probably two or three inches shorter than my six feet. I only know this from standing behind her in the same lunch line at school. She appears so much smaller now, one leg folded under her body, the other bent with her arms hugging her knee close to her chest. It's amazing how similar all of the Trombley girls look, especially through the years. It's as if Morgan handed down her shape and hair styles and expressions to Eleanor, who then left the small lanky build of her youth for Addy to fill. From the back, I could easily fool myself that it's Addy sitting in this chair, the way her long double braids rest heavy on the back of her deep purple hoodie. A slight shift in Eleanor's profile, though, makes it obvious there's a mature beauty to her cheeks and lips. I'm so used to seeing that mouth smile, and right now it's far from it.

"I'm really sorry, by the way."

I am still an idiot.

I scrunch my eyes shut and pinch the bridge of my nose. It's such a cliché thing to say, and probably the last thing she wants to hear. The minute I hear my own voice I wish I could eat the words. What else is there to say, though? *Welcome to my garage?*

"Thank you, and it's okay. I know it's awkward." She's kind enough to let me off the hook. We both shrug when our eyes meet, and I drop my bag from my shoulder, setting it on the ground near the entry into the house.

My fingers tingle nervously because Eleanor is staring at my hands. I shove them deep into my pockets and form fists, pushing down to stretch my arms that now feel the brunt of her stare.

"I can go—"

"No!" I bark out before she can excuse herself. She eases back into the chair, maybe a little startled from my quick response.

"Sorry, now I'm scaring you." I breathe out a short laugh and it draws another brief smile from her.

"It's only fair," she jokes. My chest shakes with another laugh.

It gets so quiet suddenly that I can hear the small crackling sounds our house makes when the heat is running inside. My eyes dart around for something to do or an idea for something new to say, but before I utter my next dumb thing, Eleanor fills the silence.

"So that's really yours now?" She gestures toward the Bronco. I move to the passenger door and grip the handle, peering inside at the well-worn seats.

"Guess so." It's a far cry from the Bronco in that photo. I'm half tempted to show it to Eleanor, but it feels presumptuous somehow, that she would be interested.

"It's pretty cool. I mean, it's no green Volkswagen Beetle, but..."

I smile at her joke.

"I always thought your car was cool," I respond, turning back to face her. I'm surprised when I see she's stood from the chair and is moving toward me.

"It's a manual, and the clutch is sticky. I wear my knee brace more when I drive than when I tumble on the track." Her head cocks to the side as she wears a wry smile.

"Well, this is an automatic, but that doesn't mean it runs. I may need to borrow your knee brace for the times

I'm going to have to push it," I joke. This time, her laughter makes an airy, sweet sound.

"Can I get in?" Her eyes glance to the side, to my grip on the door handle. I'm pretty sure my palm is sweating.

"Sure, I guess." I give the interior another inspection. It's pretty dusty inside. "I can't guarantee you won't take a spring to the back of your thigh, but . . ."

I pull the door wide enough for Eleanor to lift herself inside. She stands on the running board, which thank God doesn't break off with her step, and peers inside the cabin for a few seconds before sliding fully inside.

"It's roomy. I bet you could camp in this thing." Her gaze moves from the driver's seat to the large back, the second row of seats folded down in the back. The carpet from the very back is covered in grease stains, probably from my dad's old tools and his last attempts to get this thing running.

"What do you say? Should we take it for a pretend drive?"

"Huh?" I startle, meeting her waiting gaze. She leans her head to the left, lips parted in a soft smile that is void of her reality. How could I not indulge?

I nod and rush around the front of the Bronco to the driver's side. This door is a little tricky, so I put my foot on the running board to brace myself as I pull the handle open, a trick Jake and I figured out last night. I grab the handle inside and pull myself in, wishing I could pop in the key and cruise away with the girl of my dreams. But the key is on my desk inside, and turning it in this ignition won't do a damn thing anyhow.

Eleanor pulls her door closed, so I do the same. I grip the wheel and straighten my arms, leaning my weight back in my seat. I've seen my dad sit like this. It's one of the few early memories I have of him tinkering on this thing, before his real work took over.

I sense Eleanor's weight shift and feel her eyes on me before I turn to confirm that they in fact are. She's managed to tuck her long leg under her body again, her bare knee popping out through the rip in her jeans.

"Where would we go?"

I must look shocked because she starts to laugh at whatever expression is on my numb face.

"Not right now, Jonah. I mean, if we could just back out of this garage, peel down the street." Her open palm paints an invisible line from me to her side of the windshield. "If we could just *go,* where would that be? Anywhere in this whole world, where would that be?"

My brow lifts with my rapid blinking eyes.

"Oh, well . . . *hmm.*" I'm not great at imagining things beyond the practical. Part of my father's genes. We aren't really dreamers.

"Maybe Tommy's?"

Her laugh is immediate and loud. I'd be embarrassed if it weren't so surprising to hear. There's a raspy quality to her laughter, one I didn't expect, especially given how little she has to laugh about.

"I give you the option of anywhere in the entire world, and you want to drive four blocks to the hot dog joint. That's classic, Jonah. Truly." She grazes my arm with her fingertips as she continues to be amused by me, and I laugh along with her on the outside. Inside, I'm logging this memory of the time I both made her laugh and she touched me intentionally. Every time she says my name, too—a memory is logged. I shouldn't be surprised she knows my name, given we have "known" each other for years. It's just that I've never heard her actually *say* it before.

"Okay, so I should think bigger?" I force myself to relax, twisting to the side in my seat in an attempt to match her. I lean my shoulder into the seat back and grab the strings from my hooded sweater, busying my hands with the frayed ends.

"At least beyond town limits," she demands.

Her arms cross her chest like an expectant teacher waiting for my answer to a question I didn't hear in class. I tighten my lips and look down to the space between us to avoid her stare while I think of something that doesn't make me sound like a loser. I could say Hawaii or Rome, but that's not the point of this. It needs to be a real escape, one that these wheels could accommodate.

"I always wanted to hike in the Blue Ridge Mountains." I lift my gaze with my answer and breathe a sigh of relief that she smiles in response. She approves. It was the only thing I could say that would not have been totally made up. I wouldn't say I'm pining to go there exactly, but my parents used to camp there before they had me, and Grandpa Hank always talks about the fishing. I've never done either of those things—fished or camped. Seems like a guy my age should try it once.

"Blue. Ridge. Mountains." She sighs out the words, staring up at the ceiling as she sinks deeper into the corner where her seat meets the door. Eleanor is a dreamer. My mom's eyes dazzle just like hers are now. They haven't in a long time, but they used to often—when she read me bedtime stories, when she planned road trips and vacations for the three of us, when she fantasized about getting a family dog.

"We'd camp, right? With a tent? Or . . . back there?" She

reaches over the seat and points to the back of the Bronco. I swallow as I dare fantasize about a camping trip with Eleanor Trombley that involves the two of us sleeping side-by-side in such tight quarters.

"I mean, there are lodges and stuff—"

"No, we'd camp for sure. That's the only way to do it. In the summer." She folds her arms over her chest again and flits her eyes as she looks at what must be an imaginary scene above her head.

I run my moist palms over my jean-covered thighs in an attempt to stem my nerves. It works for exactly four seconds. My heart is beating out random rhythms and my mouth is so dry.

"I have fishing rods. Oh, and sleeping bags. We have *so* many sleeping bags. Before Morgan moved out, we used to beach camp in Michigan, on the lake. My dad even bought a stove you plug in to that little cigarette lighter thingy." She leans forward and taps the space where the Bronco's lighter is missing.

"The twelve-volt," I say.

"Sure." She giggles. It's the one technical automotive word I know, and only because it's how I charge my laptop in my mom's car.

Eleanor's gaze drifts away again, but the smile lingers for almost a minute as we sit in silence, basking in this pretend world she's built based on some whim that came out of my mouth. It almost feels real, and that makes me want to dive under the hood and get this thing running.

The longer the quiet lasts, the more the pressures on the other side of the garage door seep in. Life outside of this cabin is muted, and I can't help but think that the minute we open our doors, the sounds of chaos will be waiting for us. The idea weighs on Eleanor too. I see it in her heavy eyelids, her dropped shoulders, and the tight grip her hands have on her opposite arms as she hugs herself.

It's only in this stifling quiet that I regret not asking her where she would go. It's too late to do that now. The mood has passed. That's the thing about daydreams and fantasies —they're fragile. One miscued thought allows reality to breach a carefully constructed bubble.

Eleanor pops open the door, pausing with one leg inside and one leg out. Her heavy braids glide over her shoulder as she twists back to look at me one last time.

"Thanks for letting me hide in here a while, Jonah."

We exchange tight smiles that mask all the things we really think and want to say. My inner voice pleads with her to stay. Hers tries not to scream and cry.

"Anytime, Eleanor. Maybe I'll see ya tomorrow?" The question feels ridiculous the moment it leaves my lips. My dream girl slips from the seat completely and offers me a polite smile in response that my gut tells me is charity.

I leave the shelter of the cab and move toward the garage button to open the door for Eleanor so she can head back out into a wild filled with wolves ready to eat her. I don't know anything more than I did before she showed up, no news about her family or how they're holding up, nothing about the investigation or when she might again show her face at school. I didn't ask any of it even though the questions ran through my brain like ticker tape. I want this to be the place she comes to hide. That, and it's hard enough for me to talk to her about normal things, let alone the awful tragedy she has to live with when she's at home.

I press the garage door button with my thumb and take in her silhouette as the bright sunlight from outside overtakes the dim bulbs in the garage. She turns to walk backward and holds up a hand to say goodbye as her feet shuffle away. I do the same, my hand poised to close the door and keep the wolves out when she's gone. Thankfully, though, I hold out for one more second.

"See ya tomorrow, Jonah."

CHAPTER Five

I didn't really believe Eleanor would be waiting in my garage the next day. It helped keep the disappointment at bay when it turned out that she wasn't. She was right about the media being moved to the corner of our street, though. By the time I left for school Tuesday morning, the police tape was down. And when I got home, the cameras and big media trucks were gone too. Every now and then, someone stops by to do a report from the sidewalk or to take a photo, but for the most part, life outside our house in the space between where our property ends and the Trombleys' begins is back to normal.

The shift in public attention is a welcome change in my household, but not because of the inconvenience of having to navigate through the media trucks while coming and going from our house. The media sparked more friendly household arguments than normal, and mostly because Grandpa Hank had a thing for the National Network News correspondent, Monica Correa, who camped out with her crew for two full days. My mom says the old man verged on getting a restraining order slapped in his face. He took her coffee seven times in the forty-eight hours she was here, and each time he failed to take what my mom said were clear hints that she was not interested in his old war stories.

Like the rest of the world, Grandpa Hank has been left to watch Monica's reporting on TV. Not that there is much new to report about the "Mystery on Cedarwood Lane." That's what Addy's case has been dubbed by the media. I'm not sure who was the first to coin the phrase—probably Monica—but it caught on. I'll never be able to say my address without it jarring some memory. Every report feels the same, but we all hang on every word when the news is on. I think everyone in Oak Forest is praying for someone to announce "She's been found!" The police are pursuing nothing but vague leads, though. It must feel so hopeless for the Trombleys.

While I wasn't surprised that Eleanor didn't join me the last three nights that I lit up the garage to remove parts and wires from under the Bronco hood, I am a little surprised by how quiet everything is across the street. Nobody has come or gone since the chaos left. Morgan's SUV is still in the same place she left it when she arrived over the weekend. The Volkswagen hasn't budged from the curb, tracings of paint left on the windows from last week's football game. Maybe the Trombleys went out of town to get away. It's understandable. Maybe they're hiding inside, keeping quiet. That seems hard to believe; it's been a full week, and nobody can be that still and quiet for that long.

Things around here have definitely changed. Quiet, almost eerie, is kinda the new norm. Halloween came and went, and not that our street filled with high school families and empty nesters gets a lot of trick-or-treat traffic, but this year was virtually silent, other than one or two superheroes and ghosts that strolled by. Grandpa and I doled out a few handfuls of candy and ate the rest. I do wonder if people avoided our street, skipping it for others that were not covered with crime tape a week ago.

I stare out my bedroom window one last time, eyes fixed on Eleanor's across the way, waiting for some movement, some show of light, before Jake's horn snaps me from my intense focus. My eyes dart to the street below where my friend has his arm slung out his window, his palm up as if he's been waiting around for me all day. He hasn't; he just pulled up. He's impatient, which is part of the reason he fails a lot of tests. He speeds through things to get them done. He tends to do this with girlfriends too, and a part of me wonders if his reputation is rubbing off on me. Of course, this is how I make excuses to myself for the complete lack of attention from girls at school.

Grabbing a piece of toast from my grandpa's plate as I dash through the kitchen, I thank him as he hollers "Hey" for swiping his breakfast. He waves a hand at me and grumbles as I dart out the door and dive into Jake's car just before he hits the gas and peels away from my house.

"Why do you have to do that?" I shake my head as I rush to click my seat belt in.

Jake cackles.

"I know it pisses Hank off."

I grimace and cock my head to stare at him. "Why is pissing my grandpa off such a sport for you?"

"I dunno," my friend says, a quick shrug.

I shove half of my toast in my mouth and finish zipping up my bag where it rests between my knees. It takes Jake less than four minutes to get us to campus, a drive that should be twice that if you actually stop at intersections.

From a safety standpoint, I'm better off walking, a statement my grandpa makes to me every time Jake drives away from our house. It's just that the walk takes closer to thirty minutes, and it's starting to get cold. It's a tough cost-benefit analysis when Chicago winter sweeps in.

Jake is busy scanning the parking lot for people he knows, and doesn't see the Volvo station wagon parked near the main office. I'm not sure how I missed the Trombleys pulling out of their garage this morning. They must have left during my rushed shower. I'm immediately hit with a sense of comfort and dread at seeing their family car parked at our high school. I'm glad they haven't fled completely, but their presence here means something. I'm just not sure what.

Or why I am so invested.

That's a lie.

I know *exactly* why I'm invested, and she just stepped through the office door with her head down, waves of blonde hair shielding the sides of her face while her hoodie covers the top.

"What, do you have Elle radar or something?" My friend's palm slaps my back and I wince, both from the sting and from getting caught staring. Also, I hate that he knows her well enough to call her Elle. That's me being honest about my jealousy. Doesn't make this moment feel any better at all.

"I haven't seen them out in a while. All week, really." Jake's distraction made me miss seeing Eleanor get in the car. I also missed seeing her parents come out behind her. They're pulling out of the parking space, about to head the opposite way Jake and I are going.

"Gemma says Elle's gonna switch to online learning for a while. Must be what they're meeting about." Jake slings his arm over my shoulder and pulls on my neck, giving me an awkward sideways bro hug as we head toward the center of campus and leave our view of the parking lot behind. I hate that he knows people in Eleanor's circle and I have to rely on him for information. This is my honest jealousy rearing its head again. Still makes me feel like shit.

"I guess it's not easy to show your face at school when your family has been the leading story on every news network for the last week," I mumble. Jake isn't paying attention anyhow.

"Hey, catch you at lunch, yeah? It's on me today, early birthday present!" He peels away and slides his palm against mine before spinning right in step with Gemma, the girl he got his info from, probably while making out with her in his car. Seems he's moved on from Charlotte Hickman. Normally, I'd chastise him for being such a douchebag playboy, but Charlotte really isn't very nice. She's pretentious, but maybe I'm jaded because she's also two spots ahead of me in class rank and her family is filthy rich from owning two burger joint franchises.

I nod a goodbye that nobody sees, every ounce of Jake's attention now on his latest infatuation. I wish I'd brought my dad's notebook again today. It's been a good distraction *—aka excuse to be anti-social.* I still don't understand most of the notes written in it, though the fact I'm buying my first part today with the money Grandpa Hank gave me speaks volumes about the progress I've made.

Not everything in that notebook is about the Bronco, though, and I suspect that's the *real* reason they gave it to me. Turns out, Randy Wydner had a secret passion for poetry, or maybe song lyrics. I have yet to figure it out, but I found several scribbled-out, half-finished attempts tucked inside those pages, sometimes on the back side of diagrams he'd drawn to perfect scale. It's as though he is two different personalities sharing the same page.

I won't be finding any of those gems today, though. No, today I won't have much of a choice but to let Jake drag me along with his crew—*and Gemma, probably*—for lunch. At least it's Friday, which means half-price milkshakes at Tommy's. I'll just drown my lack of conversation skills in a large strawberry with a stubborn straw.

One of the biggest reasons I avoid going out for lunch with Jake is because it is *literally* the cool thing to do at Oak Forest High. I can count on one hand the number of times my friend has taken his lunch in our school cafeteria since getting his license at the end of our sophomore year. *Lucky bastard has a May birthday.*

The minute he got access to keys and a credit line from his mom, he declared he would never again eat food off a tray. I hate to break it to him, but every place he jets off to for our forty-minute lunch break serves their meals in bags . . . placed atop trays.

Lunch with Jake is such a popular ticket that his car is typically overcrowded, like beyond the recommended number of passengers. Normally, I end up sandwiched in the back, my knees hiked up to my ears because of the hump seat while two couples make lap seats on either side of me. It's so uncomfortable that usually people don't make out at the stoplights—*usually.*

I got to Jake's car early today, so I rejoiced internally when I scored shotgun. And then Jake coaxed Gemma onto my lap, insisting we share a seat belt for the drive to Tommy's. Most guys would probably thank him for being put in this position. Gemma's hot. Her mom was a model in Ghana, and Gemma is the spitting image of her, all the way down to her long, toned legs.

I remember all the girls were fascinated when her mom came to talk to us for career day in junior high. She brought the replica of her Miss Ghana crown. I was more fascinated with her story of being one of the first women from Sub-Saharan Africa to become *the* face of several designers in the high-fashion industry.

I'm probably the only seventeen-year-old guy to think about these topics in this situation, and I'm probably nuts for doing so because, back to point A: Gemma is hot. And she's into Jake. Of course, my other thoughts during our drive are about her trajectory if my best friend has to hit the brakes. My grandfather's voice plays through my mind for most of the trip.

Jonah, you're better off walking.

Something about an awkward car ride like that brings people closer, I guess, because ever since we got to Tommy's, Gemma has been talking to me non-stop. Prior to our commute, I think she thought my name was Jason. It's funny because I could literally write her short biography. It's like that for a lot of the people in Jake's circle, though, and to be fair, I've never taken the time to give them my story. I always think mine would be so boring in comparison.

"I hear Elle's parents are basically at each other's throats blaming each other. It's so bad that Morgan had to step in and pretty much be the parent. I heard she's skipping next semester so she can stay and help at the house, make sure Elle graduates and all that. Morgan and Elle don't get along, though, and it's like, this totally wretched vibe. I just . . . I feel so bad, ya know?" Gemma dips one of her fries in ranch then pops it in her mouth, which means I have about eight seconds of silence while she chews. Everyone at the table nods as if she just shared something profound, not a bunch of gossipy-sounding surface-level stuff.

She gets to call her Elle, too. This one doesn't feel fair.

"The media's gone," I add, feeling as though I should.

Everyone nods again, but less interested by my contribution.

"I wonder if her family is going to be on *Dateline*?" This question, from one of Gemma's friends, spirals into an entirely new loop.

I take advantage of my distracted company and pull out the notes app on my phone to read through some of the things I copied over from my dad's notes. Read together, the lines read like a beatnik poem, random phrases linked by nothing more than the fact they're words. But there's something about each little line that is somehow really beautiful.

"Whatcha got there, Romeo?" Jake snatches my phone and his eyes rake over the words, his mouth puckering with the need to burst out in laughter at my expense.

"Asshole!" I growl. I'm not very assertive, so this out-of-character move gives Jake enough pause to tone down his volume, but he still keeps my phone, eventually reading one of the lines back to me.

"Face like Milky Way, all lit up with potential." He spits out a puff of a laugh and I grab my phone back while he's too busy being a dick.

I push my phone in my back pocket and instantly regret my lifetime of friendship with Jake. I can't dodge his curious stare, though, so I finally hold out my palms with a "What?"

"You writing her a poem, Jonah?" A divot forms

between his brows and his mouth hangs open in anticipation of my answer. He's dead serious, and because of his reaction I know there is no way I am ever writing a girl anything and sharing it with him.

"They're things my dad wrote. I copied it from the notebook. Just random stuff in margins and sometimes on receipts." I shirk off the penetration of his stare because I sense the way it shifts from teasing to pity. He clears his throat after a few seconds and I glance to him, his mouth a tight, apologetic line.

"Sorry, man," he says, sliding his palm forward a few inches on the table for effect. I shake my head and get to my feet.

"It's fine," I say, clearing away my trash.

I decide to pass the last remaining minutes of lunch waiting for the others while sitting on the back of Jake's car. He doesn't drive anything fancy. It's a sedan that only makes the obnoxious noise it does because he talked one of his friends into jacking with the tailpipe, something he has suggested we do to the Bronco a dozen times. He just can't fathom not wanting attention. Part of why our friendship works is because I gladly give him any that drifts our way. I am happy to not share spotlights.

I'm busy calculating how fast Jake's going to have to drive to get us back to school on time when a delicate hand slinks up my arm and squeezes at my shoulder. I shiver from it, even in my layered long-sleeved T-shirt and hoodie. I jerk to the side and am met with Gemma's hand holding out this bright blue and yellow hair tie.

"I'm good. I keep it kinda short," I joke, running my hand through my hair. When Gemma's hand lands on top of mine, I tense. No, I petrify.

"It's a cute length," she says, a raspy giggle added at the

end. I'm starting to see why Jake has become so helpless in her presence. Granted, I'm pretty sure he gets compliments like this on the daily.

I pull my hand out from under hers, which I realize a little too late maybe offended her. It definitely embarrassed her because now she's sucking in her bottom lip and looking down and off to the side.

"Sorry," I say at the same exact time she does.

We both breathe out a laugh.

"Here," she says, handing me the hair tie that started this whole thing.

"*Oh-kay?*" I take it from her and stretch it out with my fingers, not quite sure what I'm meant to do with it.

"For Elle—Eleanor?"

I nod, but my puckered smile and scrunched eyes must give away how confused I still am. Gemma waggles her head and laughs politely, tugging at the elastic band still in my hand.

"I made them for us, for tonight's game. Just didn't feel right that she doesn't have hers, even though she won't be here. I want her to have it."

Gemma has more depth than I gave her credit for. I nod again, eyes clearer, and tuck the satin cloth into the front pocket of my hoodie. I keep it there, clutched in my fist, as I slip into my friend's car and make room for a girl I find to be a little less of a stranger, and a lot more genuine. She hunkers down on my thigh and leans sideways into my chest. I put an arm around her because I feel obligated to do something to keep her from flying through this windshield, but I note how her eyes never leave Jake's presence as we rush back to campus. It's pretty clear she really likes him, despite being liberal with her flirting. I hope he doesn't break her heart.

CHAPTER *Six*

It's cold enough outside that I can hear the announcers at the high school football field. Their voices don't carry far enough to be clearly audible, but when they shrill with excitement, joined by a roaring crowd, I can tell when our team is doing well.

Jake has quit asking me to go to the games. I usually make it to at least one football game every season, and this year I got it out of the way early with our home opener. It's the crowds that get to me, mostly. Besides, I need to save up my inner super strength for basketball season so I can watch Jake play. And since tomorrow's my birthday, I don't think forcing me out of my comfort zone is something he could justify.

Sounds like I missed a good one tonight. From my last count of the distant blare of trumpets and pounding snares and base drums, we've scored four times this hour. Of course, there aren't any sounds for the opponent's side, so it could be a high-scoring game on both sides. We aren't exactly known for our defense—or for football, period.

I've had the garage open the entire first half. Once again, the street is quiet and peaceful. Other than a few tiny spray paint marks the police left on the roadway, there isn't a single sign of the full-blown media feeding frenzy at the end of my driveway. That doesn't mean things are back to normal, though; far from it. The Trombley house is dark, minus the dim glow of the single-bulb porch light next to their front door. Morgan's SUV is pulled all the way up to the closed garage. So is the Volkswagen. There is no spirit paint to celebrate the exciting game happening down the road. No need for any of that since Eleanor isn't on the sidelines. I've been waiting for her to at least come to her window or step outside. Maybe I'm naïve but I have this sense that she misses it, her life from *before.* Perhaps that's exactly why she hasn't come outside.

My hands are buried in the front pocket of my hoodie as I lean against the back of the Bronco and stare across the street, drumming up the nerve to cross it and ring the Trombley bell. The mere thought of it brings acid up my esophagus. One hand grips the hair tie Gemma gave me, the other clutches the six twenties from Grandpa Hank. My mom is home, so her car is mine to take if I want it. The parts shop is open for another hour, so I could make it there in time and maybe even figure out how to install an alternator. I hope it's basically the opposite of how it's removed, but I'm not counting on anything being easy with this thing.

Deciding I owe it to Gemma to deliver her gift—*and maybe owe it to myself to prove I'm not afraid of being Eleanor Trombley's friend*—I push off from the bumper and take several long strides down my driveway. I'll use the parts store closing soon as an excuse if I feel trapped. I'll just make a delivery if her mom or dad answer. I'll find the right words; I'll be kind and they'll think I'm a good friend. So will Eleanor.

And then my finger is on the doorbell and all of those positive affirmations I filled my head with drop to the ground and wither away, probably into the roots of the dead hedge that lines their front walkway.

I think about hooking the hair band on their doorknob, but my inner debate takes way too long and the iron knob I'm staring at twists from someone else's doing on the other side of the door. Met with Mr. Trombley's pale face and sunken eyes, I find myself only able to stare back with my mouth hung open.

This is awful.

"You're here for Eleanor, right?" His voice is raspy as if he just rolled off some barstool after a serious whiskey and cigar bender. That rawness is from emotion, though. I recognize it, and thanks to my grandpa, I'm also able to sniff out the whiskey.

I must have nodded in response, though I can't feel my face and I don't recall reacting. Regardless, Mr. Trombley's large hand wraps around the edge of the door as he leans behind it and shouts, "Elle! You have company!"

I mull over uttering an apology, even going so far as to mouth the word *sorry* before he pulls the door wider and meets my panicked gaze again.

"She'll be right here," he says, monotone and lifeless. He immediately leaves the space, turning and sliding his feet along their wooden floor. His slippers are too small for his feet, his socked heels hanging off the back. I wonder if he wore those shoes to the school this morning and I just didn't notice.

I take a step back, not wanting to hover at the entry while I wait. I feel like an intruder, breaking up their quiet moment to grieve. The buzz of television is almost always on in my house. My grandpa either has the news on or one of those home improvement shows. He likes to watch the couples fight, he says. The Trombley house is stiflingly silent. It's the kind of quiet one can practically taste, thick and acidic, and the pull into this darkness is strong. Even as I stand here forcing my legs to step back more, I lean in, curious and perhaps wanting to feel what they feel so I can understand. Maybe I *do* understand.

The quiet is rich enough that I can hear Eleanor's feet pad down the wood-planked stairs inside. The warning sound helps me brace myself for making eye contact, not that I'm ever fully prepared to meet her gaze head-on. Where her dad's eyes were dark and lost, hers are clear. She's pulled herself closer to the sun, even more than the last time we talked, the night we planned a camping trip that will never come to fruition.

"Let's go to your house," she says, pulling the door closed behind her. She passes me on the porch steps and pulls her jacket on as she makes her way down the walkway toward the street.

A little stunned, I look back at the shut door behind me, expecting her father to come storming through it at any minute, fists in the air as he yells, "Come back here, young lady!" I count to three, but the door doesn't budge.

"You comin'?"

I turn back to find Eleanor waiting in the middle of our street, arms wrapped around her mid-section to stave off the growing chill. Drums thump in the backdrop from the football game she should be cheering at. She ignores them, but they must be scratching at her.

"Yeah, sorry." I don't know exactly why I apologize; it just seems right.

I jog the few steps it takes to catch up to her then mimic her closed-off position, stuffing my hands in my hoodie pocket again. In that brief blip of time I'd forgotten the entire reason I came to see her in the first place. I remember the second my hand finds the satin fabric. I'm less sure about giving it to her, though. Maybe I'm assuming too many things and projecting onto her, but I don't think the football game is what she wants to be reminded of. Instead, I grip the cash from my grandfather and wad it in my palm, pulling my fist out to show it off as I walk sideways to look her more in the eyes on our march up my driveway.

"Wanna come with me to buy an alternator?" This has to be the absolute smoothest line ever uttered by a teenaged boy to a girl.

An amused smile pulls up the side of her mouth as her eyes zero in on my fistful of cash.

"I would love to go buy an alternator with you, Jonah." She isn't even kidding a little bit.

"Yeah?" My reply is mixed with a breathy laugh. I follow it up with, "Cool," realizing that having said that I seem anything but cool. Rather than apologizing again, though, I shove the money into my pocket and fish out my mom's set of keys.

Eleanor heads into my garage, reaching the passenger door of the Bronco when it dawns on her.

"Duh," she laughs out. "Guess that's probably why we're going to get an alternator, huh?"

"Among many other parts in my future," I add.

Our eyes meet for a long second above our matching smiles.

"It's a really nice Chevy Malibu. I think you'll find the lumbar support to be quite nice." I gesture toward my mom's car parked behind the Bronco. Our garage isn't clean enough to handle two vehicles inside it, which means I have a few weeks to get this mess under control unless I want to spend the winter scraping ice off her windshield.

"I do like a good massage chair in a vehicle," Eleanor says, carrying on my joke.

I pull the door open for her and flash a guilty smile that I speak through.

"I didn't say massage chair. This ain't a Lexus."

My self-effacing humor draws another laugh out of her as she drops into the seat and pulls her safety belt over her chest. She wriggles into the faux leather that still has an ink stain on it from a major backpack explosion I had in eighth grade.

"Bring on the massage," she demands, clearly joking.

I give her side eyes.

"I never promised—"

"I demand a massage," she cuts in, reaching out for her door and shooing me out of the way so she can close it. She continues to shuffle in her seat as if something magical is about to begin, and I look to the ground, shaking my head while I laugh my way to the driver's side.

"You might be crazy," I say as I get in.

She shrugs it off with a smile, leaning forward and patting her hands on the dash as I turn the ignition. She takes control of the radio the moment it's on, tuning in a country station I doubt has ever played through these speakers. I'm in awe at the difference between her from her dad, and from the version that stumbled into my garage a week ago.

I'm also aware that she lives in a bubble, riding a distraction and pretending life is normal. She's missing out on major rites of passage because her family has been rocked to its core. I may not have been close with my dad in a typical way, but I still feel every ounce of the void now that he's gone. Addy's void is never far from being felt. Hers just comes with the added pain of hope.

"You like country music?" We've driven a full block with her singing along to the current song before she asks this.

"It's all right, I guess." I lie for her benefit, but to be fair, I've never really given country a chance. It's not a big Chicago sound, and most of the things I listen to are in the top billboard charts. If it's on the pop station, I've heard it.

"You're missing out. I'm going to school you in the art of country music, Jonah Wydner. Prepare yourself." She leans into the center again and turns the volume up a little more. I maybe recognize this song from commercials, or maybe from the background on *Monday Night Football.* It's upbeat, and not at all the stereotype I often associate with the genre of dead dogs and pickup trucks with flat tires. What intrigues me more, though, is the way Eleanor sounds singing along with it. There's a slight lilt in the way the lyrics fly from her lips. It's oddly, pleasurably, heartbreaking. I glance and catch her smiling back at me through the verse.

"You ever do choir or anything like that?" I ask. My voice shakes a little with nerves this time, and I mask it with a cough. This entire scenario is surreal and I'm starting to feel it. I also realize her parents have no idea where she is, where she went. Her car is at home, but she is not. They have to be worried. *Is she worried they're worried?* I keep all of those thoughts and questions inside to protect the bubble, but they bounce around my brain like a pinball.

"I don't have the time. Cheer takes up most of my afternoons and I do student council stuff in the mornings. At least, I did." Her eyes flit down to her lap then move to stare out her window. I'd forgotten she was on student council too. I'm wondering if that's something they let her participate in from home, at least to keep it on her college resume.

"I guess it's a pretty full slate, huh?"

"Yeah," she sighs out. Reality seems to be pushing in on her all of a sudden. It makes her shoulders drop, and she's no longer singing with the radio. Thankfully, we're a block from the auto parts shop.

"I mean, I was going to sign up for advanced shop class, but my schedule is just so—" I let go of the wheel briefly to hold my palms outstretched to signal something exaggeratingly big. It's a clever enough joke to draw Eleanor's attention back to the inside of the car, to me, and it gains me a fleeting smile. "Where would I fit welding metal and running circular saws in amongst all this studying and writing unnecessary essays for extra credit I don't need."

"Maybe you can give some of that extra credit to Jake," she adds.

My lips form a puckered smile and I shrug one shoulder.

"It wouldn't be enough to help him." Poor Jake is going to have to be the butt of this joke. I'm sure his ego will be fine. Besides, he's passing his classes, and that really is thanks to me.

We arrive at Toby's Auto Parts before another bout of quiet has a chance to settle in and take over Eleanor's fragile spirit. I rush around to her side so I can be a gentleman before she opens her door, but she waves me off, insisting she can handle opening a door on her own. I doubt this will stop me from trying to impress her with simple little gestures. I'm still blown away that we're breathing the same air right now.

My nerves take over my face as soon as we walk into the store as I realize I have no idea where to look for what I need. The only thing I've ever purchased from Toby's are windshield wipers and wiper fluid. Those things are on an end cap, and I had to get help picking out the right wipers. I'm about to embarrass myself, badly.

Thankfully, Eleanor peels off from me to wander different aisles while I walk up and down sections that *seem* they might have engine parts out and ready to take. It only takes a trip down two of those aisles for me to swallow the hard truth—I am going to have to ask someone for help. Taking advantage of still being alone, I step up to the service counter and lean over as far as I can without lifting my feet off the floor in an effort to gain the attention of the guys in the back. It takes two coughs for someone to rear back in a chair and make eye contact with me, and the man who looks like he could be my grandfather's brother—*I guess that means my great-uncle*—sidles toward me, hitching his pants up on either side as he walks.

"How can I help you?" He pulls the reading glasses from atop his head and slides them up the bridge of his nose before typing on his computer.

"I need an alternator." My voice cracks with my request, and things get a little fuzzy in my periphery. The flop sweats are hitting hard, and underneath the counter, my knee is bobbing like a meth addict. This, of course, is when Eleanor joins me.

"For what?" The man—whose name is Dale, which I read on his shirt—dips his chin to peer at me over his glasses. The slight smirk that joins his query is a pretty clear signal that he knows I'm clueless. The glance to my left, toward Eleanor, that follows, is an even clearer sign that he sees I'm here with a girl who is *way* out of my league. And then finally, the way his eyes, full of pity, flitter back to me and land on my face, tells me he probably won't be as helpful as I need him to be in terms of making me sound like I know what I'm doing.

"Seventy-two Ford Bronco." My hand squeezes the cash in my pocket while visions of my five-year-old self slapping cash haphazardly on the counter for candy run through my mind. The grumbled response I get from Dale is not reassuring. Neither is the way he shifts his weight and pulls his glasses down more.

I swallow.

"One-twenty? One-forty? Preference?"

I swallow again. My mouth is dry. So. Very. Dry.

"I—"

I'm interrupted with the swift smack of Dale's fat palm on the worn laminate counter top in front of me. It startles both Eleanor and me back a step, and my mouth snaps shut while my eyes widen.

"Hey, you Hank's grandson?"

Thank you, sweet baby Jesus!

"I am," I answer, eager that maybe I'm going to be spared more embarrassment.

"Jonah, right?" He shakes his finger at me, backing up and peering down at some mystical space beneath his computer and register.

I nod.

"That's me."

"Ah, yeah. Here it is." Dale's enormous body disappears behind the counter as he crouches and when he stands, he slides a box toward me with a yellow sticky note slapped on the top and HANK scribbled on it in fat marker.

"No charge. And tell that goddamn card hustling grandfather of yours that we're square now, and I plan on raking him over the coals next week." His hands cup the sides of the box and hold it just tight enough that when I reach to take it, it doesn't move. He doesn't let go until our eyes meet and I nod to agree to his demand.

"Yes, sir."

Box tucked under my arm, I stride out of the store a little buzzed by what just happened. I'm frightened and a little insulted. I'm also lucky I got the part I needed without breaking down completely and begging for Dale's help or running back home to take photos and bringing in my dad's weird-ass notebook.

Unable to help myself, I head for Eleanor's door first, pulling it open and getting a playful chastising glare from her as I do.

"I'm fully aware you can open your own doors, but I think if I didn't do this with Dale staring at me out that window he'd come out here and punch me in the nose." I'm only half joking.

Eleanor's crooked smile deepens and she nods, accepting my gesture and getting in the car.

"You're probably right. I should tell him I was promised a massage chair!"

"I never said—" She pulls the door closed, cutting me off again.

My face tingles from the stupid grin my lips form. In a million years, I never would have imagined I could be more attracted to Eleanor Trombley. Every word that leaves her mouth proves that wrong. Every. Single. Word.

During our drive home, I explain to Eleanor the history

of how my grandfather came to live with us and his regular poker games in our garage. It all comes down to cost-savings for all of us, and even though they bicker, my mom and he love each other like blood relatives. I realize while I talk that he skipped having his regular game yesterday, and I'm not sure whether it had to do with the Bronco's arrival or Eleanor's sister going missing. Grandpa Hank's friends are all like Dale, blunt and a bit pushy. He was maybe sparing the sweet girl he let into the garage from their probing questions.

"How come Dale didn't recognize you right away?" she asks as I pull into my driveway. I shift into park and kill the engine, riffling through the faces I've seen join my grandpa's games and give up.

"I avoid the man cave when they come over. I maybe would recognize one or two of his buddies. I can only imagine the stories my grandpa has told them about me!" I laugh at the thought as we get out of the car. I'm not the manly kind of grandson a war vet brags about to his friends, I'm sure. But I guess my dad wasn't that stereotype either, and Grandpa Hank would never poke fun of my dad.

"Think they'd let us play sometime?"

I stop in my tracks a few paces ahead of her at her suggestion.

"Dear God!" It's the only response that makes sense. It makes Eleanor laugh harder than she ever has in front of me.

"Jonah! Don't be such a chicken. I'm actually pretty good, you know? I bet I could get you another free alternator from Dale." She taps the box in my hands with her perfectly manicured fingernails.

My mouth curls, mostly because this feels flirtatious

and I feel dumbstruck. "I kinda hope the alternator goes right on the first shot," I say.

She waggles her head side to side then peers up at the dark sky, a thin screen of clouds covering most of the stars.

"You know what I mean. I'm gonna ask your grandpa if I can join in on the fun, next time I see him."

My stomach tightens because I am pretty sure she's not kidding. I can already hear the laugh he's going to belt out until he realizes she's serious. I run a palm over my face to regain feeling in it and eventually just shrug an *okay.*

I open my garage and set the new part on the bumper of the Bronco. The distant sounds from the football game break through the quiet air, and when I turn to face Eleanor, I catch a slight grin on her face as she tilts her head to listen more closely.

"Hey, I almost forgot something," I say, not completely sure it's the right time for this. I reach into the front of my sweatshirt and clutch the hair tie from Gemma. I hold it out in an open palm as I take a few timid steps closer to where Eleanor stands in the middle of my driveway. I'm guarded, prepared for her to sour at seeing a reminder of her earlier life. I'm thankful when she doesn't.

Her lip ticks up and she takes the material from my hand, our palms grazing slightly on the exchange. I curl my fingers up the moment my hand is empty and stuff it into the depths of my front pocket.

"Gemma made these," she explains. I pretend I don't already know.

"She asked me to give it to you," I say.

"It's a stupid tradition, but she makes them every year before we get ready to compete for cheer." She stretches the tie around her hand, flexing it with her fingers a few times before sliding the hood away from her head with her other hand.

The strangest grin spreads on her face as she backs away a few steps while twisting her hair up on top of her head with the new tie. She starts to clap with cupped palms and bends her knees before popping them into a locked position as she begins to cheer. It would seem weird if I didn't understand exactly what it was all about. About a week after my dad was gone, I spent an entire night working my way through every difficult math problem in my SAT study guide. I'd already taken the test and scored fine, but in that moment, I was determined to sign up and take it again, to get a perfect math score just like he had. The feeling passed and I never took the test again.

"We'll fight 'til the end! That's what makes Badger pride! Let's go! Fight! Win, win, win!" Her commands are loud and metered, marked by stiff arms in the air, regular claps and a jump at the end that brings both of her legs straight out to either side, a feat that I normally find amazing but am in near disbelief at seeing pulled off in jeans.

"Go Badgers!" I shout, probably the only time I have ever shown school spirit like that.

"Yeah!" She nods, clapping again. She goes through a few more various jumps then pulls her arms in close to her chest and bends her knees before launching herself backward into a full tuck, her arms never wavering and her feet sticking to the ground in the exact same spot they left.

She's so good. This is her thing. Like math is my thing.

"You aren't going back at all?" The question comes out before I have time to weigh the consequences of asking.

Eleanor doesn't react immediately, and the smile from

her one-woman cheer is still in place, but it's rigid and locked there to keep the acid brewing beneath it inside.

"I don't know," she says, a tinge of sadness touching the corners of the smile.

She spins in place with her head tilted back, eyes to the sky. Her arms outstretched, her fingers flex wide then grip into fists before coming in and resting over her eyes. That's when the maniacal laughter morphs into sobs. A seal has been broken, and I maybe broke it.

It would have done so eventually, but goddamn it, Jonah, did you have to be the one?

"El—"

Her hand jets toward me, an open palm begs me to stop. I snap my mouth shut accordingly and rock back on my feet, pushing my fists even deeper into my front pockets because I don't know what to do. I want to help, but that's exactly what she *doesn't* want. And maybe this is why she spends time with me. I'm not a reminder of anything from before. I'm neutral, familiar enough to carry on. Harmless.

As if on cue, the echo of the high school crowd cheering breaks into our space and pulls Eleanor's attention in their direction. Her hands drop to her sides, fingers unfurling until they hang limp. I feel utterly helpless in comforting her and my chest squeezes because of it.

"Do you think we won?" Her question comes out with a sad, breathy laugh.

"Nah," I respond. "We are probably cheering because the bloodbath is over."

She laughs a little harder at my sarcastic response. Clueless to what I'm doing, I clap like she was a minute ago. She spins slowly, eyes drawn in with that expression that says "What the *f* are you doing, Jonah?" But she's not frowning, and that's all I need to keep going.

"We tried really hard—"

I clap and bend my knees.

"We lost the game—"

I do the same movement, and the ridiculousness of it makes her lips puff out an uncontrollable "Ha!"

"Badger Pride is not enough! It turns out, we aren't very good . . ."

I'm fully committed to this now, and I attempt some sort of jump to match hers, which she reacts to by placing both palms on her own cheeks as she mouths, *Oh, my God.*

"But that's okay because people will still pay ten bucks every week to watch us be decent, okay, maybe kinda bad . . ."

I'm caught up in my own search for snarky rhymes when Eleanor jumps forward and stomps her feet right in front of mine. I freeze mid-clap as she takes over.

"And we'll still talk about going pro one day, even though we've won four games—ever." She nods to me as if I should know the next verse. I shake my head and offer another clap and jump that makes her smile grow.

"But maybe come back next month and watch our basketball team. They are better. A little," I ramble out. Eleanor nods with wide eyes and a grin, mouthing, *Yes!*

Without warning, her hands reach for mine, placing them on her hips. For some reason, the first thing I notice is the feel of the denim belt loops on her jeans. I'm sure my mouth is open wide like a fool, but Eleanor snaps me to attention by leaning in and whisper-shouting, "Ready?"

"No." I chuckle.

"We've got this," she says, nodding at me until I nod

back. It's a big fat lie because I don't even know what I'm nodding about.

Her knees unlock, and I bend mine in sync as she counts backward from "Three, two . . . one!"

With some strange innate instinct, my hands grip tight at her sides as she pushes up from the ground and I lift her up to the sky. Her knees move to my shoulders and I lock my arms around her legs as her entire weight is braced on my not very macho frame.

I glance up, praying to myself not to drop her, and the bottom of her zip-up hoodie tickles my nose and chin. It's difficult to see from my vantage point, plus I'm virtually having a heart attack while standing here, but I'm pretty sure her arms are V-shaped above her head like a superhero ready to jet off into the sky. Her hair tie falls loose as her chin drops to her chest and it lands in the tight space between her body and mine as we make eye contact and she signals with a short nod for me to let her down.

The feel of her body sliding down mine as my arms loosen just enough for her weight to return to earth sears through my chest, leaving a scar behind as I make mental notes of every single everything—the way her jacket lifts and shirt rolls up enough on her descent to reveal her belly, the exact route her hands take as they move from the sides of my neck to my shoulders as she braces herself, the curve of her back and the way my hands seem to know exactly where they fit.

But mostly, it's this moment we're in together, blue eyes to green, inches apart, a quiet that is achingly uncomfortable. It doesn't last nearly as long as I want it to, and when she breaks free, cold air sweeps into the growing space between us much too fast. My hands find their way back into my pockets and hers ball at her sides before slowly banging against her hips with what I hope isn't regret.

I bend down and pick up the hair tie that had fallen to the ground.

"Here," I say, tossing it to her. We're too far apart for a direct handoff.

"Thanks," she says, holding it up before sliding it onto her wrist. Her hair spirals into wild waves around her with the slight breeze. She's beautiful like this, and if I were another guy and this were another time and place, I would tell her that. Instead, I just stare at her like a foolish boy with a foolish crush and add this to my log of favorite Eleanor Trombley moments.

"So when does the alternator get installed?" She tilts her head toward the garage.

"Oh, uhm." I twist where I stand and glare at the box still resting on the Bronco's bumper, as if I have to think about it that hard. "Tomorrow, I guess. Jake's supposed to come over around two. My mom's making burgers for my birthday, so maybe three?"

I turn back to her and am relieved that she's staring at the box too. That damn alternator is like our reset button, letting us both pretend there wasn't a quiet weirdness ever, at all.

"Do I get to come over for birthday burgers?"

Internally chastising myself for not immediately inviting her, I fumble out a quick, "Oh, I mean, *yeah!* If you want, that would be cool. But, don't feel like you have to come, if you don't—"

"Burgers at two, then?" she interjects, halting me from digging a deeper hole, a sideways hole that would probably only lead to *another* hole. I glance up from the ground I've been staring at to find her head tilted to the side, bottom lip held between her teeth and eyes wide in expectation. *She wants to come.*

"Yeah, burgers at two," I say.

"Hey, maybe I can talk to your grandpa about getting in on that poker game?" She starts to walk backward, a smirk on her lips that makes it little hard to tell whether she's being serious or not. Drums beat in the distance, and I know from experience that the glow of lights over the rooftops at the end of our street will dim in minutes. The game is done.

"My garage is your garage," I say, gnashing my back teeth because I don't want her to see me wince at my own lameness.

"I mean, if that were the case, you think you'd give me your code," she says.

"It's seven," I say. I can tell by her quick laugh that she thinks I'm joking. "No, seriously. I put that keypad in for my mom and messed up the programming, so if you just hit seven a bunch of times, eventually it will open."

"Wow. Seems safe," she teases.

Her feet hit the end of my driveway and she stops backing away, giving me hope that maybe she'll walk forward and decide to stick around a little longer. I'd stand out here and make self-deprecating jokes until morning if she let me.

"So, two?"

I stare at her, tempted to correct her that the garage is seven, but I know what she means. She means burger time.

"Sorry, yeah. Two," I confirm before scrambling for more words. "I mean, you can come earlier, too. If you want. My mom works at the brake shop in Old Town in the morning and my grandpa and I are usually up early enough to have breakfast with her before she leaves."

"What *kind* of breakfast?" Her head cocks to the right. *She's sincerely considering joining us.*

"What's your favorite?" I swear to myself that if I have to ride my bike for miles to get actual quality breakfast for Eleanor in the morning, I will.

Miles. On a BMX.

"I make the best pancakes in the entire world," she pronounces.

"Well that's weird," I reply. *I'm about to lie.* "I've been told *I* make the best pancakes in the entire world."

I hold her gaze in a challenge, the real Jonah trapped inside me, screaming that I'm getting us in over our head because I can barely time microwaveable dinners right.

"Oh, Jonah," she practically sings while pointing a finger at me briefly with a *tsk*. "I really hate that someone's been lying to you. Guess I'll see you at seven, then. I'll bring my best recipe and you try your best with yours. Grandpa Hank can be the judge."

"Deal." I nod.

Shit.

My knee bobs with nerves, and I swear she notices before she turns and heads into the dark house across the street. I remain in the garage for twenty minutes with my mom's keys in my hand, staring at Eleanor's window and waiting for any sign that she's staring back. When I'm pretty sure she isn't, I shut the garage behind me with the usual series of sevens and hop into my mom's car to hit the grocery store for pancake mix before it closes.

Some recipe.

CHAPTER Seven

I'm not sure where I got that dose of swagger last night, but it was incredibly fleeting. My alarm went off at six, and I've been riffling through various cooking blogs for the last thirty minutes in search of easy tricks and tips to "take your boring pancakes up a notch." Too bad I don't have wild blueberries at my disposal, or farm-fresh hand-churned butter, or nutmeg. *What is nutmeg?* I have cinnamon, and that's going to have to do.

On top of feeling out of my element in the kitchen, I'm also anxious about what I'm wearing, and that my hair is combed. Is it *too* combed? Am I trying too hard? Grandpa's heavy steps are getting closer, which means he's going to find out that Eleanor's coming over, and he's going to tell Mom, and—

"Shit!" I jerk my hand from the griddle and suck on the side of my pinky finger that grazed it. That thing heats up fast!

"What, you couldn't wait for your birthday breakfast so you decided to get started without me?" Grandpa follows up his curious question with a round of coughing. When he regains his breath, he reaches for the fridge handle, but I slap it closed.

"No eggs today," I announce. I'm maybe a little abrupt. I'm nervous, but also, Eleanor cannot witness the egg situation.

"Well *par-don me*!" He holds open palms and waggles them to play up how offended he is but quickly turns his attention to making coffee.

"Sorry, I'm just . . . I'm not sure what I'm doing, and well . . . Eleanor's coming over."

"Eleanor's coming over?" My mom's voice echoes my words and my eyes flutter closed as I stand at the sink running cold water over what I feel may be a blister forming.

"Ah, so that's why you're wearing the new shirt," Grandpa Hank teases.

"It's not new," I retort. That's a lie, sorta. I bought this over the summer but I just haven't worn it yet.

"So is it the cool thing now to keep your tags hanging from the collar?" I feel a slight tug on the fabric hugging the back of my neck. "Relax, I got it."

The sound of the kitchen drawer sliding open is followed by my Grandpa's throat clearing. I glance to my side in time to see him unfolding his reading glasses from his pocket and sliding them on his face as he comes at me with scissors in the other hand. At this rate, I won't be shocked if somehow he slices off a chunk of my hair while he's at it.

With a quick snip my tag is gone, and at least one problem is solved. There are still plenty to choose from, though, so when my mom questions what I'm doing with her mixing cups and the glass bowl and the cinnamon, I freeze up and take a few steps back from it all.

"I have no idea how to make pancakes. I got this mix because it says 'easy' on the box, but I'm worried it's boring, so—"

"So you figured you'd add cinnamon. Ah, I got it. Not bad, actually. Let's see." Now both my grandpa and my mom are inspecting my work with their glasses on. My mom reads the back of the box for the mix I bought and corrects some of the amounts I've poured. A quick check of the clock on the microwave sends a new round of panic-induced nausea through my system at the realization that I only have ten minutes until Eleanor arrives.

"Are you supposed to wear your shirts in that order?" A new critique fires in from Gramps.

"Huh?" I shift my focus from my mom at the counter to my grandpa on my other side. He tugs on the gray thermal shirt I'm wearing under my black short-sleeved button down. It's one of those fifties-style gas station replica shirts. I always wanted one but didn't think I was the kind of guy who could pull them off. My grandpa isn't helping to cure me of that doubt, but it's too late to run upstairs and change.

"That's the look," I grunt back with a huff, and my frustration amuses both of them. "You guys are not helping!"

"Aww, birthday boy is upset," my mom teases, putting on her baby voice as she winks at my grandpa.

I decide then to just give up and I plop down in a chair at the opposite end of the table, my pinky finger marred by a skin bubble and my mom taking over work on the pancakes I confidently bragged about making last night. At this point, I should just welcome my grandpa's runny eggs.

The buzz of at our door is the nail in my coffin, and I

contemplate remaining glued to my chair and letting my mom or Grandpa Hank let Eleanor in. But the fear of them setting up an even worse scene than the one she's going to get is enough to motivate me to stand and move to the door, cutting my mom off with a quick, "I got it."

At least it smells good in here. That's the last thought I have before I open the door to find a downright gleeful Eleanor Trombley waiting on the other side. She's holding her own portable griddle in both hands and a variety of plastic containers are balanced on top, each containing actual ingredients. No mix in sight. Her hair is twisted into sloppy ponytails on either side of her head, and she's wearing a huge yellow sweatshirt that's several sizes too big so it fits her more like a dress over her black leggings and fuzzy black boots.

"It smells amazing in here!" she announces upon entry. I exhale the breath I've been holding because at least I got the aroma right.

"Here, let me get that," I say, taking the griddle from her.

"Thanks," she says, a closed-mouth grin following up. Before I close the door after her entry, I survey the house she just came from. Nothing has changed from the way it's looked over there for the past few days. The windows are all still drawn shut, cars unmoved, and everything about the house feels either sleepy or vacant. Yet somehow, Eleanor just walked out that front door wearing sunshine yellow, and nobody over there seems to care enough to object.

"Welcome, Eleanor. Thanks for joining us." My mom clearly has the pancake situation handled; I see three cakes already going on our griddle behind her. She also found the perfect tone and words to welcome Eleanor. I think the

Trombley girls have been in this house twice in my lifetime, and both instances were while selling us Girl Scout cookies. Eleanor seems at ease in here, though, as if she's been coming over here to hang out for years. It's odd but also comforting. I like it—her wanting to come here—even if I don't fully understand it.

I set her griddle down next to spot where my fraudulent pancakes are sizzling and she moves in to begin sorting out her ingredients.

"Well, a girl can't back down from a full-on pancake challenge, can she?" she says over her shoulder.

My mom's eyes scan to meet mine behind Eleanor's back and I mouth *Please* while holding up prayer hands.

"I see, well, you look pretty serious," my mom says, poking at a box of something Eleanor has just sat on the counter. "Jonah, you may be outmatched."

I blow out hard and laugh.

"I'm really all talk anyhow," I admit, sort of.

"*Mmm*, yes, you are," my mom says as she passes me and presses a soft hand to my cheek.

Too hungry to wait, Grandpa Hank takes the three cakes my mom finished making for himself, and I finish up the batter, pouring out two more while Eleanor hums next to me as she eyes the levels of everything she measures.

"Where'd you learn all this?" I tilt my head toward her mixing bowl.

"Oh, culinary. At school. Did you take it?" she asks.

I shake my head.

"I mean, if I'm too busy for shop class . . ."

Her head shakes with a soft laugh at my joke.

"Right. Well, you missed out," she says, dotting my nose with the tip of her finger. I watch it come at me and get cross-eyed. "Miss Dupont was a pastry chef in New

Orleans before she moved here, so we made *a lot* of cookies and croissants."

"That sounds delicious," my mom says, settling into one of the chairs at the table behind us.

"But I can solve for the derivative, and if I had not doubled up on advanced college math classes, where would you be?" I say to my mom, holding my palms out to my sides in jest.

"I suppose I'd have to live . . . *derivativeless*," she punches back.

Because Grandpa Hank loves it when Mom goes after me instead of him, he lets out a full-mouthed belly laugh.

"Shut up and eat your pancakes, old man," I fire back.

With his plate only half finished, he slides it away from him and takes a napkin to his mouth.

"I think I'll hold out for the superior pancakes, if you don't mind," he says, winking at Eleanor, who stirs things in her bowl as she takes in our regular morning routine.

"Hey, *I* made those pancakes!" my mom announces, play-slapping Grandpa on the arm as she completely blows my cover.

"Jonah!" I get a similar arm slap from Eleanor, leaving me with no choice but to come completely clean.

"Fine! I'm a fraud! Oh, my God, it feels so much better to have that out in the open." I sink back into the counter's edge and roll my neck while everyone laughs at my expense.

After a few longs seconds, the kitchen gets quiet again, enough that we all zone out to the whir of Eleanor's mixing. She turns her back to us, probably because we're all staring at her. In my case, my complete attention is focused on how hard I think she must be working to seem normal. It has to be exhausting.

"Are you guys like this every morning?" she asks, finally snapping us out of our silence.

"Oh, every day's a little different, but yeah, for the most part," Grandpa coughs out.

He excuses himself from the table to head to the powder room for his first coughing round of the day. When Eleanor swivels her head to look at me with worry, I shake it off.

"He's okay. I mean, classic chronic respiratory disease for sure, but nothing that seems to keep him from smoking cigars on Thursdays." I shrug with a smile to give her added reassurance. Honestly, though, I don't love how cavalier my grandpa is about his health. I don't think my mom does either, but he's stubborn as hell, so we pick our battles.

Eleanor's first round of cakes are ready in minutes, and Grandpa Hank makes sure he's back to the table in time to take the first few for himself. Eleanor turns her attention back to the griddle to make another round while the three of us dive in and agree through glances that these are, in fact, the best pancakes we have ever eaten.

"Do you cook for your family often, Eleanor?"

I drop my fork at my mom's question. Every conversation topic feels rife with danger. I clear my throat and apologize quietly while I toss my sullied fork in the sink and get myself a new one. I fear my worry about my mother's question is right given the long pause before Eleanor responds, but when she finally does, it doesn't seem as if talking to us about her family is hard for her at all. And she doesn't dance around the hard truth.

"I used to, last year. I've been so busy this year, though, with all of the senior-year stuff." She lifts one shoulder casually as her back remains to us. She flips the cakes over one at a time, this round made up of smaller ones so more fit on the cooking surface. "I actually miss it. I tried making dinner a few times this week. I was just trying to help out, but my parents aren't, well, they aren't so good."

I rejoin my family at the table and meet their heavy gazes.

"We're so very sorry," my mom says.

There it is again. *Sorry.*

"Thank you," Eleanor responds, still keeping her hands busy by sliding the cakes around. "It's been hard. And I can't really talk to them about things because they just aren't . . . good." She nods slowly with her words.

"I bet it's nice having your sister there to help," my mom adds.

Eleanor's laughed response is unexpected and quick.

"I guess. She's taken over making decisions, which is good because I don't know what to say when the police give us updates and offer suggestions. Morgan has always been better at that stuff."

"What stuff?" I ask, biting my tongue the moment I speak. It felt natural, though.

"Oh, like, being in charge, I guess." Eleanor laughs. Scooping up the remaining cakes, she brings the piled flapjacks over to the table and sets them in the middle. My mom stands to get her an extra plate, but Eleanor shakes my mom's offer off.

"Thanks, but I'm not very hungry," she says.

My mom pauses and Grandpa and I immediately look down at our food. No matter how normal Eleanor tries to make us believe things are, she's not strong enough to fake it all away.

"Well . . ." Mom clears her throat and returns to her

seat, catching me with a quick glance as I look up. "Thank you for treating us. And for celebrating Jonah's day."

"I'd give you a card or something but I already bought you a car," Grandpa mumbles. "So happy freaking birthday, kiddo."

His brashness breaks up the building uneasiness, and I relax back into my natural ways a little more.

"I'm pretty sure we already *owned* the Bronco, and to be technical, you didn't buy me any parts yet. I met Dale yesterday, and he says you're even now." I roll my eyes jokingly and glance to my side to make sure Eleanor is amused too. She's smiling.

"You're seriously calling in poker favors for car parts?" My mom glares across the table at my grandpa with her palms flat on the tabletop on either side of her plate. Both Eleanor and I cover our mouths to laugh.

"And you called my poker nights nothing but debauchery. *Pfft*," Grandpa Hank says, waving his hand in dismissal.

My mom glares at him hard until he must feel it because he lifts his gaze to meet her waiting stare and immediately lets out a laugh.

"So how does one get an invite to this poker game," Eleanor slips in. My mom turns her focus to our guest and hangs her mouth open.

"You all are useless. I'm running an underground casino in the garage and you all just . . . let it happen." Mom slices through the air with her hand before standing to take her empty plate to the sink.

"Eleanor, you are welcome here anytime. Thank you for breakfast, and if he doesn't let you sit in on that *boys* club he has in our garage . . ." My mom pauses to emphasize her next words by pointing at my grandpa. "You let me know. I have *ways* of making him understand."

"Ha *ha!*" Grandpa tilts back in his seat to laugh. My mom pauses behind him on her way out the door and leans down to kiss the top of his head before calling him an old fool.

When Jake turned eighteen, his teammates kidnapped him at midnight and took him to a strip club. Me, I lost a pancake showdown and displayed my weird-ass family dynamic in front of the girl who, until lately, I haven't been able to utter a full sentence to. I honestly think I come out ahead.

"I love your family," Eleanor says, leaning toward me and taking my fork off my plate, stealing a taste of my breakfast for herself. I push it closer to her without saying a word, and she finishes every last bite.

CHAPTER *Eight*

Grandpa takes over cleaning up after we all finish eating and mom's off to her weekend job. He says he's doing me a favor for my birthday, but I know better—he's sending me off to spend time with Eleanor on my own. True to form, he adds a waggle of his thick eyebrows when she leaves the kitchen, just to make me sweat.

I sent her up to my room without me to get her away from Grandpa, but now that I'm standing in the hallway watching through the cracked opening of my door while she inspects every element of my room, I regret giving her free rein.

I doubt she'll notice it, but I have a picture of her amid the collage of random things I think are cool that I taped to my wall right next to my night stand. Even more pathetic? It's a picture from last year's yearbook that I photocopied at my mom's office. It's blurry and pixelated, but it's the only photo of her I have. There is no way I will come across as anything other than a sad obsessed puppy dog if she sees that.

My nerves grow as she gets closer to that area of my room. I decide to head off trouble and burst into my room with enough fanfare to bring her attention to me completely.

"Sorry, I was talking to my grandpa for a few minutes," I give as my excuse.

"I was just scoping out your library." She points over her shoulder at the makeshift bookcase I built with cinderblocks and two-by-six boards. Just one more impressive display of how I spend my Friday and Saturday nights.

"Notice the dearth of cooking books on the shelf." My joke earns a quick laugh.

"I was looking at the Bradbury. You have a lot of his," she says, moving closer to the books and running her fingertips across the spines. "I thought Green Town was a real place for the longest time."

She's referencing *Something Wicked This Way Comes*. This little slice of a shared experience sinks into my chest. I smile because of it, mouth stretched wide enough that I can feel the heat on my cheeks, a blush put there because I'm excited.

"I tried to find it once. Seriously, I totally wanted to go to that carnival and investigate." My words come out like those of an excited child, and my mood shifts to being embarrassed. I look down at my feet as I stuff my hands in my pockets and kick at the thick pile of my carpet. I end up in my desk chair, partly to draw her attention this direction, away from her picture, and also to give my nervous body some shelter. It does very little to slow the drumming in my chest, though, especially when Eleanor sits on the end of my bed, folding her legs up to make herself comfortable.

"I would have gone with you. I mean, it would be easier with the Bronco, but we so could have walked there." Her eyes animate as she leans forward and rests her chin in her palms, elbows propped on her legs. I'm puzzled by how one person could be that flexible, but even more, how she can make an expression so dreamy that I'm practically able to see her imagination at work.

I cross my leg and lean back, threading my fingers behind my neck as I spin slowly in the chair.

"Where do you think Green Town would be?" I muse. I try to appear as relaxed as her. The difference between us is I'm completely faking it.

"Definitely south of the city. *Way* south. Somewhere with lots of woods, and really old homes and narrow streets." I can tell by the wondering way she describes her version of a Ray Bradbury setting that she's a legitimate fan and I grin at the ceiling, nerding out.

"You know, he based Green Town on his hometown, which is north and closer to Chicago," I say, showing off my trivia knowledge. I drop my chin and meet her waiting steely eyes that pin me and cause me to shift and look at her sideways with caution.

"Yeah, well he was wrong. That's not how it looks in my head. It looks like woods, and big trees and lots of fog. A suburb, ya know?"

She isn't wrong. That's exactly how I imagine it, too.

"Yeah," I muse, leaning back again, and dropping both feet to the floor as I stretch my body in the chair. "You're right."

"Can I have your phone? Just for a sec." She holds both palms out toward me when I lower my chin to look at her.

"Uh, okay?" I lean to one side and pull my phone from my front pocket and toss it on the bed in front of her. If she asked for my wallet next, I'd probably give her that too. And then my keys, and then she may as well steal my identity.

"Passcode?" She's cradling my phone, thumbs poised to type as I spill out the numbers for my birth date. She must realize it because she laughs and whispers, "Cute" as she unlocks my phone. She could be doing anything right now, and I'm letting her. Of course I am.

After a few seconds of typing she sets the lock screen back on my phone and holds it out for me to take. I give her a squinting stare as I take back my phone, curious what that was all about. Before I can ask, the sound of my bed springs squeaking with her movement draws my focus back to her, and I completely forget about my phone.

"We should really make this trip, Jonah." She's shifted to lay sideways on my bed, her comfort growing as evidenced by my pillow she stuffed under the crook of her neck.

I swallow down the instant lump in my throat and croak out, "Yeah?"

"For sure. I mean, not to Green Town; it's not real. But to the Blue Ridge Mountains, like you said? I looked at pictures online after you mentioned it, and it looks beautiful. I bet you can actually breathe there. *Gah*! What I wouldn't give to just . . . breathe." She rolls to her back, letting her arms flop out at her sides so she covers the expanse of my mattress.

My throat lump is back. It came back fast, and this time it's a little too big to swallow.

"You need water?" I rise but one of the buttons on my shirt snags on a wooden groove from my desk, jerking my shirt and my entire left shoulder down as I stand. I cough out as it chokes me and Eleanor smiles out a soft laugh at my performance. I do my best to regain some balance as I move to my door, hoping like hell my suddenly numb legs don't drop me to my knees in front of her.

"I'm good. Thanks, though," she says, her head falling to the side, flat on my bed . . . *where I sleep.* Her eyes land on me as she tugs on the bands around her hair, and I excuse myself before I see her waves and curls spread out on my blanket.

My feet hit the stairs and only pick up speed with each step until I sound like a cattle stampede heading for my Grandpa. He's settled into his daily paper read at the kitchen table, but thanks to my crash-bang entry, he flattens the paper to the table and meets me with wide eyes and his thick eyebrows pushed up to where his hair probably should be, when he had more of it.

His mouth closes into a wry smile as I pass him by and head straight to the cabinet for a glass. I'm gulping down water a second later.

"What the ever-loving hell, Jonah. Please say you aren't running away from a bug or a spider. That's not going to impress the girl."

I refill my glass for one more round before turning to face him. I've never really had anyone to talk to about these kinds of things. Jake listens in his own way, but he doesn't get what it's like to be me. If he had a girl he was into on his bed, he'd be next to her in seconds, probably seducing her a minute later. But this is Eleanor, and she's special beyond words. She's also not in the kind of place emotionally for anyone to be making moves or whatever.

I lick the moisture from my lips while I think, eventually setting my glass on the table and taking the chair next to my grandpa.

"What do I do?" I stare at him with the most serious expression I can muster, eyebrows up a tick and mouth pulled in tight. He studies me for a few seconds, squinting, and I make sure he knows that I need *real* advice. "I mean it. You know that Eleanor has always been *the* girl. But this is not how I wanted to really get to know her. Nothing is normal about any of this, and I am probably just a convenient friend for her right now. But she's also Eleanor, and honestly . . ."

I breathe out a short laugh and let my head fall into my open palm, arm propped on the table. "I don't care if she's using me for a distraction. I don't care at all because I like spending time with her. But maybe that's selfish? Am I a dick for wanting her to keep coming over here while her family is literally reeling across the street? Am I—"

"Stop it, Jonah." My grandpa wraps his hand around my arm, tugging it gently from under my head so I'm forced to sit up straight and look him in the eyes. He twists to sit sideways in his chair, so I do the same. Leaning toward me, he places a palm on either side of my face.

"If you like spending time with that young lady, then you spend time with her. She wouldn't come to see you if she didn't want to. And her reasons are whatever her reasons are. If you can be a good friend to her when she truly needs one, then maybe when she heals from this crazy business her family is going through, you'll have built a really close connection."

I blink for the first time as he pats his right hand against my cheek then sits back in his chair.

"And it's okay that I think she's beautiful?" My chest burns from uttering such honest words.

My grandpa's mouth tugs high on one side and he laughs softly while giving me a subtle nod.

"A beautiful girl is a beautiful girl, pretty when she's laughing and just as pretty when she's not. There is never anything wrong with admiring God's work, my grandson. Never a thing at all wrong with that. You just remember to respect it too."

He reaches for his paper and shakes it out straight again, shifting in his seat to lean back comfortably. My grandma died about ten years ago. I have vague memories of a funeral, and I have heard stories about her from my mom, mostly about how she was a saint of woman who kept Hank in check with his smoking and gambling and swearing and all other baggage that comes along with an army veteran who also spent years working with the same group of guys for the Chicago Metra downtown.

I rap my knuckles against the table twice then stand, my strength a little renewed. I pause right before I round the corner toward the stairs and look at the top of my grandpa's head as it peeks over the edge of his newspaper. He refuses to adapt to digital news. He likes the feel and the smell of the ink, he says.

"Thanks, Grandpa," I say.

"Don't mention it," he coughs out. "Oh, and Jonah?"

I rock back a step and meet his eyes, the paper bent on one side in his hand.

"If you *do* see a bug in front of that young lady, smash it with a shoe. Don't be a chicken shit like that friend of yours."

I grin.

"I won't, Grandpa. Size elevens right here," I say, lifting my leg and tapping on the toe of my sneaker.

I smile my way back up the stairs, ideas running through my mind of things Eleanor and I can do to pass the time while we wait for Jake to show up and my mom to get back home. We could rent that old movie of the Bradbury book, or maybe surf the Internet for camping sites in the Blue Ridges, or she could try to teach me one of her dances. I'm horrible, so it should make her laugh. I love to see her laugh.

All of my brainstorming gets put on hold when I reenter my room. Eleanor lay just where I left her, only now she's curled up on her side, knees drawn in to her chest. Half of my blanket is pulled around her body as she clutches the edge in a fist against her chest to keep herself wrapped like a taco. Her lips hang open, the bottom one making it look like she's pouting as she takes long, hypnotic breaths.

I tiptoe into my room and close my door until it's only open a crack. I move to my window and draw my shutters closed one section at a time, pausing before completely closing the last set to peer over at the Trombley place. Another car is parked in the driveway next to Morgan's. It's a Mercedes, an expensive-looking one. Lawyer maybe? I close off my view and glance at the sleeping beauty over my shoulder. I wonder when she last slept peacefully. I wonder if she's sleeping peacefully now.

Scanning my room, I search for something to occupy my time, landing on my copy of *Something Wicked This Way Comes*. It's askew from where Eleanor left it on the shelf. Taking it in my hand, I sink down to the carpet and crawl in slow motion toward the bed, hating that my knees pop when I move. Eleanor doesn't seem to wake, so I lean my back against the side of my bed and cross my legs out in front of me. Her soft breath sighs just to the right of me, and before I crack open my book, I allow myself the privilege of staring at her this close. Her lashes are gold, like her hair, and there's a trail of freckles that spans from one cheek to the other, crossing over her nose. It's like God sprinkled her with cinnamon, my one and only pancake ingredient. I wish I could cover her better, or give her another pillow. But any movement might pull her out of whatever dream she's managed to find, and in her sleep, she seems to be smiling.

I let her be and pull my phone from my pocket, switching on the flashlight so it's just bright enough for me to read. I balance it against my chest and bring my knees up to lay the book flat and open against my thighs. And while sweet dreams hopefully carry on behind me, I dive into one of my favorite fictional nightmares.

CHAPTER Nine

Eleanor sleeps right through the hamburger festivities. I made sure she could. I read the entire length of my book over four hours sitting as still as possible so as not to disturb her. I may not be able to look to my left for the next couple days thanks to the awesome crick in my neck, but it was worth it.

In total, she slept a good nine hours. Jake ended up bringing Gemma with him for my non-eventful eighteenth birthday party, and she took a few trips up to my room to look in on Eleanor while we ate. I've been dodging the probing stare of my best friend most of the day, but now that we're alone under the hood of my Bronco, it's impossible to avoid the question I've been anticipating.

"Elle's been coming here a lot." This is Jake's way of testing the waters, seeing if I have some exciting revelation to spill. I don't know how it is with girls, but I know the idea of girl talk, and this, this is the guy equivalent of that —*Jake style*. He wants to know if we're hooking up, doing shit, and not just kissing or whatever. I know it's disrespectful as hell, but he doesn't mean to be. His brain only has so many modes to shift to, and emotional support doesn't fit with his logic.

"Yeah, she's been over a few times." I keep my eyes fixed on the wrench I'm making careful quarter turns with on a bolt I'm not sure holds a major purpose.

"Like, she really came over this morning, huh?" He's a foot away and if I wanted to, I could knock out his teeth with a quick jab from my right elbow. I could pretend the wrench slipped.

"She really did. I mean, you saw her, right? Not a hologram." He can't see the face I'm making, but I'm pretty sure my sarcasm-drenched response painted a thorough picture.

"And she slept in your bed. *All day.* And you . . . you read?"

I stop turning the tool and close my eyes as I let out a deep sigh. I'm going to do this just once and if I have to do it again, I'm going to threaten to stop tutoring his ass.

"Yes, Jake. Eleanor Trombley came to my house to have pancakes with my family and then slept the rest of the entire day in my room, and I sat there and let her." I stand and turn to face my friend as I flatten the wrench under my palm on the edge of the truck. His smirk is annoying, but the longer I stare the less prominent it is in his suspicious expression.

"Okay, dude," he laughs out, holding his hands out like a guilty criminal pleading innocent. "It's just weird is all. That's all I'm saying. I mean, you are in love with this girl for what—your entire life? And now, here she is, glued to your hip, and you read a fucking grade school book?"

"Her little sister is missing, Jake. How do you not understand that her being here, needing a place to escape, is only to avoid what is probably suffocating her over there?" I point beyond him out the garage, where the sun is setting on a still very dark house. "She's not here for some loser like me to hit on her. *Christ*! She's hurting, Jake. She's fucking lost. And am I glad she stumbled here for help? Yeah, of course. And what does that say about me?"

The obviously pretend coughing sound seizes my breath, and both Jake and I turn to our right where Gemma and Eleanor have entered the garage through the back door. My lungs feel like they are deflating into raisins inside my ribcage, and my mouth feels fat and numb like it does when the dentist shoots it up with Novocain. Even the end of what I said was bad enough and never meant for Eleanor's ears.

"Mind if we join you boys?" Gemma does her best to dress up a really crappy situation, and I'm thankful for it. Still, as my eyes graze over Eleanor's face, I can't help but feel pained when she quickly averts her eyes.

"Of course. Make yourself at home. Maybe some tunes, too, yeah? Jonah? What do you think?" Jake is trying to erase the last two minutes, but my blood is still boiling because of him. I turn to meet his eyes with a hardened deadpan expression.

"Come on, birthday boy. Loosen up," he continues, patting a stiff hand on my bicep. I flex from the touch and regret not taking my shot with my elbow when I had it.

"Whatever," I mumble.

Jake immediately jogs to his car in my driveway and pulls out a small speaker from his back seat. He sets it up at the edge of the garage and connects it to his phone, putting on a playlist of the current top hits. Gemma sings along with the song that starts halfway through, and at least four more songs play before anyone actually speaks. Thank God it isn't Jake. I'd be happy if he never spoke again.

"You think you might be able to drive this thing to school second semester, Jonah?" Gemma asks.

I unbury myself from the space under the hood and calm myself with one last deep breath. My pulse has settled since I flew off the handle, and Jake is starting to show some remorse. He does it in little ways, becoming overly helpful with everything—running inside for a drink when he sees my water is empty, handing me tools before I need them, telling me my ideas are good when they're just guesses. This is Jake's way of saying sorry.

"I think I'll be happy when it can make it to the gas station," I joke. Jake laughs more than necessary, and I roll my eyes toward him.

"Dude, you can stop. I'm not mad anymore," I say under my breath. He holds out a fist and I drop mine on top to seal the apology acceptance.

"I bet this thing can hit the highway by Thanksgiving," Jake pronounces.

I quirk a brow and he holds out his hand, wanting to shake on it. That's three weeks away, and I don't see how that's possible. There are too many mysteries under this hood, like wires that look as if they've been rat food and lead to nonworking parts.

"I think you're delusional, but what are the terms," I say, glancing to his open palm.

My friend chews at the inside of his mouth for a moment until his lips pucker in this *ah-ha!* expression that jacks up my nerves.

"We get this baby running by Thanksgiving and you, Jonah Wydner, self-proclaimed-loner, have to come to prom."

Shit.

"Because nothing screams 'I am not a loner' like going to prom by yourself," I respond. My entire body is hot with embarrassment because I'm not even exaggerating a little.

"You won't be alone. We'll all go together—one big group. In this thing!" Jake's hand lands on the top of the Bronco in a sturdy declaration that makes me punch out a laugh.

"So that means we have to *keep* this running long after Thanksgiving." I anticipate a lot of upkeep on this truck. I've actually been toying with the idea of maybe selling it once it's working again, but I don't want to have that conversation with my mom and grandpa until I actually get enough results to make it a viable option.

"I mean, if it's so impossible, what's the harm in making a little bet. I'll even buy your prom ticket," Jake says.

"And if I'm right and this plan fails miserably?" I question.

There's a long pause in conversation, the void filled with the very song that Eleanor sang during our trip to the parts shop. It's as if karma's introducing her to the conversation.

"Jake streaks the gym after his last basketball game," Eleanor says.

My eyebrows shoot up to match my friend's upon hearing that suggestion. Gemma spits out her water and laughs loud enough to cause it to echo in my garage. We all turn to face Eleanor as she sits with her legs twisted up in the green folding chair.

"I would honestly pay to see that happen. Your white ass flying through that gym. I mean, come on." Gemma leans to one side hanging her arm over the back of her chair as she crosses her legs slowly in temptation to Jake.

She stares at him with one brow higher than the other for a few long seconds and he doesn't break her gaze once, even as he accepts the terms.

"Deal. Jonah, you better start pricing out tuxes because ain't no way I'm getting naked in the gym—unless I want to."

We all laugh at his attempted bravado, and Eleanor is the first to call him on his ridiculous argument, shouting above our collective laughter, "What does that even mean? Who wants to be naked in the gym?"

"This guy," I say, pointing to my friend, setting off a new round of laughter.

To prove how unfazed he is, Jake pulls out another folding chair, places it in the open part of the garage, and promptly stands on it. He rolls his hips and tugs up the bottom of his sweatshirt and T-shirt underneath, swinging them in cowboy-roping-style circles over his head after pulling them off. It is one of the saddest-looking strip teases to ever be performed, no doubt, but it has all of us laughing so hard that it might be hard for a passerby to discern whether we're in pain or not.

Point proven when the music cuts off and our good time comes to an abrupt halt as Jake flirts with unsnapping the button on his jeans.

"Oh, party *foul . . .*" My friend's voice fizzles when he sees Morgan Trombley standing at the entry of my garage, his speaker in one hand and the batteries in the other.

"What is wrong with you, Eleanor?" It's as if Morgan doesn't see the rest of us at all. Her eyes are red, almost glowing, and locked on to her sister's.

"I'm just visiting my friends." Eleanor's voice is almost a whisper, and her body somehow becomes smaller in size, everything about her shrinking before my eyes as she squirms to fold herself into a tighter ball.

"Aunt Renee and Uncle Kevin have been here all day. They're asking about you, wanting to see you and make sure you're all right. We all thought you were in your room, sleeping. That's all you do, sleep! We were worried, and instead you're *here*?"

I bristle at her comment about my house as if I'm some den of sin just because one of our teenaged friends makes us laugh with a strip tease. Also, I can't believe that all Eleanor does in her room is sleep.

"Hey," I say, moving forward with an open palm to stop Morgan's verbal assault.

"I'm sorry, but who are you? Why are you talking?" She scolds me fast. I'm so shocked by her words that I'm left with my mouth hung open, unable to form the right response. I'm mentally riffling through the facts, that the Trombleys are grieving, that they are worried and stressed to unnatural heights, that Morgan is only doing what she thinks is right to keep anyone else from going missing.

But Eleanor slept for an entire day at my house, which means she doesn't sleep at hers. Or maybe I'm all wrong about it, and maybe she should be with her family right now. I don't know what's right.

"He's my friend, Morgan. It's his birthday, and I wanted to feel normal for a little while," Eleanor finally blurts out, standing from her chair and glaring at her sister with fire in her eyes. "So much for that lasting, though."

She folds her chair and leans it against the other folded chairs with a bang, quickly crossing her arms around her chest and marching toward her sister who has come to take her home. The two of them have a short standoff, staring at each other at the entry of my garage, eyes glassy and jaws locked for battle until Morgan breaks, bending down to set Jake's speaker on the concrete. She pockets his batteries and passes her judgmental gaze over the three of us, ignoring Jake's retort of "Hey, those are mine."

"I'm sorry, Jonah. Sorry, guys." Eleanor grimaces, her voice a far cry from the defiant one she used a second ago. She follows in her sister's steps while the three of us hover at the garage entry and watch her melt back into darkness.

Jake and I manage to get a lot done in the couple of hours he and Gemma stick around after Eleanor leaves. Probably because no one is talking. Or singing. Or dancing. Nothing but the cricket-like sound of wrenches broken up by the occasional masculine grunt from Jake or me trying to loosen impossible bolts.

When Jake gets a text about a party at one of the other ballplayer's houses, we wrap up work for the day. He asks me to tag along, but we both know that's not happening. I close down the garage after he and Gemma leave and go inside to cut myself an extra piece of birthday cake from the pan of chocolate goodness my mom made. I can tell from the missing gaps that Grandpa's cut a few extra pieces of his own.

Plate in hand, I scale the stairs to my room, my house quiet and dark minus the rhythmic snore from Grandpa's room. Mom will be up early again for her weekend job, so she's long been asleep.

I close my door behind me and head to my desk, flicking on the small lamp to the dim setting. I open my laptop to the latest scrolling stream of dumb videos to amuse myself while I eat, but the call to look out my window is too strong to completely ignore. Shutting my laptop down, I open my shutter slats and survey the windows of the Trombley house. Dark, every single one of them. The cars are all in their same positions, the new one probably belonging to Eleanor's aunt and uncle. I look on at the quiet scene while I eat bite after bite of my cake, mentally replaying Morgan's visit to admonish her sister for leaving the house. I still have Eleanor's bowls and her griddle in our kitchen downstairs. How did nobody see her leave with all of that stuff?

I'm deep in these thoughts when my phone buzzes against my hip. I pull it from my pocket, expecting some picture from Jake or a text about how I'm missing out on all the fun—*I always am*—but instead it's an unknown number and the word *hi.*

My phone flat on my desk, I prepare another forkful of chocolate cake while I stare at the singular, tiny word and wonder who's messing with me. I tip my head up as I take the bite and am drawn to the flashing glow coming from the window across the street. It takes me a few blinks to realize what she's saying—*S.O.S.* I flash my desk lamp off and on twice just to let her know I see her, then feel my phone buzz on my desk again.

ELEANOR: *It's me. I forgot to tell you I sent myself your contact info earlier.*

This is why she had my phone. My lip tugs up with the slight, dumbstruck smile. Eleanor Trombley wanted my number.

ME: *I was about to tell Jake to stop f'ing with me.*

She sends back a laughing emoji.

I look from my phone screen back to my window and decide to clear room on my desk so I can swing my shutters open fully. It takes a few minutes for me to shuffle around my clutter, and I get another buzz on my phone while I finish putting my lamp back in place.

ELEANOR: *Redecorating?*

ME: *Ha ha.*

I glance back up from my phone to the now clear view out my window. Eleanor lifts her hand and I do the same. It's pretty late, not quite midnight. She slept all day so I doubt she's tired. Her sister has no idea what she's been doing in that room all day and night. My guess is virtually nothing. She's been thinking, and thinking can be poison when you're going through the kinds of things her family is.

I pull my phone up to my desk so I can type while keeping an eye on her. I'm compelled to make sure she's there and looking back, this strange feeling in my gut that losing sight of her might put her at risk.

ME: *Morgan still mad?*

Eleanor stares down at her lap; I'm guessing she's reading my text. Her shoulders sag and I imagine the sound of her heavy sigh. The dots on my phone tell me she's typing or thinking, so I watch and wait patiently. I practically jump when I feel the buzz under my hand, lifting it to read her response.

ELEANOR: *She's always mad lately. Everyone is something. Dad is a zombie, my mom is manic, my aunt and uncle came over to cook and clean for whatever reason, and Morgan is the boss.*

ME: *I'm sorry.*

I send my pointless apology for things I can't control.

ELEANOR: *Don't be.*

ME: *I know, but I still am. Just cuz.*

ELEANOR: *Thanks.*

I stare at our text string and wish I could fix it. Words.

That's all I have to give her. I can't help find Addy. I can't cook worth a damn, not that cooking helps; clearly it doesn't based on her comments in our texts. I can't find them a lawyer to demand more justice, or a psychic, or pay for a TV commercial pleading for whomever to bring Addy home. I don't even know if someone has her sister to begin with.

I don't know if she's alive.

It's the one thought that simmers in the background of everything since news broke that Addy is missing. I wake up and look out the window and wonder how Eleanor is, *and if her sister is alive.* When I saw her family at the school, I wondered if they'd found out . . . *if Addy is alive.* It's in the background every time I look into Eleanor's green eyes. I see her, and I see her sister, and I let the thought ring in my head. It must be ringing in hers, too. I bet it's what keeps her up at night.

My phone buzzes.

ELEANOR: *I made you a birthday present.*

Like a switch flipping, I mentally move away from the dark thoughts. First to flattery then to guilt for being flattered when I should feel empathy. My thumb hovers over the keyboard on my phone while I'm stuck on how to respond. I envision a crocheted scarf or hat; my mom got into that for a while after Dad died. I have a closet full of afghans from her two-month yarn binge. Before I can type anything, though, a link pops up on my phone in our text string.

JONAH'S NEW FAVORITE PLAYLIST

I know, even as I open the link, that I am about to be assaulted by some twangy-ass ear-candy. I chuckle the second the first chord plays.

ELEANOR: *You love it?*

I mean, how can I not? I don't think I will ever be transformed into a country music fan, but do I love that Eleanor compiled what looks like two dozen or more songs into a playlist just to share some little bit of herself with me? Yeah, I do love that.

ME: *Already got me thinking about whiskey and pickups.*

What it really has me thinking about is her, and how happy she was sitting next to me in my mom's car, singing her heart out, voice of an angel. I switch my phone's mode over to my earbuds and pop one in my ear so I can listen a little clearer and turn the volume up a bit.

ELEANOR: *That first song is about a guy working on a Bronco.*

My brow pinches because I didn't hear any of that at all, not that I was paying close attention. I restart from the beginning and put my other earbud in so I can really concentrate, and from the very first lines, I get it. I mean, the guy in this song is clearly a little older than me, and he sounds as if he actually knows what he's doing, but the sentiment and meaning in these lyrics strikes an open wound I didn't realize I had. He's working on a Bronco that he wants to give to his son. I'm not sure if she realized how much these words would resonate, but the impact is profound. I play the entire song through and start again from the beginning, searching for the lyrics so I can read along with the music this time.

ELEANOR: *You like it at least?*

I pause the song halfway through, realizing I left her hanging.

ME: *I do, Eleanor. I like it very much. More than I thought.*

ELEANOR: *Good. Happy birthday, Jonah.*

Her light goes out, but I stay here, by my window, in case she's still looking out. I don't want her to feel alone.

I resume the sound on my phone, and for the first time, maybe ever, I experience a deep, satisfying ache that stretches inside my ribs and pushes down inside my body, pinning me to my chair with a force stronger than gravity. It's painful, but it also feels as though it's supposed to be. I don't realize until the song finishes that my cheeks are wet. Tears are streaming down them, and I start to wipe them away with the edge of my sleeve. I stop halfway, though, deciding that I want to feel the cold air dry them on its own, so I know all of this is real. I miss my dad. I miss him like hell, even the parts I never got to know. And I hate that he's not here to show me how to do any of this—the Bronco, college . . . *life.*

CHAPTER *ten*

I've always liked Sundays. I get the memes that complain about the day being too close to Monday, but I've always looked at it differently, I guess. I see it as *one more* day. We could have been screwed with six-day weeks and only one day of rest. Yeah, yeah. I know that the whole earth calendar, moon-sun cycle doesn't work out mathematically any other way, but for the sake of my argument, I choose to be thankful for a year divided by sevens.

I choose to love Sundays.

Today begins like most Sundays for me—breakfast with Grandpa Hank, a battle of will to stomach his eggs, and a dose of daily news. Typically, he and I divide up the Sunday paper and trade sections as we read. He insists on the actual news print, which normally I criticize because it's wasteful and the ink feels gross. But on Sundays? On Sundays, he is right.

Today's *Tribune* comes with a heavy story inside, though, and it takes us a while to uncover it buried in the local section. It's Addy's story—a plea for help to find a missing Oak Forest grade-schooler who seems to have vanished into thin air. Morgan wrote it, and I wait while my grandfather reads through it first before daring to myself. When he spins it around to face me and pushes it forward, I know he's signaling that I would want to.

Most of what Morgan writes are things we know. Her words are powerful—the way she describes the empty hole left in their hearts, how their nerves are forever raw because of all that is unknown. She gives details about Addy, mostly descriptive, but there are some new things I didn't know—things that a sister would. Addy sings her words, and it's more than just a nervous behavior, but rather part of a mild Tourette syndrome. Stress makes it harder to understand her, and by now she is no doubt in serious distress. Ten days off her medication, her tics are likely more prominent as well, mostly her right arm jabbing out at the elbow when she walks and a scrunch-like blinking habit that accompanies every turn of her head.

"Did you know Addy had Tourette's?" Grandpa asks when he sees I'm more than halfway through the story.

"I didn't even realize she was nine until the news broke last weekend," I admit. How little we know about the people who share our space is eye-opening in times like this. The thought strikes me that I should probably make a point of mentally noting important details about all of our immediate neighbors, and maybe I should share some of our details with them. It's a miracle people are ever found after they go missing.

"You get to the end?" My grandpa peers at me over the rims of his reading glasses, his mouth a hard line that leads me to believe there's more to be revealed. I shake my head and he glances down at the paper in front of me. "Let me know when you do."

I swallow and prepare myself for something heavy. It's pretty clear that the next few paragraphs were written with some help from investigators, details about leads and things for people to be on the lookout for. It isn't until the very last paragraph that I understand why Grandpa wanted me to finish completely. The last person who saw Addy anywhere at all was Eleanor.

I fold the paper and toss it on the pile of sections we've already read, then lean forward to rest my elbows on the table and shove my fingers into my morning-crazed hair.

"Damn." It's the only appropriate response.

"Uh huh," Grandpa mutters in agreement. "You know that's all that poor girl is thinking about—all of the things she doesn't remember, things she should have done differently, or stuff she maybe should have said."

My head feels heavier in my palms and I shift a little to press them into my squeezed shut eyes. It's probably selfish to correlate all of this to my own experience, but I do it anyway. I do it because for me, it has never been the things I wish I did or said, but more the one thing I wish I hadn't before my dad was gone forever. I was in a mood, and dad was leaving for work in a rush. He was always in such a hurry to get back to that job that didn't appreciate him. I don't even fully remember what he was promising me to look at when he got home that night. It might have been a paper, or maybe it was a college program I was considering. All I know is in that minute I didn't believe he gave a shit about me and my future at all, and for once in my life, I said my inner thoughts out loud, *just* loud enough. He died about two hours later.

In a rare bout of spontaneity, I hurry from the breakfast

table, pulling my phone from the pocket of my well-worn navy blue sweatpants as I rush up the stairs, taking them two at a time. I throw my gray hoodie over my Harvard Math Dept. tee shirt and shove a beanie on my head to tame my hair. Before I chicken out, I punch a quick text to Eleanor with my thumbs while I work to stuff my socked feet into my gym shoes without untying them. The heels get bent under my feet but the shoes are on enough to hobble down the stairs as I press send.

ME: *Hey. Are you awake? If so, do you wanna get out of here?*

It was a gamble when the idea sparked in my mind. After the way Morgan tore her sister away last night, Eleanor might be on family lockdown, despite the fact she's already eighteen. She might also really be sleeping all the time, and asleep right now. But I went with my gut, and my gut said she was lying in her bed staring at nothing and torturing herself with all of those words her sister wrote in the paper—especially the last dozen or so.

A blast of cold hits my face the moment I swing open our front door. I puff out a short smokestack of fog from my mouth and clap my hands together a few times to bring blood to the surface. The act is also a bit of a bolster for my confidence as I shuffle down our driveway, shoving my toes in with every step until the heels of my shoes right themselves. By all accounts, I'm wearing nowhere near enough for this morning's chilly forty-one degrees, according to my phone app that's about as reliable as the Cubs pitching rotation last year, or so Grandpa Hank always says. It may very well be colder. It doesn't matter, though, because I'm doing this, and there is no backing out now that Eleanor is rushing down her driveway to meet me in the middle of the street. She's wearing an equally hurried outfit.

"Thank you for rescuing me." That's how she greets me, eyes wide and relieved. I hope she's as enthusiastic when I tell her I don't have a working vehicle to take us anywhere.

"Metra ride?" I hold up my all-day pass and the rider card my Grandpa uses that I'm sure is good for at least a dozen more trips.

"Yes, please!" Eleanor takes one of the cards from my hand and pockets it, practically skipping through the middle of the street in the direction of the closest station. "We better hurry if we want to catch it on the hour."

I shrug and pick up my pace to match her, and we both even out into a decent-paced jog. While a mile-long run isn't much for Eleanor, it has me panting pretty hard by the halfway point. On the bright side, I'm not cold anymore. We pick up our pace when we see the train pulling up at the Oak Forest station, and we get through the gates and board the train in what feels like the nick of time. On instinct, I take a seat with my back to the window and Eleanor does the same, plopping down in the space next to me.

As the train chugs forward I snicker, the last ten minutes catching up with me all of a sudden.

"What's funny?" For some reason, seeing the dent between her brows when she asks me that question makes me laugh even harder. I hold out a finger while I catch my breath, both from running and from laughter.

"Morgan is probably going to kill me," I finally manage to say.

Eleanor sits back in her seat and unwraps the thick yellow scarf from her neck while she seems to stare out the opposite side of the train in thought.

"*Hmm*, no. You'll be fine. Me? Oh, I'm dead." She swivels her head until our eyes meet and holds a serious expression in place for about two full seconds before we both spit out in laughter.

We're near the front of the train, so the conductor checks our passes first and we spend the first stop getting comfortable. I take my hat off for a few minutes to cool down from my run, but when I catch a glimpse of my reflection in the window—what looks like feathers jetting off in various directions from my head—I promptly pull it back on, leaving just the few curls at my forehead out to let my skin breathe.

"You see today's paper?" Her question comes out of the blue, but I have a feeling she's been sitting on it for a few miles.

She glances my way and I nod when our eyes meet, offering a short lopsided and sympathetic smile.

"Morgan is doing so much. A few of the local news stations are coming over tonight for interviews and to get updates on the case. She has all of Addy's pictures pulled out and ready to show. She even has one of her in the outfit she was wearing when I—"

She doesn't finish the thought and I don't make her. It's the outfit Eleanor saw her in. I didn't pull her out of her house to rehash the things that are torturing her, though. I took her away to let her mind rest and to give her an escape from that feeling I sense is gnawing at her day and night. She feels responsible. I get it because there are days when I feel responsible, too, as if I said something just cruel enough to literally break my father's heart.

"Are you serious about playing poker with my grandpa? You know he's a bit of a shark, right?"

Eleanor shifts to face me, and her bent knee ends up

resting on the edge of my thigh. I will myself not to look at it but it is literally the only thing I can think about.

"You know it's card *sharp,* right?"

I don't answer right away because, well, Eleanor's leg and my leg are having a moment. When she snaps her fingers a few inches from my face I feel as though I maybe slipped into a catatonic state for a second or two. I didn't. Her effect on me is just that powerful.

"Card sharp?" I managed to hear enough to play along. "That's ridiculous. It doesn't even make sense."

"Oh sure, because little card sharks swimming around the ocean makes all the sense in the world." Her mocking tone stuns me for a second. She may be able to handle herself at my grandpa's card table after all.

She shifts back so she's sitting straight again, and I mourn the loss of her knee but only for a beat as she replaces it with the feel of her arm against mine and her head leaned in as she shows me the screen of her phone. She pulls her gloves from her right hand with her teeth so she can work her phone screen, and I watch in wonder as she types CARD SHARP in to the search engine and totally proves she's right. Technically, both are right. But her term was first.

"You and I would be really good at trivia," I predict.

She clicks her screen off and tucks her phone away, smirking at me from the side.

"Maybe if we end up at the same college we'll do one of those trivia nights at the bar and win a free round or whatever," she says.

I let the visual of that sink in and can't deny wishing for it to come true.

"Maybe," I mumble.

The train makes several stops through the suburbs as it

inches closer to downtown. Neither of us are dressed for that kind of an afternoon, though, so before we get too far into things, I suggest we get off at the Singerville stop because of the nice downtown and the bus line that goes to the state's biggest shopping mall.

Eleanor agrees, and we spill out of the train and back into the cold Chicago winter. The sun is out today, a rarity, and it is probably the only thing keeping the temperature tolerable. It helps when we walk quickly, so we seem to speed walk everywhere we go. Our first stop is for hot cocoa at a bakery in the downtown. The hot drink warms us enough to make it to the bus line, and once we get inside the closest department store, we're treated to a flash of warm air the moment we pull the glass doors apart.

"This is my favorite mall in the entire world," Eleanor says. "We came here last year for junior prom shopping. I mean the dress was all right, but this place has one of those arcade restaurants and we went there for lunch. That's what I *really* remember."

"Shippy's," I say with a nod. I've been there once with Jake. It was for his birthday, maybe his tenth, so it's been awhile. I doubt the place has changed all that much. Skee-ball and pop-a-shot and dance-off games for tickets. "Wanna see if it's open?"

Her eyes light up at the suggestion, and I thank Grandpa Hank silently for the extra cash in my pocket thanks to his poker skills and being owed a free auto part. He refused to take it back and told me to "have a good time." I believe today qualifies.

Eleanor nods emphatically and I gesture toward the escalator, a little embarrassed by the way she's skipping next to me like an excited child. I'd never say anything, though. My hermit status is worth risking for her happiness.

When we get on the escalator, our strides are totally in sync. The result is a tight space that brings our bodies side-by-side and touching on the shared step. I begin to utter "Oh, sorry," but before the apology finishes leaving my mouth I freeze at the feel of her fingers reaching in between mine. It's strange how my hand just knows where to go, how my thumb knows it belongs on top and her pinky belongs on the very bottom. Our digits thread together like puzzle pieces meant to fit. Again, like in the train, I fight the urge to stare at the place where we touch. Eleanor is holding my hand as if it's completely normal and not at all new or strange or shocking. *It's very shocking to me.*

I play along, though. I focus on making my hand feel natural, on willing my palm not to sweat, and on fending off the need to twitch with nerves. It lasts for the escalator ride, and our hands slip apart as she rushes off at the second floor, darting into Shippy's ahead of me. I form a fist to capture the warmth and feel of what just happened, then join her at the hostess stand.

"Party of two?" The girl working up front is dressed like a nurse from World War II. It's part of the theme here, and I've never understood the correlation. I dig it, though.

"Yes, we're together," Eleanor responds.

And I suppose for today, right now, we are.

CHAPTER Eleven

Sixty dollars on skee-ball feels like a bargain. I don't even care that all I have to show for it is this wicked dragon temporary tattoo that, yeah, after Eleanor pointed it out, does look more like a pigeon. I gave most of my tickets to her so she could get the giant smiley face pillow. Maybe she slept better with it. I slept better knowing she had it.

We got home as the sun was setting, and I slipped in right before my mom got home so I was able to eat Sunday TV dinners on the couch with her and my grandpa while we watched an old episode of *Star Trek: The Next Generation*. I've seen them all, some twice. Still feels like a necessary Sunday ritual.

I texted Eleanor after to make sure she wasn't in trouble with Morgan, but I never heard back. I found myself checking my phone all day at school today too. Nothing. It has me worried and my head is taking things in all sorts of directions. Does she regret spending time with me? Holding my hand? Or was her family upset with her for running off? She never once texted anyone to let them know she was gone. From what I could tell, though, nobody called or texted her either.

My dad's notebook was my distraction and excuse for not being social at school today, but I did manage to hold conversations with Jake and Gemma once they got back from lunch. Without giving them details—or giving Jake an excuse to give me shit for spending the entire day with Eleanor again—I learned enough to know Eleanor wasn't in major trouble or hurting or upset. Not enough to tell Gemma anyhow. They spoke last night about cheer. She said Eleanor doesn't want to quit, but she doesn't think she has a choice.

For the entire rest of the day I contemplate how stuck she must feel, to the point that instead of heading straight home from school, I find myself here, at her front door—the one place that literally scares me to the point of quivering in my shoes.

"Ring the bell, Jonah. Man up! Come on." I whisper what I think my grandpa would say to me in this situation. The words feel much more urgent when they come from him, but if I keep this up, someone in Eleanor's house is bound to see me talking to myself. I'm already enough of a weirdo; don't need to add more evidence in Morgan's case to stop Eleanor from spending time with me.

I'm about to press my index finger into the glowing button when a pair of chilly hands reach around my face and cover my eyes.

"Guess who?"

It's obviously Eleanor. Also, I am pretty sure I just yelped and it was not a manly yelp whatsoever.

"Sorry, I couldn't resist," she says as I turn around and

swallow down the bile that shot up my throat like a rocket when she startled me.

"Noted. Paybacks though." I grimace in jest and let her think that one day there's a chance I may get her back. I couldn't muster the courage to ring her doorbell. Pretty sure I won't be able to spring out and yell boo.

"You just get home from school?" She tugs on the strap of my backpack.

"Oh, uh, yeah. Easy day. You start the online stuff yet?"

"Yeah, I basically finished the entire week's worth of homework today. Not sure I'm going to be college ready with this method." She scrunches her face and I think to myself how much Jake would love to trade academic situations with her.

"Is it a Bronco night?" Her hands are shoved in the back pockets of her jeans and she reminds me of . . . *me.* Maybe she's nervous asking me that question, inviting herself into my garage. How do I tell her she is welcome to observe or interrupt my life at any point she wishes?

"I don't know. Jake's starting basketball workouts because their season starts in December, and it's hard to do some of that stuff on my own. My Grandpa isn't really able to slide underneath and stuff." I'm not making an excuse, but I can't invite her over to watch me fumble about the engine like a fool.

"I have two capable hands," she says, holding out open palms that are probably a lot more qualified than mine at making that thing run.

I lift a shoulder as if to say "Why not?" and Eleanor loops her arm through mine, gently urging me to leave her front walkway and head toward my house. I notice the driveway is getting fuller, a minivan now tucked up into the last bit of space next to her aunt and uncle's car.

"Full house?" I ask, pointing at the minivan as we slip between the line of cars on our way down the driveway.

"*Too* full. More like crowded," she says, her mouth tight and pinched at the corners as she glances toward me. "My grandparents are here too. You'd think it was Christmas, but no, it's just . . . *something else.*"

Her words trail off at the end. I gather she doesn't want to make guesses at how that statement should end.

It's just a mystery.

It's just a kidnapping.

It's just a possible homicide.

"Maybe it will be a miracle, so, sorta like Christmas." I shrug, but she slows her pace, which slows mine too since we're still linked at the arms. I kick myself internally for saying something so hopeful. It's clear that's not what she wants to hear or think. I understand. I didn't want to hear empty promises after my dad died. People constantly told me "It gets easier," and that phrase never quite fit. It only made me feel guilty for not falling to pieces. If anything, it's gotten harder the more distance I have from losing him.

Stopped in the middle of our street, Eleanor steps to face me, her hand sliding to my elbow, where she clings to the sleeve of my flannel. "Jonah." She stops after my name, and it's obvious she planned on following it up with more. Her mouth hangs open for a few long seconds and her eyes dart from meeting my gaze to somewhere else entirely. She snaps her mouth shut again, forcing a closed-lip smile in its place instead and nods.

"You're right. There are a lot of maybes up in the air." She nods again, almost as if she's convincing herself of her words. I let that be the end of that, out of fear of saying something that will only make it worse.

Eleanor lets go of my arm when we reach my garage,

and I think of how pathetic I will seem when I don't wash this shirt for several days. And when I sleep in it. I can feel her anxious energy behind me while I punch in the sevens to open my garage and I get so rushed to busy ourselves with the Bronco that I end up spilling the contents of my backpack on the garage floor as I free my arms from the heavy burden.

"Why did I expect to see dozens of calculators come flying out of that thing?" Eleanor jokes as she bends down to help me corral everything back into the unzipped pouch. She pauses with my dad's notebook in her hand and turns it over a few times as she studies it.

"Is this the magic notebook?" She lifts her gaze and the shot of her green eyes knocks me on my ass, literally. I fall ungracefully and make an actual *harrumph* noise as air gets knocked out of my body from the impact on my tailbone.

"I wouldn't call it magic. Maybe . . . *insightful?*" I finish stacking papers and folders to slide back into my bag while she takes a seat on the ground across from me and flips through the pages. She comes across the photo and pinches it at the edges to get a closer look. Her smile spreads into something spectacular, and I'm as caught looking at her as she is looking at this odd little memento from my parents' story.

"Your mom looks exactly the same. And is that your dad?"

I nod.

She glances up again.

I swallow.

"You look like him," she says, her grin somehow pushing a rosy color into her cheeks.

"Maybe," I say, taking it from her between my thumb and finger. I stare at the image for a few seconds, the first time I've really looked at it since I initially found it, and for some reason I pair it in my mind with the song on the playlist Eleanor made for me.

"That song you sent me, about the guy and his Bronco?" My mouth goes dry. I look at her and I know I'm doing a poor job of hiding my emotions. I decide in a breath that it's better to just let the tears well up in my eyes than it is to actually reach up and wipe them away.

"I thought it might resonate," she says, filling in my thoughts for me, as though she knows I won't be able to fully voice them.

"It did," I say through a breathy laugh as I look back down at the picture in my palm. I stare at it without saying a word, long enough that the quiet becomes obvious and heavy. I can't seem to get myself unstuck.

"Hey, have you ever watched the sunset from your roof?"

I pull my brow in tight and smirk at her abrupt and out-of-left-field question. I look up and close one eye to show my confusion, which makes her laugh.

"I know. Random, right? But seriously, have you?" She's so excited about the prospect I hate to tell her that I have. It's been a while, though, and maybe going up there with Jake to throw water balloons into the street doesn't count.

I shake my head no and commit a tiny lie.

"It's settled. Come on," she says, taking the photo back from me and tucking it safely inside the pages of the notebook. She slips that into my bag, secures the zipper then insists I follow her to the side of my house where the eave is at its lowest.

"We climb," she says, and I stop hard and let out a punch of laughter.

"Oh, yeah. No. *You* climb. I get ladders," I say, moving

beyond her toward the side of my house where our tools are piled on top of each other in the shed.

"Suit yourself," she says, jumping the few inches it takes to reach the eave. She pulls herself up easily and I watch in awe. I think she may actually be more athletic than my best friend, and I would harass him about that if not for the fact that I still intend on using a ladder.

It takes me a few minutes to fumble through the mess in the shed. I can't complain because I'm the one who left it that way. I figured I wouldn't have to see hedge trimmers or the mower again until spring. I wasn't counting on a beautiful girl talking me into a trip up the roof.

By the time I get the ladder settled and scale my way to the top, Eleanor is already perched at the very highest peak of the house, her back resting against the brick chimney.

"It's a little slick so watch your step," she hollers.

I run my finger along one of the shingles and feel the dampness. It was pretty cloudy all day, which made things cold and moist. Still determined to join her, I crawl up on my knees, my weight balanced on either side of the pitch of the roof. I'm sure she walked to her spot like a gymnast on a balance beam, but I have to find my center before I can make any forward progress. My hands held out at my sides, I slowly work myself to a standing position but I keep my back hunched until I test the grit of the shingles under my shoes.

"Oh, my God, you're never going to get here at that pace," she laughs out, hopping to her feet again as if she's on flat ground. She's beside me in a matter of seconds, holding out her hand. I take it, and not because I don't think I'll find my footing but because somehow, holding Eleanor's hand, I'm a whole lot more, well, everything.

We walk sideways along the ridge of the roof, stopping

at the spot near the chimney, and we both sink down with our backs against the bricks and our legs stretched out before us. I shove my hands inside my sleeves for warmth and Eleanor does the same.

"The sun goes down so early in the winter. In California, they get an entire extra hour. It's not fair," she says, crossing her arms over her chest and adjusting her back against the bricks in a bit of a pout. It's cute, and she catches me laughing at her.

"What? You don't ever wish you could zap yourself to California for just a little while?"

I laugh a little harder at her follow-up question, which makes her shift to face me, head cocked to the side waiting for my answer.

"I mean, sure, I guess. But more for the beaches and ocean and schools like UCLA. And palm trees. *Gah*! How cool do palm trees seem?" I look out at my front yard and the bare-boned sticks left behind after our elm tree lost all its leaves. "Besides, we really have about the same amount of daylight hours as California. You just have to wake up earlier here to take advantage of the full spectrum."

A few quiet seconds pass before I turn to meet her stare. Brow pinched and mouth open, she's looking at me like I'm a green alien spouting off Lord Byron or something. I did use the term *full spectrum*. Probably not a very cool moment for me.

"What?" My voice comes out in a nervous chuckle. Thankfully, her puzzled expression morphs into a more amused one as she shakes her head.

"Of course you know the number of daylight hours in California."

I swallow behind my tight smile and her lip ticks up as her eyes flinch. She's read right through my bluff.

"Wait a second," she says.

Oh, God.

"You know *all* of them, don't you? You know every state's sunrise and sunset times, don't you? Jonah! Do it, tell me! What is the sunset time in Cali today?" She pokes my side with her elbow a few times in an attempt to egg me on, and I laugh off her suggestion, mostly because she's right and I feel like an enormous loser somehow having this skill. It was a boring summer in fifth grade and I was really into climate studies, which then got me hooked on earth rotations, and well—

"Fine. Four-fifty-four, okay? That's what time the sun sets in California today. Give or take."

Eleanor practically cackles.

"Give or take. As if four-fifty-four could be a rough estimate. That's rather exact, Jonah."

I roll my eyes, and I'm only partly playing. I'm actually a little embarrassed. I really was guessing, but I know I'm close. It was probably fifty-five after at the start of the month, and surely the time has slid a minute by now.

I glance to my side and find Eleanor looking it up on her phone. I try to interrupt her search by pushing her screen away, but she stiff arms me then holds up a finger.

"Come on, I didn't know you were going to make fun of me," I say.

Eleanor snaps straight up at my plea, holding her phone against her chest while her face takes on a more serious expression.

"I'm not making fun of you. I think you're amazing!"

I breathe out a laugh at her compliment, not fully bought in to its sincerity. I bring my knees up and prop my elbows on them, shielding my eyes with my hands from both the sun and Eleanor's expectations.

"Two minutes off. Amazing," she says.

I shrug. "Like I said, give or take."

"And what's our time?" I can tell she's already looked it up by the way she cups her phone to hide the screen from me. I don't need to cheat.

"Two minutes off, you said?" If I'm going to show off one of the many ways I'm like a robot, I might as well be good at it.

"Two minutes. It was fifty-six after," she answers.

"Okay, so that makes it about four-thirty-seven or thirty-eight here."

Eleanor punches my arm in her enthusiasm.

"Thirty-eight! Holy shit, you're good at this. Do New York!" she begs.

My chest is tight, but my embarrassment fades a little. It helps that she seems to be enjoying this. I rummage through the logic I created when I first committed these things to memory, and I know that New York falls somewhere between home and the times on the West Coast, which seems weird but is true. I rub my temples while I calculate and Eleanor teases me that I'm doing it for show.

"I'd guess around forty-five after," I relent.

"Exactly!" She punches my arm again and this time I rub it. It didn't really hurt, but my action is enough to get her to stop quizzing me. I'm also aided in my effort by the chatter that comes from across the street, drawing our eyes toward Eleanor's house.

"I bet they won't even see me," she says.

I'm doubtful because where we're sitting we're in pretty clear view. It's hard not to notice people sitting on a roof in our neighborhood. The angles are steep, which practically puts us on display against the dark gray shingles.

"It looks like they're all going out somewhere," I say.

"*Mmm*, yeah. They're meeting with a private investigator. My grandparents are paying for it. He was over the other day." Her mouth falls into a perfectly straight line and she blinks slowly as she takes in the action below. They all pile into the van and I'm on edge, expecting Morgan to cup her hands around her mouth and yell at her sister to get away from the creep—*that's me*—and join her family where she belongs. None of that happens, though. Morgan climbs into the driver's seat while her parents ride as passengers. I join Eleanor in staring at the glow of the van's taillights as they back out of their driveway and head down our street.

Mentally working out the right words to soothe what I imagine she feels—cut out, ignored, helpless, angry, guilty —I decide that nothing I say would help with any of that. I would just be spilling out words. So instead, I change course and ask something personal.

"Are you and Addy really close?" I take care not to use the word *were*. I stumble over my words a lot of the time, but not this one. It's important that I leave Addy very much present and alive.

It takes Eleanor several seconds to answer me, though I can tell she's rummaging through pleasant memories by the way she smiles at her hands as she kneads them in her lap.

"Addy does this thing where she puts on my cheer uniform, like, if I'm wearing the home one she puts on the away version. I have to pin it, and if I'm not there to get the pins in she just ties up the loose waistband with hair scrunchies, like this." She pulls free the tie that was holding her hair up in a knot at the base of her neck and twists it around the bottom of my sweatshirt. It essentially turns my hoodie into a crop top that's tight around my ribs.

"I think this might be my look," I joke.

Her raspy laugh makes an appearance. She laughed like this during skee-ball. It's simply the best sound in the world.

"Addy would approve," she says through a wide smile. Her eyes blink as she turns her attention to her less crowded driveway, the blank spot where the van was parked probably the same spot she saw her sister last. "She wasn't wearing my away uniform that Friday, when she disappeared."

She glances up at me and I see the guilt threatening to ignite tears.

"Was she out of scrunchies?" I try to inject a little humor into our conversation to help her not fall apart. I can tell she doesn't want to. It's one of those things that people like me, people who have lost someone, recognize. And Eleanor, she isn't ready to lose it. Not now.

She sniffles and puts on a practiced laugh.

"Probably. Those suckers are always getting lost," she says, tugging the one on my shirt free and wrapping it around her wrist.

"Well, it's probably because you go around putting them on men's sweatshirts," I say, leaning into her. I've grown bolder with little shows of affection. I'm careful, though. I don't want her to think I mean anything that I don't, or that I want something more than just spending time with her.

"How much time till sunset?" She flattens her palm on my thigh with a friendly slap as she asks me this question and I'm grateful I don't tumble from the roof.

"Oh, uh." I fumble my phone from my pocket, risking losing my grip due to my nervous hands. I eventually click the screen on to get the time. "Maybe half an hour."

"Perfect," she says, meeting my gaze and offering a smile and a nod as if she's communicating something. I just don't know what. "Tell me about that picture. The one of your parents."

I suppose it's fair that I talk about a raw topic since I made her share a little bit about her sister. I'm about to dive into how different the man I knew as Dad seems from that picture when my voice is robbed of power by the feel of Eleanor's head on my lap. She's spun to the side and flattened herself along the pitch of the roof, her hair spread over my jeans in all directions. At first, I can only see her golden lashes, but after a few blinks, she opens her eyes right on mine, and I'm hit with my kryptonite.

"Okay," I breathe out, leaning back and tilting my head enough that I can see the wisps of clouds across the sky. They're starting to catch the golden color of the sun as it drops. I have no idea how to pretend this is normal, but I can't very well leave my neck craned like this through sunset. This angle also only makes the rapid pulse of blood racing through my body sound even louder.

I right my head and let the dizziness settle in my brain, willing myself not to look down at the beautiful creature staring up at me unless I absolutely have to.

"I don't think I've ever seen that side of him," I say.

"Well, he was a lot younger, so probably not." Her voice almost tricks me into looking down, but I don't fall for it. I chuckle at her comment and force my gaze straight ahead at the line of winter trees.

"That's not what I meant. It's just that he didn't seem like that kinda guy. He was always so . . . serious." Dozens of memories of my father race through my head like a picture slideshow, and he's serious in every single one. Even when we were celebrating and having fun, there was always an undertone to his expression. His brain was always working.

"You get that look sometimes," she says. My brow grows heavy at that thought, which in a way proves her right, I suppose.

"Do I?" I still keep my face forward, especially now that it's stoic and pensive.

A gentle laugh calls up from my lap. Damn her, I want to look. I spare a short glance and force a smile.

"Not all the time," she says. I look up before I get trapped. "But sometimes, when you're in intense thought. And when you're quiet."

I pull in one side of my mouth, a little disappointed in myself because I am serious. I don't mean to be. It's a default because most of the time I don't know how to act. I'm more uncomfortable in my surroundings than I am serious, I think. But to everyone else, I suppose I look a lot like my dad did most of the time. Detached.

"You also look like he does in that photo a lot of the time. Happy?" I can't tell whether she's trying to ease my bruised ego or if she's being sincere. I look down at her again because sometimes people need to see eyes to understand true meaning. Hers show something very honest, and incredibly gentle.

"You haven't seen me that much." I wasn't expecting to say that, but those are the words that come out. I've thought them often over the last few days that Eleanor and I have grown closer. I'm her solace, and I'm okay with that, but she and I weren't much of anything before she wandered into my garage.

"I see you now." She smiles up at me and I reflect her expression as best I can, nodding.

"That you do," I say, my voice a hoarse whisper.

I get stuck on her image just like I feared I would. Small hairs tickle her face as the breeze picks them up. Her cheeks are peppered with dust from heaven, and her skin is soft like cotton sheets. I find myself moving my focus from her eyes to her lips, over and over again, noting details I've never been granted access to before. Her front teeth scrape against her bottom lip naturally, and a tiny mole or birthmark dots the space just above her lip on one side—a beauty mark like famous women before her; like Marilyn Monroe.

"Have you ever had a girlfriend, Jonah?"

I'm frozen on her nose as she asks this question, and I'm glad I'm not looking her directly in the eyes when she does. My eyes widen. I know it's obvious; my eyes stretch enough that I feel it at my hairline.

"I guess, maybe one or two. Really more like dates gone bad. I never really clicked with someone, I guess." My voice cracks during my response. Of course it does. I squint and spare myself meeting her eyes.

"I've had a few . . . boyfriends," she says through quiet laughter. She rolls a little on her side, looking out toward the street and the dimming sky. Somehow her position feels more intimate like this, her cheek resting on my thigh, hands nestled under her chin. I'm struck by it, and without thinking I reach forward to catch the stray hairs blowing across her face. It's a tender touch that sweeps them behind her ear, my fingertips grazing her cheek with a feather light brush. Unfazed, her eyes drift shut then open on me with a slight shift of her head.

"You aren't missing much. For me, at least, it wasn't all it was cracked up to be. Being *with* someone." There's an emptiness to her words and a depth to her eyes as her stare lingers for a few extra seconds. I'm wounded by what she says, and I can't help but feel shot down before ever getting in the air.

Also, she's never picked anyone worthy of her time or attention. I've watched her dates pull up at the curb and they're douchebags, every single one of them.

"I could see that, I guess," I mutter. I'm thinking out loud.

"*Hmm?*" She sits up, stretching her arms up over her head and bringing her legs in to hug her knees.

"Your comment, about it not being all it's cracked up to be. I can understand why you'd say that, based on . . . your history." By the end, I'm slurring, desperate for a way to erase my words from existence. They just keep coming, despite the nonverbal cues I'm getting—falling eyelids, dipping chin, slumping shoulders. I let some of the bitterness into my head and I'm not getting any of this right. I can see in her eyes that I'm not. She's instantly guarded.

"I'm not making sense. Just ignore me," I say, still earning a scowl. I swallow the dry knot of regret choking me and push on.

"Hey, I almost forgot. I got you that invite to the poker game, for Thursday. My grandpa says he isn't spotting you any cash, though, so if you need, I can give you some of mine. I have forty bucks, and—"

"Explain what you mean by *history.*" She's pulled her feet in closer to her body and is hugging her legs tighter. I can't help but think it's a move to somehow inch herself a little farther away from me.

I roll my neck and blow out a heavy breath before letting my face fall into my hands. Rubbing my eyes, I groan. "I didn't mean it in a bad way."

"Oh, you meant it in a good way? I mean, it's *my history* after all. Go on." She holds out a palm, sweeping the air between us. She's clearly overreacting, and I know it's because she's exhausted and heartbroken, but she keeps pushing. I'm bound to make this worse.

"It's just . . ."

Here I go, making it worse.

"You don't really pick the best guys. Sometimes they don't even walk you to the door. And you—"

"You watch me come home from dates?" She stands as she says this, and I look to either side of her, panicked that she'll lose her balance. That dose of adrenaline mixes in my system along with the instant burn of feeling caught being creepy, and my chest feels as if it's been excavated and filled in with concrete.

"Not always. I've just noticed sometimes. And I didn't mean anything about you. It's the guys. It's always the guys." I'm too frazzled to get the right words out, and my stumbling attempt has only resulted in Eleanor walking away.

"Please don't go," I call after her.

"I'll see you later, Jonah." It's clear by her tone that she has no plans to anytime soon, and later might mean never again.

"Fuck!" I breathe out, probably loud enough that she heard it. Add this to the words and outbursts I can't put back inside. I press my palms to my eyes and rest my head against the brick. The sky is close to pink now, and two minutes ago, I'd be in awe. Now, I just want it to be night and then morning—a fresh slate and a chance for a redo.

I pull my phone from my pocket to send Eleanor a text that I can only hope clears up the muddy words I vomited out a moment ago.

ME: *I'm really sorry that came out so wrong. I only meant that you deserve a better boyfriend. That's all. Nobody's been worthy and that's probably why it hasn't been all it's cracked up to be. Having a boyfriend, I mean.*

I hesitate before I hit SEND and consider adding more. I want to tell her I'm not a loser who stares out my window at her, but aren't I really? I want to tell her that I would never let her walk to her door alone after a date, and I would always be early and always have her home on time. I stop myself, though, because as pathetic as my confessions sound they also sound like a job interview. I'm just lucky she wants to sit in my garage and up on the roof sometimes. I can be satisfied with that. And if she's gotten what she needs to find her strength in these dark days and decides she's done with my company, then I have to be satisfied with that too.

I make my way along the roof, never fully standing because now that the sun is nearly down, I'm even less sure on my feet. I leap from the middle of the ladder onto the ground and decide to leave my shortcut out in case I'm lucky enough to experience a repeat tomorrow. A short text in response buzzes at my side, and for a beat, it gives me hope.

ELEANOR: *It's fine. I'm just tired.*

I know it's not, and I know she is.

And that message was more of an ending than a beginning.

CHAPTER *Twelve*

Eleanor has kept to herself. I guess I've done the same. No texts sent either way, and no late-night visits to the garage. I don't even know what I'm doing on the Bronco at this point, other than fumbling around with wires and constantly checking my periphery, hoping she'll show up. I spent the last two nights under the hood for no other reason than to make sure she saw the garage lit up and open for her if she wanted company.

It's the same tonight, only now there's an empty chair at Grandpa Hank's poker table that she should be sitting in. He'd be irritated by a no-show under other circumstances, but I'm pretty sure everyone in this garage can read the anguish on my face as I pace around the tight space and constantly monitor life across the street.

"Maybe Hank Junior here can take the young lady's spot until she shows?" Dale's suggestion makes my stomach lurch. I don't know poker very well, but I'm also pretty damn sure Eleanor isn't coming.

"I think that's an excellent idea. Jonah, come on, have a seat," my grandpa says, patting the open chair next to him.

I roll my neck and let my gaze fall on the empty space, reluctantly dragging my feet toward it. I plop down in the chair and instantly feel like a child at a kid's table. I think maybe my chair is shorter than the others. It seems to amuse them all, tight smiles held back with sucked-in lips, waiting to burst. Dale can no longer hold it in when I lean forward and rest my elbows on the table, which is basically at chin-level.

"Okay, *ha ha,*" I say, standing and dragging the stunted chair away from the table.

"It's Hank's fault. Don't blame us," my grandpa's buddy, Gary, says through a gritty laugh. "He switched it out while you were moping around the driveway."

"Nice. Real nice, Gary. Thanks for that color commentary. I appreciate it," I mutter, flipping open a normal-sized chair and pushing it close to the table. I'm a little more motivated to get good at this game now that they've pissed me off. None of these guys like losing, even though it's only twenty or forty bucks a night.

"Deal me in," I say, resting my elbows on the table again, this time like an adult.

Grandpa smirks at me from the side of his mouth, probably thankful I got the lingo right and didn't embarrass him. He runs me through a refresher course while he deals; three of a kind beats two pair, a full house beats a flush, and if I get a flush these old bastards are going to assume I'm cheating.

The first seven or eight hands go by with me dropping a couple of bucks and folding each time. I endure their razzing, and get called a few terms I've never heard before, my favorite being *gollumpus.* I Googled it when grandpa cracked open a new case of beer from the garage fridge and handed out cold ones to everyone, including me.

"Clumsy?" I cock an eyebrow at Gary, who tagged me with the term.

"I don't know. We always called dumb shits that name in the army. And no offense, Jonah, but you're playing like a dumb shit," he says. The table erupts in a round of coughing-laughter. These unhealthy assholes think they're so funny.

"Yeah, yeah. Just count your chips, Gary," I fire back. I open my beer and shoot my grandpa a quick glance for permission.

"I gave it to ya, didn't I?" he says.

I look over my shoulder at the closed door that my mom never steps through when the garage is full of these men. I'm a rule follower. Always have been, and even when I stray outside the lines—like the time I helped Jake TP the house of his eighth grade basketball coach—I always find a way to go back in and make it right. I woke up at five in the morning that day to clean up his yard before he saw it.

But there comes a time when following rules starts to feel all wrong. I've been feeling that a lot lately, since the stupid fight with Eleanor, and maybe before that. I'm about to graduate and I'm supposed to go off to school somewhere and have this great college experience. Left to my own devices, I don't think I'm prepared to be very adventurous at all. I'm not even that excited about the prospect of a dorm room, or a roommate. Especially not a roommate.

Drowning in my self-pity, I crack the tab and tip my head back while taking a massive gulp. I drain a third of the can and slam it down on the table as a show of commitment.

"You all right now?" Grandpa asks.

I nod at him and pour every bit of energy I have into making the most statuelike, impossible to read face I'm capable of. It's not like I've only been a rookie, losing these first few hands. I've been studying too. And I realize a lot of this game has to do with math, and *math* . . . that's something I can kick Gary's ass at.

The first round post-beer is easy. I luck out by getting dealt a pair of aces, and I know from my understanding of odds, and the fact the third ace was flipped on the turn, that I am sitting in a pretty good position. Dale folds, which means he doesn't have anything worth moving forward with, and I can take a pretty solid guess at what types of cards he had. Their friend Jimmy is a terrible bluffer, and I know he's full of shit by the way he plays up his hand. Honestly, Jimmy's the real *gollumpus* at this table.

I write his hand off and do my best to study my grandpa and Gary through the river, and force myself to remain calm when the other ace gets flipped over. Using my newbie status to my advantage, I let the two old men hike up the amount in the pot with their little game of one-on-one, and when it comes time to call, I don't know if they actually realize I'm still in the game. They both flip over their three-of-a-kind hands, Grandpa's higher than Gary's. With his arm poised and ready to sweep the chips into his pile, he gives me a sideways glance and raises a brow.

"Go on, throw down your cards," he says. The simmer of laughter at the table, ready for me to lose again, bolsters my confidence. My face as guarded as it was when this hand started, I toss down my two aces on top of the other two and flit my gaze to meet my grandpa's stare.

"Son of a bitch, would ya look at that!" he barks out.

He leans back in his chair, his hand falling away from the chips that are, in fact, now mine, and I swivel my head to look at Gary, who is as shocked as my grandpa.

"You little shit!"

Somehow, the trash talk comes out more like a huge compliment, and just like that, I'm ushered into their club —no longer the punk kid who was sulking over an unrequited crush, but an honorary senior citizen and gambling degenerate who fills the voids in his life one dollar at a time.

The game went on for three hours—and two beers. I could have pushed it and had a third, but I like being relaxed while still having my wits about me.

I help Grandpa clean up the garage, plugging in the box fan to air out the space so my mom doesn't lose her ever-loving-mind over the cigar smell. He heads in first, and before I close up the garage, I stand at the entrance with the light off and give one final, hopeful look at Eleanor's window.

Her house has been quiet all night. Both the van and her sister's SUV were missing for most of the afternoon, and they still haven't returned. Maybe her family decided to stay somewhere else after all, like with her grandparents. I'm not even sure where they live. I didn't ask because asking Eleanor questions about her family feels too invasive. All roads lead back to Addy.

I finally shut the door and give up for the night, doing my best to find my way back into the house and through the downstairs without making too much noise. I grab my backpack from the kitchen table because I have some reading to finish before my first hour. The glow of the television gets my attention before I make it to the stairs, so I pause and back up toward Grandpa's easy chair where the remote rests on the arm. I didn't see my mom curled up in the chair from the back, and I startle at coming upon her when I grab the buttons.

"Jonah?" She stretches out sideways on the chair, her legs unfurling over the arm.

I'm grabbing my chest, sweating from A: her scaring me, and B: I smell like beer.

"I thought you were upstairs," I say. *Please don't sound buzzed.*

"I must have fallen asleep watching the news. They might have a lead on the case. For Addy?" she explains.

That's where the Trombleys are. I feel selfish somehow for feeling slighted by Eleanor not being home or answering my texts.

"Did they make an arrest?" I slip past Mom and move to the couch, noting that the only thing showing on the television now is a rerun of *Friends*.

"They haven't said. Just that they would probably hold a press conference in the morning. They wouldn't do that if there wasn't something new to talk about." My mom rubs her eyes and rights herself in the chair before leaning toward me and wrapping her hand around my arm affectionately.

"So tell me, did you clean them out in poker?"

I lean back and laugh.

"I didn't do too bad. I think Gary might ban me from playing with them," I say.

"Oooh." Mom winces as if she feels bad for Gary. He's her least favorite. He's the one who brings the cigars.

"I'm pretty sure Grandpa knew I was counting cards,

though." I shrug and lean to the side, pulling out six twenty dollar bills. I did better than I thought, tripling my money.

My mom chuckles, then reaches toward the coffee table where her coffee has gone cold.

"I can warm that up or make you a new one," I say, taking it from her. Partly it's an excuse to get out of close quarters before she really starts to study my red eyes and sniff my breath. I've already decided to lie and blame Gary for spilling a beer on my shoes.

"Maybe tea instead?" She leans her head back and watches me round her chair.

"Sure," I say, carrying the mug into the kitchen and giving it a quick rinse.

"Your dad used to do that, you know. Count cards."

I smile behind her while I heat some water and fish out a tea bag from the cabinet.

"He did?" I mean, I would guess if he was ever in a gambling situation, he deployed his skills. I would think pit bosses wouldn't be too keen on him at blackjack tables, but I don't recall a time he and my mom ever went to a casino.

"Uh huh," she confirms. "So I'm sure your grandpa noticed you counting cards. How do you think he gets so lucky?"

I pause my dunking of her tea bag at that realization. Grandpa's been holding out his math skills on me. Either that or he decided as a young lad that he would follow the dark side of math. Can't say I blame him. A guy gets more chicks on the dark side for sure.

"I found a picture in Dad's notebook." I'm not sure whether it's the beer buzz or the moment, but I decide it's time to share the photo with my mom.

"Oh yeah?" She hangs an arm over the back of the chair.

I snag my backpack from the floor and reach inside,

feeling between the pages for the photo. I hand it to her and her face instantly lights up with recognition.

"My God, do I remember that day." One hand rests on her chest as she stares at her younger self in the small photo in her palm. "We were so young and so in love. You know, your dad wasn't just numbers and formulas. That man, he could be downright romantic."

I twist my lips, playing grossed out. Oddly, I'm really not. I'm curious. I want to know about these other sides he had.

"Did he ever write you poetry?" I'm assuming so given the short stanzas I found in his book.

"He did," she says through smirking lips. "But those are for me and me alone."

My mouth sours again, and this time I'm not quite kidding.

"Okay, fair enough." I hold up a palm.

My pocket buzzes as I stand, and I pull my phone out to see a message notification from Eleanor.

"You should keep that," I say to my mom, knowing full well I'm not prying that picture out of her hands tonight.

I retrieve her tea from the kitchen and set it on the table for her. She's already lost to memories of my dad, though. Happy ones that press a smile into her face.

I read the message from Eleanor on my way toward the stairs, but before I climb, her words hit me hard.

ELEANOR: *Jonah, I need you. Can you come outside? Please.*

And here is the difference between me and those other guys who won't even bother to walk her to the door after taking her out. One word, and I drop everything. I leave my bag at the bottom of the steps, ignore my mom's worried questions over what has me in the sudden hurry, and bust through our front door. I leave it wide open behind me and rush toward Eleanor as her legs try to carry her weary body my direction. When we meet in the center of the road, her weight collapses against my chest as she throws her arms around my neck and climbs into my embrace, giving me all of her to care for and hold.

I don't understand, yet despite that I lift and cradle her while she buries her face and lets go of suffocating tears. Her hair is a tangled mess, covering her face and eyes and sticking to her arms that are too bare for how cold it is outside.

"Eleanor, what's wrong?" She shakes her head and cries harder.

I look over her shoulder as I hold her, toward her open garage. Morgan stands in the open doorway at the back, a dim light showing her form. This is a deflated version of her sister, different from the one who marched into my world a week ago and tore Eleanor away from my company.

"Elle, you need a jacket or a sweater. It's too cold out here." I can already see the bumps forming on her arms.

She adjusts her grip around me, holding tighter. She isn't heavy, and even if she were, I could hold her like this forever if I had to, if that's what she needs.

I look to her sister again, waiting for a command or advice. An explanation at the very least. But instead, she backs away and lets the door slam closed, leaving the garage wide open for the world to see and steal from.

"Let's get you inside," I say at Eleanor's ear.

My mom has made her way to our door, prompted by my abrupt exit. I carry Eleanor to my house and my mom opens our door wide as I enter. We make eye contact and do our best to communicate without words. This is a gift you're left with when you lose someone you love; you can say volumes to those who understand just by the shape of your eyes. Mom's are heavy, sloped down with concern and panic of what to do and how to fix this. Mine are probably the same.

"You want to go to my room?" I ask.

Eleanor is wordless and too distraught to even bother to nod. Her entire body is quaking and the tremors get stronger with every ragged breath she sucks in.

"Can you bring up some water, or tea maybe?" I hold my mom's gaze for a few seconds as she looks to Eleanor then back to me. I can tell that Mom is trying to piece together the cause of this and drawing tragic conclusions. Her eyes start to water, and I don't think I can handle her falling apart now.

"Mom?" I snap her to attention and she runs her sleeve over her eyes as she swallows down her worst thoughts.

"Tea, yes. I can do that." Mom nods toward the stairs and I take her direction, climbing them slowly so I don't drop Eleanor. I am not Jake, and this is not a position I have ever been in before, except maybe the time I gave Tabitha Worley a piggyback ride in fourth grade because she dared me to. I dropped Tabitha.

I kick my door open and carry Eleanor to my bed, sitting on the edge, unsure of where she wants to be and whether she wants me to stay here or leave her alone. Like the melting of wax, her arms unwind from my neck and her legs fold together as she moves to the space at my side, her entire body leaning into me until I scoot back enough to turn myself into a pillow for her to cry into and be held.

Hot tears roll from her cheeks onto my thighs, soaking through my jeans. Her chest is in a constant struggle for air, her mouth gasping between quivered lips. She is desperate to breathe.

"*Shh*," I hum as I untangle wet strands of hair from her reddened cheeks with one hand while rubbing the other in circles on her back. This is what my mom used to do when I was sick to my stomach, and I don't know . . . it just feels like the right thing to do.

Eleanor turns closer to me, her knees curling up and her balled fists tucked under her chin while she shakes. My mom walks in with the tea and I meet her gaze with my own, picking up in the exact same place we left off downstairs. Mom sets the tea on my night table and crouches down so she's on Eleanor's level at my other side. I've only seen this helpless look on my mom's face once before, when she was told to come to the hospital where my dad had been taken. He was gone—*gone*—before she got there.

"Honey, would you like me to tell your parents you're here?" My mom's voice is gentle and measured. This territory is both new and familiar. Things are . . . *fragile*. For all of us.

Nearly a minute passes and my mom asks again.

"Eleanor?" she says, finally drawing a slight head shake from the broken girl glued to my lap.

"It's fine. It's okay. They're doing the same thing, over there. All of them, it's . . . it's fine." It's clearly not, despite what Eleanor says. She rubs her clasped hands under her nose, then brings them to her forehead, shutting her eyes and shaking with a new round of sobs.

"I'll make sure it's okay that you're here. You can stay as long as you want," my mom says, meeting my eyes again as she stands. I give her a tiny nod and continue the pattern of circles on Eleanor's back after she leaves.

"She wasn't there, Jonah. They went to get her, but she

wasn't . . . she wasn't there." Quaking in my lap, Eleanor peels her eyes open and stares forward to the open door and dark hallway where my mom disappeared. Her words are a partial puzzle. This must have to do with the news my mom mentioned.

"I'm so sorry, Elle."

My hand changes patterns, circling counter-clockwise now, as if that's what will make all of this better for her.

"Elle," she whispers, her eyes still fixed on the nothing in the darkness.

I breathe in slowly through my nose, and I'm sure she can feel my chest and diaphragm expand. I called her Elle. I've done it twice now. It seems right, as though we're close enough for such things. I'm not quite sure why it's the way her name came out, honestly. It just is.

"Yeah. I'm here, Elle," I say, my voice nervous and tender.

Her tears slow, but the stroke of my hand continues. Eventually, her eyelids grow so heavy they can no longer fight the will to look out into the blank space in front of her. She's asleep enough for me to move without waking her, letting me support her head and guide her closer to the center of my bed. I pull my old quilt from my closet and spread it over her body to keep her warm, staying by her side long enough to tuck her hair behind her ear. No matter how hard I try, though, I just can't erase the divot permanently centered between her brows.

CHAPTER Thirteen

It takes me a few minutes to wrap my brain around where I actually am. Our sofa has never been the greatest place to nap, let alone attempt a full night's sleep. I gave up my bed willingly last night, though, to someone who needed it a whole lot more than I did.

Mom helped me bring down some extra blankets when she got back from the Trombleys' house. It was Morgan who came to the door, her torn-up eyes and defeated posture reminiscent of her sister's. The entire family spent the day with a victim's advocate, sitting in a board room at the Oak Forest police station while investigators descended on the first solid lead in Addy's case.

Someone's security camera picked up a white car driving down a nearby street around the right time. They were looking for vehicles that didn't *live* in our area, and this particular license plate fit the profile. Police tracked it to a home owned by a single woman in her late forties who lived near the Missouri state line, almost four hundred miles away. When they got to her home, it was filled with cats, animal feces, stacks of old magazines and newspapers, and trash. The white car and the woman were gone, but they found one of Addy's skates in the garage among a pile of random objects like tools and old children's toys. According to neighbors, the woman hasn't been home in more than a week.

Nobody saw a little girl.

The smell of coffee lifts me out of my haze and I turn to find my mom working in the kitchen.

"How was your sleep?" she asks.

I grunt through a stretch and get to my feet.

"Eh," I say, shrugging a shoulder.

"Rough morning I guess, huh?" She pours me the first cup from the fresh brew and I take it from her.

"Yeah, pretty rough," I say, running my hand along my side where the uneven couch cushions jacked up my sleeping position.

"Because of the couch or the beer Grandpa gave you last night?" she deadpans with pursed lips, then blows the steam from the top of her coffee cup.

I'm not a good liar. I've never had much reason to lie, so after a few seconds of stammering through false starts of an excuse, I give up.

"How'd you know?" In my head, I'm already blaming Gramps.

"Jonah, hon. Your grandpa buys the cheapest beer on the planet. I could smell it on you the moment you walked in from the garage." She laughs at my expense.

I should have gone with the 'Gary spilled a beer' story. I probably wouldn't have been able to pull the lie off longer than a minute anyhow.

"Sorry," I say, bowing my head and staring at the brew

in my cup. The weight of shame pushes down my shoulders.

Mom steps in close to me and kisses the top of my head. "Don't be. Your grandpa gave me my first beer, too."

I breathe out a short laugh and look up at her.

"Really," she continues, joining me at the table. "I bet if he had the means, he would have let your dad and me smoke weed with him also."

My eyes grow wide.

"Mom!"

"You're damn right I would have." I turn at the sound of Grandpa's voice as he coughs his way through a rough good morning.

"I hear your grandson cleaned everyone out last night." My mom's scornful expression has shifted into a smug one as she flits her gaze from me to Grandpa and back again.

"Ha! Little shit's a card counter just like his dad," Grandpa says on his way to the fridge.

"Just like you, you mean," my mom teases, swatting at him gently.

Grandpa laughs in agreement and goes to work pulling out the eggs and butter. While he gets started on breakfast, Mom finishes up her cup and gathers her things for work, leaving me and Gramps with a semi-serious warning not to cause any trouble.

There's a lot to catch my grandpa up on, but before I can share the difficult details of why Eleanor is sleeping in my room, the sound of her feet hitting the wood stairs draws my grandpa's eyes over his shoulder.

"That Jake idiot show up early for breakfast before school?" Grandpa asks.

Before I can explain, his mouth drops open at the sight

of a very weary and worn-out Eleanor at the bottom of the steps.

"Hi," she croaks. I think maybe she believes her lips are smiling but they aren't. She's as blank as a canvas, her face ghost white except for the sprinkle of freckles. Even her lips are pale.

"Well hi, young lady. You joining us for eggs this morning?" My grandpa looks to me for approval but I'm dumbstruck because *no! Nobody is ever here for eggs. He doesn't quite understand how bad this is.*

"I'd love some," she says, her voice faint and her body going through motions as she pulls out a chair and slips into it beside me. I stare at her until her eyes manage to find mine, and I wordlessly check on her heart and her head.

"Thanks for letting me take over your bed. I didn't mean to—"

"It's fine," I interrupt, ending with a closed-mouth smile. We hold each other's stare for a few seconds, and I can't help but sense that she doesn't know what to say or do next. Not only with me, but with everything.

"I can call off from school today. Stay home, maybe just hang out with you and watch a movie or—"

She shakes her head and mutters, "It's fine."

"One military special coming right up," Grandpa says, sliding the first plate across the table to our guest. Eleanor picks up the fork but when my grandpa turns his attention away she just pokes the barely cooked yolk around her plate.

I tap on the table with my fingertip to get her attention and when she glances up I shake my head and take the fork from her hand. Because I know she'll feel bad, I take three bites of the eggs for her, doing my best to swallow them without so much as letting them pass over my taste sensors. I silently gag a little, then put the fork down on her plate. The entire scene pushes her mouth up just a tick, the slightest hint of a smile.

I repeat this process with my plate of eggs, impressed when Eleanor knows to play along, telling my grandpa the eggs were great but she's not very hungry. I clean our dishes and check my phone for the time, struck with a touch of panic when I realize Jake should be at my house in less than five minutes.

"I really can stay home. I don't mind," I say to her.

"I know it sounds weird, but that would actually make me feel guilty." She twists her lips and as crazy as her reasoning might seem to most, I do understand. She doesn't want the attention, not about her reality anyhow. That's part of the reason she's over here and not in her own house.

"I'm not going anywhere. Was planning on working my way through the Sunday puzzle that I never finished, then Dale might come by and take a look at the Bronco. You're welcome to stay here as long as you want," Grandpa says.

Eleanor looks to me, I think for a blessing, so I shrug to let her know it's up to her. Dale offered to poke around the truck for me last night, sometime after I took a huge pot from him. I think I earned a little respect from my grandpa's crew.

"I should probably check in at least," she finally says, leaning her head in the direction of her house.

"Suit yourself," Grandpa says. I'm glad his tone is normal. If I were Eleanor, I don't know that I would want everyone treating me as though I were fragile, regardless how absolutely delicate I might be.

I meet Eleanor's gaze one last time, trying to read

whether or not she's ready to go home or just trying not to be a bother. The dim light that's shown in her eyes a few times over the last few days is completely out this morning. Her sense of hope seems to be history, as is the stupid fight we had. When she appears determined to go back to her house, I rush up the stairs and switch out my shirt for a new one and throw on a thick flannel before running my hands through my hair. It's a wild mess up there, so I shove my Sox cap on and hope things flatten out enough by fourth hour, when Mrs. Dahl will undoubtedly make me take it off. She's a Cubs fan.

Eleanor is gone by the time I get back downstairs, so I use the few minutes I have before Jake arrives to fill my grandpa in on what he missed while he was sleeping. As tough of a soul as he is, the man possesses a great deal of empathy for people dealing with loss. I remember him talking to my mom right after Dad died about how there's a unique ache that accompanies burying one's child. He was never supposed to outlive my dad. Just like Eleanor was never supposed to lose faith that her sister would be around to follow in her footsteps on the cheer squad.

When Jake picks me up, I go through everything that happened last night again, leaving out some of the details like the way it felt having her come to me, how I held her until I was sure she was asleep. He'd focus on my shit when the important part is that Eleanor is not okay. He must have filled in Gemma because by the time the lunch hour arrives, the two of them act as if they were there with her all night and I am just now learning about everything.

It's easier to let them dominate the conversation, and since only a few of Eleanor's closer friends are around, I decide not to interject and stop them from gossiping. It doesn't keep my arm from remaining flexed and primed to take a swing at anyone who says something inappropriate, though. Not that a punch thrown by me would have much of an effect, but it would be enough to get Jake on his feet with a few follow-up rounds.

No matter how many times I replay the last twenty-four hours in my head, I can't make sense of them. Nothing that is happening feels fair. How could it, I guess?

I've texted Eleanor twice so far today, just to make sure she's holding it together. She hasn't written back, which only heightens the visuals in my mind of her walking around her dark house like a zombie with no one willing to talk to her. By the time my last hour is over, I've convinced myself to sprint home and break my way into her house to make sure she's all right.

"Dude, what? Are you ditching me too?" Jake catches me halfway through the parking lot and pulls up beside me. I note that Gemma isn't in the car with him and scrunch my brow.

"Gemma skipped last hour. She faked menstrual cramps and you know Mr. Donellan," Jake says.

"Let me guess, he plugged his ears and said *lalala.*" Mr. Donellan teaches computer science and is basically afraid of human interaction and uncomfortable conversations. When my dad died, Mr. Donellan actually said the words, "There, there" to me while flat-palming my shoulder twice when I came back to school. The mere mention of the word menstruation probably made him want to dive into a cave and never come out.

"I'm headed straight home, so hop in," Jake says.

I glance around and decide that's a lot more efficient than running, especially since Gemma isn't here to side-track us with stops at her house or the coffee shop.

"So you and Gemma are like, for real, huh?" Jake and I

haven't had a tutoring session in a week so I feel behind on the latest school gossip. It almost always revolves around him and whomever he's dating or just broke up with.

"I kinda think so. I mean, it's weird, but she's always so . . . interesting." His eyes squint while he speaks and stares out the windshield. His epiphany makes me laugh.

"My God, I think you may have finally hit maturity. Yes, Jake," I say, pausing to pat his shoulder like a proud papa. "Girls are in fact interesting."

"Shut up. She's hot too," he adds, brushing me off, probably because he's also experiencing actual feelings. I roll my eyes and pull my phone out to see if Eleanor's texted me back. When I see she hasn't, I breathe in deep through my nose in an attempt to undo the knot in my chest that has just gotten tighter.

"She's fine, you know. I mean, not *fine,* but she's okay." Jake's reassurance rolls off me like water.

"Yeah, probably," I dismiss.

"No, seriously. I know she's okay. That's why Gemma skipped last hour. She went to hang out with her. They're probably binge watching that island dating show or something."

I blink at these new details, instantly jealous of Gemma. The sensation fills me up like an ever-expanding poison, and even though I'm logical enough to reason that it's ridiculous, that I'm being unfair, I can't help the feeling. All she has to do is write me back, but she doesn't have time for that because she's too busy watching dating paradise reality shows with Gemma. *Gemma didn't give up her bed last night.*

I'm quiet for the rest of the ride home, and I'm pretty sure Jake can tell that I'm simmering because he lets me be. The Volkswagen is gone for the first time in two weeks, probably because someone had to pick Gemma up from school. Dale's pickup truck is in our driveway when Jake stops in front of my house, and I vow to myself that I won't so much as glance at the Trombley place for the rest of the day.

It takes me exactly six seconds to break that promise.

"Oh hey, I know you hate parties and shit, but Gemma just texted," Jake hollers from his window, halting me halfway up my walkway. "There's a bonfire at the Molinas' place tonight after the game, and I guess Elle insists on going. You think maybe you wanna come just to keep an eye on her? With me, of course."

My eyes flutter closed and I draw a quick breath to erase the childish bitterness from my face before turning to face him. I will be the *only* person looking out for her. I know what happens to Jake at parties, and his attention span does not become acute.

"Yeah. Pick me up on your way, after the game. And I can drive home."

My offer earns me a grin from my friend, and he mutters something else about being here after eight but I'm no longer listening. I'm busy checking a window. A dark and empty window I know better than to look at.

CHAPTER Fourteen

I am probably the only teenager who is openly honest with his parent about going to a party where there will definitely be underage drinking and probably a lot of pot. I told my mom because I am going to be incredibly late. The party won't even get going until 10 or 11 p.m., and I plan on making sure Eleanor makes it home in one piece. Why she is putting herself in this environment baffles me. There is nothing about the scene outside Jake's car that says *calming and good for someone going through a trauma.*

This marks the third party of my high school experience. We roll up to the dirt lot next to the Molina house, and it's as if nothing has changed since my first party two and a half years ago at the very same residence.

The Molina family is huge, seven kids in all. Three are in college, three are in high school, and the oldest is married and lives out of state. The most talked about parties in Oak Forest happen at the Molina house. The vacant lot was once slated to become a park, but that never happened, which makes it perfect for bonfires and messes.

Plus, they're on the outskirts enough that cops tend to look the other way since there isn't anyone nearby to annoy with party noise.

The Molinas throw enormous parties every time their parents are out of town, which is at least a dozen times a year. They own several restaurants near the Indiana border and try to visit them each once a month. The Molina girls, freshmen twins, shatter every strict rule they've been imprisoned with whenever their brothers throw one of these parties. Honestly, I don't know how someone hasn't died at one of these ragers.

The music assaults my ears as soon as we step into the dirt from the peaceful quiet of Jake's car. I am already miserable. Add it to the speaker-buzzing bass sounds and a dense layer of smoke from a poorly built pit fire, and I'm basically in a circle of hell.

"Loosen up, dude." Jake walks behind me and grabs my shoulders, shaking them as if that is going to break through my social anxieties.

"I'll relax when we find Gemma and Eleanor," I say. I probably won't relax, but at least it'll ease the knot in my stomach.

"You are unnaturally responsible for her, you know?" Jake mocks me.

I scrunch my shoulders and glare at him while we make our way through the dusty field toward the blaze someone just tossed a new log on.

"I'm just being a good friend. That's all," I say, and for the most part, that's the truth.

"Whatever." Jake leaves me to stand by myself with that response while he hops in the beer line to get a cup and fill it at the keg.

"Jonah! Oh my God, you're never at these!" Slender

arms wrap around my neck and I recognize the long glittered fingernails that accompany the shrill, drunk voice.

"Hey, Mandy. Yep. Senior year and all, so ya know—*woo!*" I raise both hands and shake them with my fingers stretched. Mandy and I have gone to school together almost as long as Jake and I have, and for an entire week our freshman year, I was her boyfriend. We could not be more opposite. She said yes because Jake dared her to, and I asked because I was fourteen, a pushover for peer pressure. Plus, Mandy is a cheerleader. I'm pretty sure she cheated on me with her next boyfriend. Regardless, ever since, she takes every opportunity to flirt with me. I don't know whether it's because she regrets ever breaking up or because she likes to string people along. Things really peaked at the beginning of the school year when she took off her bra in the middle of Lit class and tossed it to me. Four desks away. I shoved it in my backpack and threw it away when I got home.

"I'm so glad you're here!" Her mouth is practically in my ear, somehow making her louder than the music that's blasting.

"Yeah!" I shout back, taking a step away to gain some space. I shove my hands into my pockets, giving her the opening to pull my beanie from my head and tug it on her own.

"Oh, hey!" I run one hand through my hair and reach for my hat with my other. Mandy dances away, though, in a series of drunken steps punctuated with a very tipsy laugh.

"Thank you, Jonah!" She blows me a kiss, swinging her arm out when she does and running it into the chest of some football player who gets her attention next.

I'm not getting my hat back.

Fuck.

"I see Mandy found you," Jake teases as he steps up to my side and hands me a cup. I shake my head but he pushes it at me, insisting.

"It's Sprite. So you don't look like a douchebag."

I grimace but take the cup. I hate that shit, like that matters. The fact I'm the designated driver should be celebrated instead of brand me as a loser.

"Gemma and Elle are by the fire, on the other side. Smoke's blowing this way," Jake says.

I glare at him, my mouth a straight line while my eyes burn from the ash.

"Ya think?"

"Shut up and drink your Sprite," my friend spits back, flicking the bottom of my cup enough that I spill most of the soda on my pants.

Great.

I remember all of the reasons I *really* hate parties the second we clear through the smoke and enter the crowd of drunken, obnoxious teenagers hovering around a poorly built fire. Cups in the air, half of them are dancing, bodies grinding together in ways I'm sure they think are sexy but are just—

And then I see her.

Eleanor is spinning in a slow circle, her arms above her head, hands twisting together from the buzz of whatever she drank, smoked or took. Maybe a little of all of that. My eyes meet Gemma's when Eleanor's back is to me and the plea for help is clear. I rush away from Jake, who's taking his time mingling with the crowd of people who seem to love him. The closer I get to the girls, the clearer the danger is. It's not so much that Eleanor is out of her mind and dancing on a table, but that she's wearing a long shirt without any pants, her body probably freezing because, even though the fire keeps things warm, it's nearing thirty degrees outside.

"Jonah, I swear, she was out of my sight for maybe five minutes. I don't know."

I sense the panic in Gemma's voice and do my best to form a reassuring smile.

"It's okay. I'm driving, and I can always take her home. Can we get her to come down from there?" I step to the side, trying to catch Eleanor's attention, but before I can, two hands pound into my chest and shove me backward several feet.

"Hey, fuckwad! Who do you think you are?" This guy is *not* one of Jake's friends. As well liked as my best friend is, he isn't the "it" guy everywhere. And the Molinas invite people from lots of places to their parties, including the junior college. I'm guessing that's where Shakespeare here hails from. He's about twice as thick as I am, but only half of that is muscle so I feel like, if anything, I can knock him over then outrun him.

"I'm her friend, and I'm here to make sure assholes like you don't take advantage of her," I shout. My voice carries enough over the music that Eleanor must hear me, crouching down so she can see me better.

"Jonah!" She sounds like Mandy, but her eyes are far more lost. There are two hearts drawn on her cheek in yellow and blue, probably a little touch Gemma gave her to make her feel better about not cheering at the game. I should have gone with her, sat by her so she wasn't alone or surrounded by people who don't fully understand what she's going through.

"Hi, Elle. Maybe let's get you some water, huh? And you

can have my flannel." I start to take it off, but she pushes my arms down and rejects the idea.

"No, I'm good. I'm dancing, and I've decided it's not my fault! I don't care what Morgan says." She stands quickly and immediately goes back to swaying her hips and giving the growing number of scumbags, including the dickhead who clearly was not threatened by me, more to look at than they deserve.

I exhale, my chest pounding with anger and frustration and worry. I'm not equipped for situations like this, but it's Eleanor, and it's not as though I can simply wash my hands of this and go home. Besides, I'm the driver and somebody has to get Jake home.

I meet Gemma's worried stare.

"Are you driving?" I notice she isn't holding a cup and her eyes look clear as day. She flashes me Eleanor's keys.

"I figured one of us needed to have our wits about us. She was insistent on coming. She texted me all day long, venting about Morgan telling her she should stay home and be with the family more, that she wasn't doing enough, especially since she was supposed to be watching Addy. I think she's really cracked, Jonah. It wasn't like that at all, and Morgan is taking it out on her because she's a bitch and that's how she deals with crises. I'm worried about her." She glances back up at her friend, the flickering glow of the flames lighting up her intense features.

"I won't leave her side all night. I promise. And if I have to carry her home, I will," I say. Gemma's eyes fall back to me, a touch of relief in them. We're miles from home, so that was an exaggeration. I won't carry her; I'll take a car, especially now that I know Gemma can take Jake home.

"I don't know what she did with her fucking pants." She

purses her lips after a vent of her own, and when she puts her hands on her hips and scans the area, I laugh.

"Let's see if we can get her to tie this around her waist, at least," I say, shaking my head and handing Gemma my black and yellow flannel. It's my favorite one, and I'm wearing a thinner long-sleeved shirt than I normally would. The blast of cold hits me, even this close to the fire, so I know Eleanor's cold.

"Hold this," Gemma says, giving me her phone while she climbs up to join her friend on the table. A round of whistles follows, and I'm afraid people will think I'm like these other assholes standing around.

"How'd you manage to make this happen, my friend?" Jake's arm flops along my shoulders and back as he steps in next to me, grinning.

"I didn't manage anything. Eleanor's super drunk, and Gemma's trying to get her to tie my shirt around her waist." I'm a little pissed that he sees this as some sexy show, just like those other dicks.

"Why isn't she wearing pants?" he asks, still a little too amused for my taste.

"Hell if I know." I shrug, glancing at his arm still slung over me. I try to shirk it off but he adjusts and leans on me a little harder. He's trying to force me to relax and fit in. I'm not in the mood.

We both look on while Gemma makes a game of it, basically tricking her friend into letting her cover her bottom half more than it is, which is not much at all. When she gets boos from the crowd, Jake's jaw tightens and I feel his fist form as his knuckles crack. If he picks a fight, I'm going to have to join him. My hands form fists in my pockets.

As the music morphs from rap and club beats mashed

together in no coherent order, Eleanor's body grows more and more listless. I start to worry that she'll collapse, and I think Jake does, too. It's either that or he's really raring for a fight because he's pulled his arm away from me and is holding his fist in his other palm, practicing his punch.

All it takes is Shakespeare to light the match.

I bolt the second his hand reaches forward and touches Eleanor's thigh. I slap it away and pull Eleanor from the table and into me. Jake takes over handling Shakespeare while I awkwardly lift Eleanor over my shoulder to carry her to her car.

"Can you get Jake home?" I shout over my shoulder to Gemma, who's following close behind.

"Yes," she answers.

When we reach the Volkswagen, Gemma exchanges keys with me and helps me persuade Eleanor to get into the passenger seat. That job becomes a whole lot easier after Eleanor vomits on the side of the road while her friend holds back her hair.

"You sure you can handle this?" Gemma's eyes meet mine as we both work to get Eleanor into the car and buckled up.

"I'll get her home. And I will make sure she's okay." I'm dead serious, and I think Gemma senses the depth of my promise.

She offers a faint smile and wraps her hands around mine as I squeeze the keys. "She's in a really bad place. Thank you for being there for her."

I nod and tighten my lips. There have been dozens of ways I fantasized about a world where I am Eleanor Trombley's person. This was never one of them.

"Tell Jake to call me tomorrow," I say, getting in on the driver's side and cranking the engine to peel us out of here.

"I'm sorry, Jonah. I got sick," Eleanor says as we drive, her voice weak and childlike. I'm starting to think someone gave her something, and I fight the growl deep in my belly that tells me I should race back to the party and tear apart every asshole there to find out who did it.

"It's okay, Eleanor. We're going home, and you can rest."

"You called me Eleanor," she hums.

I breathe in long and deep through my nose, then glance to my right to find her sad eyes waiting. I don't know how to respond. I'm rushed with a mixture of feelings. I want to yell at her for acting out, for not listening to her sister and staying home. I want to shake her sister for being so thoughtless with her words. And then I want to go back in time and call her *Elle.* That it means something to her makes me feel more than I have, maybe ever.

She's turned to rest on her side in her seat, an uncomfortable position that also makes me uneasy about driving. I'm not sure what I'm worried about more, that I'll stop fast and snap her neck or that she'll vomit on me.

We stop at a light about halfway home so I use the break to do my best to urge her to sit the right way in her seat. Tugging on her belt isn't enough, and she's too out of it to understand what I'm doing, something that becomes more obvious when she wraps her hands around my arm and brings it in for a hug like a scared child with a teddy bear.

"I have to drive," I explain, working my arm loose. She clings to it, but eventually I get it free, just in time for the light to turn green.

I pull forward slowly, entering the intersection while scanning both ways over and over again to make sure nobody is coming at us.

"Elle, I need you to get in your seat the right way.

Please?" I beg and use calling her Elle as a tool. I feel dirty that I did, but I need to soften her obstinacy. It works and her hard-lined mouth opens into a slight smile as she shifts and tugs at her seat belt until it's close to crossing her body in the right place.

"Thank you," I breathe out.

"You didn't wear a hat tonight," she stammers, reaching her left arm toward me and landing her open palm on the side of my head. Her fingers twist into my messy hair and I reach up and tether her hand in mine so I can drive safely.

"Someone stole it." If Mandy shows up on Monday wearing my hat I'm going to take it back.

"You shouldn't wear one anyway. You have really nice hair," she hums. Her fingers are trying to break out from my hand as I keep us clasped over the center console. I can't believe I'm in a position where I am literally fighting to keep Eleanor from playing with my hair.

"Thanks," I say, blushing with a sideways grin. Shitty situation or not, I'm still an absolute sucker for her compliment.

We manage to cross the highway without seeing much traffic, and by the time I pull her car along the curb outside her house, her head is nodding toward her shoulder as she fights off sleep.

"Hold on a few more seconds. Let's get you inside, okay?"

"Uh hmm," she says, a faint whisper.

I don't know where to take her—her house or mine—to sleep off whatever this is. I'm almost positive one of those assholes slipped something into her drink, especially if Gemma was with her almost every second.

"Think you can get inside?" I let go of her hand and turn to face her as I kill the motor in her car. I keep her keys hidden in my palm and I plan to keep them all night. She doesn't need to get any big ideas about driving herself somewhere.

"I think so. Morgan's up. She's . . . always . . . up." She starts to crawl out of her car after her sing-songy answer, so I race around to greet her before she can attempt to walk.

"Do you have a house key?"

"Oh . . . yeah." Eleanor pushes my hands away and feels around her hips. It's as if she just realized my shirt is tied around her and she pulls on the sleeves and begins to giggle.

"Hey, I like this one. Is it mine? Where are my pants? *Ohhh.*" Her brow furrows.

"Was your house key in your pants?" I ask. She's already stumbling her way toward her front door.

"Maybe," she slurs.

I catch under her arms before she completely crosses up her legs, and her prophecy turns out to be right as Morgan opens the door and takes two steps onto the stoop. I expect her to come running, worried, to join me in taking care of her spiraling sister. Instead, she crosses her arms over her chest.

"Shocker. You went to a party." Her eyes land on her sister with such disdain, even if I didn't care so much for Eleanor I would insist on defending her against that kind of judgment.

"You think you can help me get her inside? Maybe you can have your piece in the morning when she'll actually be able to ascertain the words you are saying?" I think I'm bolder than normal because of the pent-up aggression I'm still working out from the jerks at the party.

"I told her not to go. You should know better, too." I can

actually feel Morgan's scowl as she steps under Eleanor's other shoulder to help me guide her inside.

"You make some pretty shitty assumptions, you know that?" I grunt out as we move through the foyer and toward the stairs.

"Let's just get her to the couch," Morgan says, ignoring me completely. I know that's not where Eleanor wants to be, though. She'll only wake up worse, and she'll never fall asleep completely with her sister only a few feet away.

"I got her," I insist, sweeping my arms under Eleanor's legs and carrying her up the steps, leaving her sister trailing me. She doesn't come all the way up, and I'm glad because I'm in no mood to be considerate of her feelings.

"Thank you," Eleanor mumbles against my shoulder.

"Don't mention it," I huff.

I weave my way around the railing and down the hallway that matches mine, knowing exactly where to take her. I've only seen this room through a window, and from a distance of a few hundred feet.

It's dark inside, so it takes a moment for my eyes to adjust enough to find her bed. She reaches out as we get closer and I let her take herself the rest of the way. She flips on the small lamp by her bed, a pink one made of lace and crystal that looks as though it belongs in a little girl's room. I bet Addy loves this light.

She begins to push her shoes from her feet with her heels, so I help her get them off completely then fold her blanket over her body.

"Can I keep your shirt?" she mutters, her face smooshed into her pillow and her eyes closed.

"Consider it yours," I say, moving her shoes to the floor at the end of the bed. When I turn back to face her, I find her eyes open more than they've been the entire night. Staring at me, she blinks slowly, her face void of emotion.

"I'm sorry I'm hard to be friends with."

I lean back against her dresser with a heavy breath and pinch the bridge of my nose. Her words hurt, and they aren't true.

"Eleanor, there is nothing hard about being in your life. I'm glad you let me bring you home, though. Maybe tomorrow we can talk about . . . *this*?" I wave my hand slowly, signaling her current state.

She responds with another slow blink and I assume that's as much as I'm going to get.

"Okay, then. Why don't you get some sleep?" I step toward her night table and reach to flip off the light, but Eleanor stops me by brushing her knuckles against mine.

Frozen where I stand, I lock onto her touch and relax my fingers to let hers find their way into the spaces between. It's such a light touch, and it might be all the energy she has to give, but it's enough to refuel me and remind me why I will walk through fire for this girl if that's what she needs. Eleanor Trombley is special. Always has been, always will be. And the more I get to know her, especially all of her broken bits, the more I think we're finding each other at the exact moment we're supposed to.

"Good night, Elle," I say, squeezing her hand gently and tucking it back into her body, then pulling up her blanket.

I flip her light off for real this time and close the door almost completely before making my way back downstairs to where Morgan waits by the front door. Before she has a chance to tell me all the ways she is right and Eleanor is wrong, I break down the hard truths that a person going through something like this might not be capable of seeing on her own.

"You have to stop," I say, stepping up to face her squarely. Her mouth hangs open and her eyes squint.

"I don't mean to offend you, or . . . or maybe I do. I know you—your entire family—you're all going through hell. I can only imagine half of it. When my dad died last year, I had closure. It was a dull pain, but at least I knew that was what I was going to get. You all, you're left without answers, and the clues that come along seem like traps that are only going to make things hurt more, make the pain last longer."

I pause my lecture when her eye ticks and she shifts her hands to her back pockets as she steps in closer. I move back a step on instinct.

"My baby sister is missing, and there isn't a goddamn thing I can do about it. No offense, but you don't know shit." I think she wants to mean every word of this, but fear flickers behind her eyes.

"I know that punishing your other sister—more than she's already punishing herself—is not going to make things better for either of you. You're only going to ruin your relationship with her, make her resent you. She's eighteen, Morgan. She is missing all of those things that make up who she is. She's *choosing* to miss those things because she thinks that's what her family expects her to do, and instead of living her life she sits in her room, thinking about how she is to blame for absolutely everything."

Morgan shakes her head, but before she can tell me I'm off base, I continue.

"You think she's in there sleeping at night, but she hasn't slept in days. She's slept at my house, twice, and probably because she was so exhausted that her body couldn't go on anymore. She can't sleep here because being here reminds her that Addy is missing and you blame her for it. And if *you* blame her, then your parents must blame her, too. And now your grandparents. You all have created this environment where she doesn't feel safe in her own house. That's why she keeps going out and seeking peace and comfort *literally* anywhere else."

"Okay. Okay!" Morgan growls, cutting me off. Her eyes are glassy and she swipes the tears away with a jerk of her hand. She looks out through the open door toward my house, to the place where her sister feels safe.

After a few long wordless seconds, I dip my head and move to leave the Trombley home.

"They're never going to find her."

I stop cold at the doorway. I don't think she could have uttered a more devastating statement. I tilt my head to the side and meet her eyes. The tears are back, and they fall when she blinks.

"At this point, they're looking for a body." She shrugs, letting out a tiny humorless laugh that's only there to mask the devastation she's barely holding inside. She shakes her head and breathes out a ragged breath that flaps her cheeks. She's tired. They all are. Her eyes dip down then come back to me, her brow creasing with worry and regret.

"I shouldn't have made her feel that way, that it's her fault. Any of it. I know I'm not being fair. I've been making so many decisions, and I feel like I have to make *all* of them because my parents just can't."

If I knew her better, I'd hug her. If I weren't such a recluse, I'd step in and help their entire family. I would have from the very beginning rather than watch it all unfold out my front window. *I should have.*

But I can save Eleanor. I can make this inevitable life-altering pain survivable. I just need Morgan to let me.

"Let her sleep. She was acting out tonight, rebelling. But when she wakes up, she's going to remember that she thinks you hate her. That's when you need to make sure she knows it's exactly the opposite. You need each other. Trust me. I'm a guy with a very tiny family who values both members as much as the air I breathe." I let the thought of losing Grandpa or Mom pass over my soul, and imagining it carves a deep wound.

"Thank you for getting her home," she says. I think maybe this is the first time she hasn't looked at me like some house elf from under the stairs. I fish Eleanor's keys from my pocket and hand them to her for safekeeping, because I know if anything, I can trust Morgan to keep her sister out of a vehicle for the next several hours.

I leave her with a soft smile and head out into the darkness, crossing the street to my house where I enter through the garage. I should be exhausted but for some reason, I'm not tired at all. The palette of emotions I've gone through in the last hour have charged my mind and my muscles. Rather than waste the next few hours staring at my ceiling and flipping from side to side in my bed, I decide to do some good. I shut the door behind me and flip the main lights on in the garage before propping open the Bronco's hood. Dale and I got through about two dozen wires before he left, which leaves a couple dozen to go.

I arm myself with the wire tester and pull my phone from my pocket, resting it on the fender. With a few swipes, I open the playlist Eleanor made me for my birthday and smile at the now familiar chords that start the first song—the song about a young man working on a Bronco he hopes to one day hand down to his son.

CHAPTER Fifteen

I finished every wire I could access without some sort of yoga move. I worked on the truck until the sun was almost up, and then grunted out some sort of explanation to my mom and grandpa as I passed them on my way up the stairs. Sleep took over the second my face hit the pillow, and if it weren't for the faint buzz of my phone coming from somewhere in the depths of my blanket and sheets, I would have kept dreaming until the sun went down again.

Finally uncovering my phone, I bring it to my face to focus my eyes enough to read the text message. I sit up when I realize it's from Eleanor.

ELEANOR: *Can I come over to talk?*

I flatten my palm on the side of my face to rub life back into my skin. Staring at my screen, I switch over to the camera mode so I can see what kind of hair situation I'm dealing with. All I can do is laugh when I see the absolute rooster hawk split in two on top of my head. I push it down only to watch it pop back up. I'm not telling her *no.* I knew that the moment she asked. I just need to buy myself a few minutes of time.

ME: *Give me 5 mins to shower.*

I don't wait for her response. I rush to my bathroom with the cleanest pair of jeans on my floor and my Harvard hoodie. After the world's fastest shower, water pounding my hair long enough to train it back where it's supposed to go, I get myself semi-dry and toss on my clean-ish clothes before clamoring down the stairs.

I haven't looked at the time yet today, but I'm guessing by the way the light comes through the front window that it's mid-afternoon. I speed up my trip down the steps when I hear my grandfather having a conversation with someone, knowing there's really only one person that could be.

"This here is my world-famous hangover cure—"

"Oh, hey, I think she's good," I say, sliding into the kitchen in my socks in time for my grandfather to crack an egg in what I am pretty sure is half a mug of Pabst Blue Ribbon and honey.

"You had a late night. You need some of this, too?" Grandpa holds the mug up and I take it from his hand happily while shaking my head on my way to the sink.

"Oh, ya know? I think I'm okay," I say, pouring the contents down the drain. I hit the disposal button and turn the water on to make sure it goes down, catching a whiff of cheap beer that confirms my initial suspicion.

"Hey, that's a sure-fire recipe! And a waste of a perfectly good beer," he grumbles.

"Yes, but that concoction only works on war veterans in their seventies," I reply, leaving the cup in the sink and turning to face my grandfather's scowl. My eyes move to Eleanor standing just beyond his shoulder, hugging herself in the shirt I gave her last night.

I wasn't going to drink that, she mouths silently, her eyebrows up to her hairline.

No, I mouth back.

"I can see you. And I can read lips, dumbass," Grandpa jabs. He grunts his way around the kitchen a little longer, muttering about the beer a few more times before heading to the living room where he puts on the pre-game for the Blackhawks.

I chuckle at his behavior because I know he's over it already. My attention moves back to Eleanor, and I can see why Grandpa thought she might need a little *boost* this morning. Dark circles weigh under her eyes, the rest of her skin vampire pale. Her hair is pulled into double knots at the base of her neck on either side, and I think maybe she woke up with a hairstyle a lot like I did.

"I just—"

"Would you—"

Our breathy laughs come out in sync as we talk over each other. I lean back into the counter and extend my hand.

"You first," I say, my eyes moving to the spot where she's kneading her hands together. She's probably embarrassed about last night, and I don't want her to be. We all have low points. I am finding it hard to reconcile that version of her with the one in front of me, and the one I've spent time with over the last several days.

"I brought your shirt back." She perks up, pulling one arm halfway out of the sleeve.

"You keep it," I say, nodding toward her. It's my favorite, and yet it was somehow really easy to give away.

Her brow pinches, but her mouth ticks up with a tiny grin.

"You sure?" She's already pushed her arm back through the sleeve. She loves it.

"It looks a lot better on you," I say. That is not a lie.

"Thanks," she says, sucking in her bottom lip.

We make eye contact once or twice while a healthy dose of awkward silence settles in. I wish I could let her off the hook, but I don't know how to change subjects. Last night is clearly all the two of us are thinking about. Thankfully, Grandpa Hank breaks up the sound by yelling "bullshit" at the TV.

We both look toward the back of his head and I ease her concern with a soft laugh.

"He does that with hockey," I reassure. "What's funny is it's still only pre-game. He's probably reliving a bad call from two days ago."

I roll my eyes, and Eleanor gives me a courtesy laugh.

"Hey, wanna come hang in the garage? I did a lot of work. I think Jake may win the bet at this rate," I say, leaning my head toward the garage door.

"Can we not tell him? I was really looking forward to him streaking," she says.

"Oh, absolutely. Good plan," I agree.

Our eyes hang on to one another for a breath and I break the tension, urging her to follow me to the garage. I left things a bit messy when I finished up this morning, so I grab a broom from the corner and sweep up the wire clippings. Before I can get the dustpan on my own, Eleanor kneels with it and waits for me to push the trash into it with my broom.

"Thanks," I say.

Her eyes flit up and she gives me a tight-lipped smile that highlights blushing cheeks. She's still embarrassed about last night. I have to make this easier for her.

"So . . . how are you feeling?" I rub the back of my neck and wince at the uncomfortable entry into this topic. She pauses briefly on the way to the trash can.

"I almost let your grandpa feed me honey-beer-egg soup, if that's any indicator," she says, glancing over her shoulder with a bashful smile. She continues to the trash, dumping the mess and leaving the dust pan in the corner.

My hands slide into my back pockets and I inhale, breaking my breath up with a short laugh when Eleanor spins to face me and does the exact same thing.

"Listen—" I begin.

"No," she interjects, shaking her head. She steps closer to me and when her palms run down my biceps and tug on the elbows of my sleeves, I give over complete control of my limbs to the most beautiful girl in the world. Even at her lowest, Eleanor Trombley is a wonder to behold.

My hands fall from my pockets as she moves her hands along my forearms, eventually taking my wrists then my palms. She holds them in front of her, her eyes fixed on the act while I'm unable to look away from her face. I study the jerking motion of her lashes as she blinks rapidly, nerves and raw emotion picking up her breath.

"Why do I feel like you're about to tell me my dog died?" I joke in an attempt to lighten the mood.

She laughs as a few tears slip out.

"Oh, don't cry. I don't really have a dog. I mean, you probably would have seen it."

She laughs a little harder and I give her hands a squeeze for added strength and courage. A hard swallow moves her throat and she lets go of one of my hands to run her arm over her eyes. I leave my hand where she left it, and I'm relieved when she holds it again.

Breathing out through whistle-ready lips, she brings

her eyes to mine and shakes our hands as they stick together.

"I'm so sorry about last night, Jonah. I never meant to put so much of my shit on you, and it isn't fair." She glances down to her feet, so I tug at her hands this time, coaxing her gaze back up.

"Hey, I don't do things I don't want to do," I respond.

She grimaces.

"No, it's true. Peer pressure is useless on me." I shake my head a little.

Her eyes squint with skepticism.

"So why did you go to the party last night? You hate them. It's the one thing *everyone* knows about Jonah Wydner." She levels me with a daring look, and it's a tough call because she's not wrong.

"I do hate parties," I admit. "But . . ."

I lean back and open my mouth, cautioning her not to assume anything.

"I would not have gone if I did not want to go. At least *some* part of me." I hold the tight-lipped grin in place while she evaluates my answer to see if I'm bluffing. I'm not. Yes, I hate parties, but I went for her. I would swim through lava to keep her safe.

Her head cocks to the side but her smile shifts into something lighter, maybe shedding a little of the guilt she brought over here this morning.

"You know, it's an excellent time to climb up on the roof and watch the sun go down." Her fingers slip away as she makes the suggestion, and I find my hands frozen in place for a moment all on their own. I shove them back into my pockets.

"Is it really that late?" I lift a brow.

"It's almost four." She winces and I join her.

"I don't think I've slept this late since I had the flu sophomore year," I admit.

She laughs at my response, then hits the button for the garage door.

"This used to be a regular Saturday morning occurrence for me," she says.

"I'm pretty sure you can't call it morning," I add.

She spins on her heels as she moves out of the garage and points at me.

"You are probably right."

We cross my driveway to the very dead grass in our side yard. Eleanor leaps up to grab the eave but her fingers slip at her first attempt. She crouches to jump again but stops, spinning to face me as she points over her shoulder with her thumb.

"You been sunset watching without me?" she asks.

The ladder is still out. I haven't touched it since the last time we went up there.

"That would sound a lot better than admitting I'm too lazy to put it away, but sadly, I'm a lazy ass." I mush my lips together and shrug.

"Well, my muscles are not feeling it today, so let's just say you were planning ahead." She marches to the ladder and scales it two rungs at a time. Even at her laziest, she's got me beat.

She waits at the roof's edge for me this time, and I'm a little embarrassed because I climb ladders the same way my grandfather does—like one wrong move might break a hip. I crawl onto the shingles as she stands and holds a hand out for me.

"I can't run and leap over there like you do," I say, waving my hand just out of reach. It's like I'm about to shake on a deal and I want to make sure I know the terms.

Eleanor leans her head back and the sound of real laughter pours out with the rasp that I've missed.

"It's fine. I'll go slow," she says, taking my hand and helping me to my feet.

I sway a little, only half joking that I'm searching for my balance. I notice that she walks along the rooftop on her toes, almost like a ballerina making her way to center stage. I move with the grace of a Clydesdale.

We settle in the ridge this time and I lower myself carefully, dividing my weight over both sides of the roof. Eleanor seems to collapse into a sitting position, her legs knotted together as she perches at the apex facing me. I breathe out a laugh at how different we are.

"What?" she asks.

"Just, you can tell you do things like gymnastics and stuff. It's pretty clear I work out math equations." I shrug.

"You'd think that would make you more confident up here, being able to compute the exact angles and all that junk," she argues.

"Huh," I say, taking her reasoning to heart. I glance to my left and then my right, but before I can fully take in the angle of the descent behind me I grip the roof's surface beneath my thighs.

"Nope. There's no math logic for this," I say.

She giggles, an actual giggle. It's the best sound, like a children's birthday party with a petting zoo kind of glee. Jake made fun of me endlessly the last time I crawled up here with him. I was too shell-shocked to smack him with one of the water balloons.

A few cars pass along our street, and we both give our full attention to them, watching them come to complete stops on either end. I notice her driveway is half empty, and wonder if she's had a chance to talk with Morgan today. I hope my advice was taken to heart.

"Family outing?" I ask, gesturing to her empty driveway below. Her parents' car and Morgan's SUV are missing.

I expect a heavy sigh or for her to push my question off. But none of that happens.

"My parents are attempting grocery shopping. And Morgan is getting a pedicure." She blinks as her gaze shifts from her world below to me. "It's a good step. Important, probably. I mean, Morgan's feet are disgusting. Really, I don't know how we've all managed to live in the same house with her like that."

Her teeth grip her bottom lip as she pauses, waiting for me to laugh. I give in, understanding her need to use humor to not be real right now. She laughs with me for a few seconds, until our efforts die down into quiet again. I'm so close to her that I can only focus on one eye at a time, and as hard as it is to not to blush under her stare, I endure it, reminding myself that she's looking at me, too.

"She said you talked," she says finally, shifting her body to face the other direction, away from the setting sun.

"I gave her some advice, not that I'm qualified or anything."

We both glance to our sides, meeting in the middle for a brief exchange.

"You're more than qualified, Jonah. I think it meant a lot to her. We—Morgan and I—talked a lot when I woke up. You know, about twenty minutes before I came over here?" She laughs through her words again.

"Good," I say through my smile.

That I helped, even in the smallest way, settles the raging nerves in my chest. So many of my choices when it comes to Eleanor have me on edge. I never know if I'm helping or hurting. I only know that my intentions are always from the heart, and I guess that's all that matters.

"Speaking of trying things to feel normal . . ." She draws in a deep breath and I steady myself for whatever she has to say. It seems to be difficult.

"I want to cheer. I miss it." She nods and moves her focus to me.

I push my smile into my cheeks, making sure to show enthusiasm and support.

"You were meant to do it. And if you think you're ready, then I think you should." I can see the reservations play out on her face, her smile timid, tempered by gritted teeth. Before she can make an argument for the other side, I continue with all the reasons she should.

"It will make your days feel normal, and you're so good at it. I mean, not as good as me, but . . ." I let the quiet slip in, sensing that she doesn't want any jokes. She wants the truth.

"It's what Addy wants," I say, getting to the only thing that matters. It's been three weeks, a timeline that feels too short to do something other than sit and hope and pray.

"You mean *would* want," she answers in a quiet voice that works hard not to break. Her eyes flit to mine then back to the sky behind me.

"No, I meant what I said. No matter what, that's what Addy wants." My words are heavy with meaning, and they earn me a long stare into Eleanor's eyes as she turns to understand me better. I swallow and shake my head, never once letting my eyes shift from hers. "You can't think that way. Addy *is*. No matter what. And always."

I'm trying to both encourage hope but also edge it with hard truths, that this story—her family's tragedy—might get worse before it gets better. Morgan wasn't wrong last night. It's been three weeks. Their one solid lead disappeared with few clues. The odds of finding Addy are growing grimmer by the hour. And finding her alive may no longer be the only mission. It doesn't change the way Addy lives inside her sister's heart, though; I'm learning that slowly. My dad is more alive inside my chest now than he was the year before he passed. It's about knowing someone.

"Will you come to the games? There are only two left, and then competition. So I have someone there for me, to see me? My family…they just can't yet." Her plea breaks my heart and I can't help the way it pulls my eyes down with a tender sorrow.

"It would be an honor." A strange electricity builds between us during the silence this time, and I'm not sure whether it's because of a real connection or because I want there to be one. Eleanor is the first to look away with a glance to the side, the sky's colors reflecting in her golden lashes and off her soft skin. She's orange and pink, like a work of art—God's colors brushed on her face.

"Oh, it's show time," she says, and I think partly to change the subject and break up the intensity blanketing us.

I lean back on my elbows and turn my face to the sun just as it dives behind the rooftops and trees in the distance. Eleanor moves closer, her shoulder leaning against mine, but her body is turned to face behind me. I shake with a quiet laugh, assuming she's joking, but the longer she sits backward, the more I realize she's watching an entirely different wonder happen behind me.

"You waiting on the moon or somethin'?" I joke.

"I always watch the sunset from the other side. Sky looks like candy this way." She grins and goes back to watching the magic happen as pinks dip into purple and oranges become red. I watch it all happen in her expression—in her eyes and in the way the light hits her face. I stare at her more than I look at the sun dropping before me, because of all the things she could have said, she found a very intimate line of poetry to reference.

I hear you, Dad. And you are right. The sky does look like candy, and this girl is incredibly special.

CHAPTER Sixteen

I wasn't sure she would actually go through with it. Sunday, when we hung out in the garage with Jake and Gemma, I got the sense that Eleanor was waffling on her decision to come back to school. Her car was still parked in front of her house when Jake picked me up Monday morning, and we were running late. Jake is always running late, which makes me always running late by default.

But then it was our lunch hour, and I was getting ready to hide in my favorite window seat with my final reading for the semester—*King Lear*. Gemma approached me, her arm looped through Eleanor's as if it were just another Monday and nothing had ever changed at all.

I gave in and joined them for off-campus lunch. Like I told Eleanor, even things I hate doing I will do when there is *some* reason for me to want to. Monday's car ride of death was a must for me because Eleanor was going. Not only did I want to protect her from Jake's crash-and-burn style on the road, but I didn't want anyone else letting her sit on their lap.

I took the same seat as last time, and instead of Gemma on my thighs, it was Eleanor. It was the first time I've held her like that without it being to console her. It was greedy, but I have thought about that five-minute ride for the entire week. It might have been the only time I've been in a car with Jake driving when his lack of attention to the road was the last thing on my mind.

My Tuesday lunch was taken up with a dental appointment (*thanks, Mom*) and I decided to let Eleanor have her time with Gemma the rest of the week. Things almost felt normal, as if she never left the hallways of Oak Forest High at all. Only, in this version of my senior year, Eleanor talks to me in the hallways and I don't run and hide.

Tonight, though, will be a different test.

For us.

For her.

As shitty as our high school football team is, there is still a strange hierarchy that accompanies the Friday night games. There's an unspoken structure to where people sit within the student section, and though I always get a pass because I'm with Jake, I don't want to sit in the thick of the crowd with him. I want to be up front where Eleanor can see me if she needs a reassuring face.

"Are you sure you want to sit with the freshmen? I mean . . ." Jake doesn't quite grasp why anyone would do this. Even when he was a freshman he did not sit with the freshmen. It's harder to see things up front, at least if you're watching the game. I couldn't give two shits about our one-and-eight football team, though.

"I'll be fine. Honestly, I might even be the popular guy down there. Those fourteen-year-old girls think I'm a sophisticated older man." I tug the neck of my long-sleeved shirt as if I'm wearing a tie. Jake jerks with a laugh and rolls his eyes.

"There is nothing about you that looks sophisticated in that thing," my friend says, pointing to the hat on my head. I'm still without my beanie, so I had to settle for my Cubs hat which is, apparently, a dad-hat style. Flat brims are where it's at.

My shoulders sag with his confidence deflator.

"It's better than my hair," I say, pulling it off briefly to unveil hair that at this point is probably in need of a cut. My friend studies it for a minute and shakes his head.

"I don't know. It's really a toss-up." He turns and walks up the bleachers to where the rest of his basketball teammates are waiting for him. They're all decked out in our school colors, some of them going so bold as to paint Badgers on their chests and wear their shirts tied around their heads.

I turn to the roomy area on my right where a few freshmen girls share a bag of popcorn, and I smile when they look up at me.

"Oh, my God!" The one talking actually looks repulsed while the other two laugh, and they huddle in closer. I think they're hoping I will pass and sit nowhere close to them.

I sigh.

They get their wish as I slip to the very front row, behind the trash can. I've thought this through, and nobody hovers around that can, which means if I need to stand and lean over the rail to talk to Eleanor, I shouldn't have to fight my way through a crowd.

I wore my gas-station-style shirt over my gray long-sleeved shirt and black jeans. I couldn't look less full of spirit, but that wasn't part of my thought process. I think I look good in this shirt. Or I did, until a few minutes ago when three freshmen girls brought me down a big notch.

The drums from our marching band kick in from behind the bleachers, so I get to my feet. Cheer walks in with the band. It's literally the one programming note I have memorized. I've spent every game I've attended waiting for this part so I could watch Eleanor Trombley march in at the front of the line.

She isn't first this time, but that's okay. I think she asked for it to be that way, not wanting the eyes on her. People still whisper. Not so much the students but their parents. Gossip keeps people going, and it seems to be a primary fodder of choice for adults of a certain age and income.

I catch the grin on my face when my eyes meet hers, and I can't be certain but I think her eyes widen seeing me. I clap along with the band, which is something only band parents do it seems, but I've already started so I keep the habit up through the fight song while I stand by myself, sheltered by a trash can that smells of old soda.

"Let's go, Badgers!" The cheer squad yells in unison, but it's only Eleanor's voice I hear.

Her lips are a bright red, and her cheeks sport the same blue and yellow hearts they wore last Friday night, only this time they're accompanied by high, rosy cheeks. This is where she belongs.

I keep my spot protected, manspreading, as my mom calls it, to keep other people from sitting directly next to me. I stand for kick-off, but keep my eyes on Eleanor rather than the crappy defense that lets the other team get away with a sixty-yard return. I don't sit until she tells me to—literally. She spins to face the crowd and completes a few jumps before holding her hands at her hips and mouthing my name.

I cup my ear, unable to hear her. She steps closer to the rail and I get excited for a minute because everyone sees her talking to me. This is literally a scene out of a dream I once had.

"You can sit now!" She points with her finger in a downward motion, and my face burns red hot.

"Sorry," I say, smiling through gritted teeth. A few people near me laugh, and I let my eyes flutter as they roll behind my lids. Eleanor is still smiling when I open them again, and that is all that matters.

I decide to stay close to the bench for the first half, not that there is much to stand for at a Badger game. Eleanor seems mostly in her element, catching on to a few new routines and following Gemma from behind. She seems a little winded when the buzzer sounds and the team heads to the locker rooms for half time, so I decide to step closer to the track and see if she needs me to get her a snack or something more exciting than ice water.

Navigating toward the field is a little like salmon swimming upstream to spawn, but eventually I make it to the small walkway along the track. I lean over the fence and hold up a hand, trying to get Eleanor's attention, but her coach steps into the space between us, blocking her view. I back up into the shadow under the bleachers so I don't distract them, but the longer the conversation continues, the less sure I am that this is a good idea.

"We had to move on, Eleanor. I am so sorry for what your family is going through, but I had to look out for the team. You'll still be an alternate, but we have to be ready for regionals." These are the only words I can make out for certain from the cheer coach, and a slight shift in my position reveals a familiar expression on Eleanor's face. It's the brave one she puts on when she's trying not to let everything out. It's like a cork holding back a hurricane. Her lips work to maintain an understanding smile as she nods, but it's her feet and hands that tell the truth. Her legs step side-to-side, her hands scrunched in her uniform. Puffs of fog accent her breath coming from her nose as she repeats the same words, over and over again.

"Of course."

"Yes, I understand."

"I will, and thank you."

She was replaced. Her senior year, her defining moment, and her passion. Those words she is uttering, they are all lies. My chest burns for her.

I stay in the shadows, even after her coach leaves her to find her way to the chairs to sit alone and watch her squad —the one she captained—do their routine without her. She keeps that smile locked in place and holds back the tears, though I can see them as they hover on the precipice, waiting to fall like daggers toward her neck and chest. She claps to the music, counting along with her teammates as if she's out on the field with them doing the same flips and tricks.

When their performance ends, she stands and clasps her hands behind her back, one holding the other so tight the blood squeezes to the surface of her skin.

I dash from my spot before she notices me, grabbing myself a semi-warm pretzel and a Coke from the snack bar before heading back to the bleachers. My area is no longer open, so I hover on the steps for a few seconds before deciding to join Jake and the other seniors in the middle of the student section. I'd rather rub shoulders with people I know.

"You get lonely down there?" Jake asks.

"Something like that," I answer, knowing he's not really looking for one. I offer him part of my pretzel and he rips off one of the loops. I don't really even want it.

The conversations around me carry on amid these worlds where nothing has changed. At least two of Jake's friends comment how hot Elle is and how the new cheer uniforms are shorter than the old ones. Not one of them sees how her smile no longer reaches her eyes. I bet they don't even notice she isn't at the top of the pyramid where she belongs. For them, Eleanor was on vacation. Now she's back, and all is right in their world. Meanwhile, hers is burning to the ground.

"You're quiet." Jake pushes into my side, and I give him a sideways glance.

"I'm always quiet," I mumble, pulling another bite of my pretzel free and stuffing it into my mouth for a better excuse. "I'm eating."

"Bullshit. The food here is shitty. What's going on?" His attention is only half on me. I can tell because he keeps turning to his other side to join in with the laughter. I don't tell him this is why I hate coming to these things, because Jake loves stuff like this. When I'm here, I feel like his sad, pathetic pet that needs tending to. I'd be perfectly happy having him give me a place to sit and then ignore me, but that wouldn't feel right to him. Jake is actually a kind person who tries to do right by people despite his sordid dating history. He wouldn't feel right ignoring me, and I wouldn't feel right telling him to.

"They didn't let Eleanor do the routine. I hope she's okay, is all." As soon as I finish my sentence I know Jake didn't fully hear it.

"Oh, you think? Wait, what was that?" He shifts to give

me his total attention, but with the extra seconds of thought, I decide it's better for Eleanor if I don't make her worries known to anyone else.

"I just thought our team was better than this. That's all," I lie. It's a half-lie, actually, because I did expect us to score.

"Oh, yeah. I should have warned you. We've gotten worse since the last game I dragged you to. I hear they might fire the coach."

"Like that will make a difference," one of his friends snarks, leaning over Jake's shoulder.

"I know, right?" Jake answers, clasping hands with his friend in some sort of bro agreement. I tuck the straw from my drink into my lips and suck in a huge gulp. At least the soda isn't flat. The burn of carbonation is a pleasant distraction and I let my eyes water, thankful for the way it scratches against my throat.

I stick with Jake and his friends for the second half, and I only catch Eleanor looking for me once. I do my best to stand and raise a hand to help her find me, but her search is short. In a way, she seems relieved that I'm not there to witness her not shine. Thing is, though, she *is* shining. Simply being here and breaking through the heavy boulders tied to her spirit is a massive achievement. But no teenager wants to hear high level psychology like that when their world seems to be slipping away.

I don't stand again until the end of the game when our team actually scores. It's only because the other team's third string is in, but still, a touchdown means we aren't completely shut out, and that is cause for celebration on the Badger side of the field.

I slink out with the thick crowd, tagging along behind Jake and his friends down the steps and into the parking lot where everyone breaks up into their respective cliques to make plans for the next few hours. Jake knows better than to force me into another party, and there is no way I am letting Eleanor put herself through that after tonight. I can't guarantee she won't do something stupid like last week.

"Hey, see ya for tutoring Sunday? Test Monday, bruh," Jake says, holding up a palm as I inch away from his group of friends.

"Sounds good, yeah," I say, relieved when I'm finally free to wander by myself. I toss my empty drink cup into a trash in the middle of the lot then wait at the curb until most of the lot clears out, minus the cars belonging to players, band members, and cheerleaders.

Eleanor's car is in the very center, and if I had her keys, I'd pull around and pick her up so she doesn't have to walk far. Instead, I sit on the parking stop in front of her car, my back resting on her bumper. It takes about ten minutes for players to file out through the locker room doors. The ladies' side is on the opposite end of the building, so I keep my eyes focused on the yellow-lit walkway where Eleanor should appear soon. After a few more minutes, she comes into view, the first one out, her best friend nowhere in sight.

She's practically marching toward me, her hand working her keys into position, her pompoms clutched to her side along with a gym bag that I guess contains her uniform. She's taken out the ribbons that had pulled her hair up tight at the top of her head. Everything about her movements teems with anger. I stand before she gets to me, and I mentally run through the talking points I spent the entire second half preparing. I'll congratulate her for taking the first step. I'll soothe her when she tells me what happened, and encourage her to fight to earn back her spot. I'll offer to buy her a puppy just to make her laugh.

My mouth hangs open as she approaches, though, and by the time she reaches me, I realize that nothing I say will penetrate the walls she's put up over the last hour.

"It's all fucking bullshit. Let's go," she says, pulling her door open and throwing her things into the back of her car.

"You ready?" She lifts her head and meets my gaze, her eyes glowing with rage. I'm not sure what's better for her at this point, to be angry or to cry, which is what I know she really wants to do.

"I—" My mouth still hangs open, not sure where to go from there. I haven't moved a step. I'm still balancing on the parking stopper and she's ready to hop into the driver's seat and peel out of this place.

"Do you want me to drive?" I don't know why I think this is the best way to go.

"I'm fine, Jonah. This was a stupid idea, is all. Just, let's go home." Her brow is pulled so tight that I fear it might leave a permanent line in her forehead. Her nostrils flare as she stares at me. This is one of those moments I am destined to stand out from everyone else in her life. She'll either hate me for it or—

"This was not a stupid idea, Elle." I use her nickname, and I can tell immediately she thinks I'm using it as a weapon to soften her. Maybe I am.

"You know they replaced me, right? I saw you. You heard everything. They had to 'move on without me.'" She makes air quotes when she repeats what her coach said, but her phone is still in her hand as she does this, and her grip slips, sending her device end over end toward the ground.

"Shit!" she shouts, her voice echoing and drawing attention from the few people in the lot.

I rush over to help her retrieve her phone but she brushes me off when I get close. On her knees, gravel digs into her skin, piercing holes in her leggings. She cradles her phone in her palms and stares at the cracked screen.

"I know a guy who replaces those things—"

"Just *don't,* okay?" Her voice comes out stern, like Morgan's, and the bite in her tone makes me back up a step or two. My hands find home in my pockets as I do, and I move back to the front of her car, giving her the space she wants even if I don't think it's what she needs.

She fusses with her screen for several minutes, and I'm left to watch her try to make various functions work. She swears every time she realizes something else is broken, and eventually she tosses it with a hard thrust along the ground, busting off pieces as it bounces several spots away.

Gemma is on her way to her car and pivots to us, but I wave her off silently, begging with my hands for her to let me have this one. Gemma isn't stuck on the sidelines. She will pretend to understand how this feels, but she can never really understand.

After a few minutes, the parking lot gets quiet again. There are a few cars left, but for the most part we're alone. Nobody is parked close enough to give a damn about a girl trying her hardest not to cry.

I scan the parking spots around us and retrieve the various parts of Eleanor's phone. The sim card actually came out, which is not easy to do. I usually have to use a paperclip to get that sucker to pop out. I put all of the pieces in my front pocket and move closer to Eleanor, who has given in to gravity and is now sitting on the ground with her knees bent while she inspects the holes in her pants and the bleeding skin underneath.

I know better than to talk first. I've got all night, and they'll be cleaning the bleachers for at least an hour. Students are gross. I lean against her car a few feet from where she's sitting, and fold my arms over my stomach for warmth while I wait.

"I fucked up, Jonah. I fucked it all up," she finally mutters. She blinks at the end of this faulty confession.

"You didn't fuck anything up, Elle." I mean it, but she winces as if I've lashed her anyway.

"I did. I took my eyes off my sister and ruined everything for everyone. And how shallow am I that I care about being in some stupid dance that isn't even very good." She shakes her head, tears finally descending along the contours of her face.

"Nobody saw her, Elle. Nobody was watching, and you are not her parent—*your* parents are her parent." It's probably cruel of me to turn the fault on her mom and dad like that, but honestly, why everyone in her house seems okay with letting her carry the blame baffles me.

My words don't seem to matter; she's content to fall on the sword. Maybe it's so she can feel something other than the green poison of envy for the girl who took her place in a dance that, yes, probably *isn't even very good.* I want to see her fight, though. I know there's a warrior in there, and I feel like if she loses that, then she'll never be the same.

"Show me," I say.

She lifts her head and scowls, her mouth turned down.

"Show you what?" she spits back.

"The dance. The one that isn't even very good. Show me," I insist. I raise my arms up so they're folded over my chest, and do my best to hold my mouth in a smug line.

She laughs out once, then looks to her right, toward the locker rooms that are now emptied. The last car is about to pull through the gates. Nobody but me here to see anything.

"Don't be stupid," she utters, getting to her feet and bending down to brush any remaining gravel from her legs. "Where's my phone? Or what's left of it."

She approaches me with an open palm and I shift, shoving my hands in my pockets to keep her phone pieces safe and out of reach.

"I have your phone. It's fine. Show me." I lift my chin as if I hold some sort of authority.

She stops a few feet shy of me and shakes her head, her palms out at her sides.

"What are you doing, Jonah?" She looks to her sides again, always checking to see who is watching.

"Nobody is judging you, Eleanor. Everyone is gone. There's nobody here to see."

"I know!" she fires back.

There she is.

"Okay, then what are you waiting for?"

I hold her gaze, my head cocked to one side a tick, hers to the other. Her nostrils flare with the fire I lit, a different fire than the kind that gives up.

"Get in the car, Jonah. I want to go home." She's lying. I can read it in her eyes. Her focus wavers, darting from me to the things around me. Her hands ball into fists at her sides and rap against the sides of her thighs.

"You go. You can leave me here and I'll walk. It's fine." I shrug, my gut telling me she won't do that.

"Fine," she utters, stomping to her driver's side door, still open from when she threw her things inside. I step away to make room for her as she pulls the door shut and shoves her key in the ignition, over-cranking it so it makes a grinding sound while the motor roars to life.

For a moment, I think maybe my gut is wrong because in a matter of seconds Eleanor shifts into reverse and peels backward from the parking spot, fishtailing her tiny car forward at Jake-level speed. My hands still in my pockets, I shuffle my feet as I turn to watch her leave. Before she makes the turn, though, she skids to a hard stop. Her car sits idle, the tail lights indicating that she hasn't yet shifted into park.

Don't go, Elle.

Long seconds pass with her tailpipe spewing fog into the cold winter air. It smells like rain outside, but the chill on my neck and face makes me think it might be snow coming instead. I could freeze to death waiting her out. She's heartbroken, scared, and stubborn. And she is every bit the girl I would die for.

Her door flies open and a few more seconds pass before she steps outside. She doesn't move and she's too far for me to hear anything other than serious shouting. Her breath fogs at a regular pace, and the rings of smoke in the air match the deep thumps in my chest. I start toward her, my feet picking up the pace along with my beating heart. I head to the passenger door, but stop at the back of her vehicle when she opens her mouth to speak.

"What are we doing, Jonah?"

I hang my head and stare at the toes of my shoes, the sharp edges of her broken phone pushing into the tips of my fingers in my pocket. I move back a step so there's nothing between us.

"I don't know, Eleanor." My eyes shift from the bright lights at the back of her car to her face, holding the view until my sight adjusts to see her perfectly. "You tell me. What are we doing?"

In half a breath, she abandons her open door and rushes me, her hands hitting my chest hard enough to move me back a step before her fingers grasp at my shirt and pull it into her fists. My hands fly to her face, cradling it as my eyes close and lips part in anticipation. Her lips find mine just as she whimpers, her mouth fitting perfectly with mine in a kiss that is rushed and desperate and hungry. My thumbs slide along her cheeks, sweeping away leftover tears as she lifts herself up on her toes. Her hands move along my chest and over my shoulders until she's grabbing the back of my shirt with one hand and pushing off my hat with the other.

Right and wrong have their debate somewhere deep in my head, but my heart mutes them. I have imagined kissing this girl so many ways, but never in a million years did I expect her to be the one initiating it. Wanting to take her pain away, to leave her brave and loved, I kiss her harder, supporting her back as I arch her toward her car until her shoulder blades rest against the side panel.

Both of her hands push into my hair—the stupid dad hat lost somewhere in the parking lot—as I dip my mouth into the curve of her neck and nip my way up her cold, soft skin until my lips finds her ear.

"I'm sorry," I say, not knowing why but feeling as if I should apologize for taking advantage of this moment, for giving in, and for letting her give in, too. My teeth graze along her earlobe while she lifts her legs and wraps them around my waist.

I grab under her thighs to support her weight, lifting her so she's above me, holding my face and kissing my mouth as if I'm her dream, too. I kiss her until my lips are raw. I kiss her until the football field lights shut off. And I kiss her until the maintenance crew's pickup truck echoes on the other side of the lot, threatening to lock us inside. We leave before they can. I drive us home in her car. And when we get there, I kiss her more, in case I never get to again.

CHAPTER Seventeen

I can't stop smiling.

I smile through Grandpa's eggs, and I *never* smile through Grandpa's eggs. I've also been downright chipper while Dale barks at me and calls me a half-dozen unflattering things as we work our way through the new wiring harness for the Bronco. Apparently, the work I did on my own has to be redone, which a different version of me would feel is a massive waste of time. Today's Jonah, though? He thinks mistakes like this are opportunities for learning. When I say that, I think Dale wants to punch me. The happier I am about everything, the more irritated he becomes.

"We're going to need more connectors. I don't know how you got things so jacked up, but we're basically back to square one on this stuff." Dale pulls his hat off and runs a hand towel over his sweaty head.

Okay, I'm starting to feel a little bad. I'm still really freaking happy, but there's a tinge of guilt that I've ruined Dale's Saturday.

"Show me what to get and I'll make a run." I step up to peer under the hood while Dale shows me exactly what he needs, being a little more precise than necessary—and maybe a little condescending—but who cares, because last night I spent a good three hours making out with Eleanor Trombley.

"Did I hear you say you're running out?" Grandpa steps through the open garage door with his morning paper tucked under his arm.

"Yeah. Dale's sending me to Toby's for parts," I holler.

"Dale's not sending the dipshit anywhere," Dale barks out. "Kid made a mess and now he has to clean it up is all. And I'm not going to the place I work on my day off." Dale's testiness amuses my grandpa, who laughs his way forward until the three of us are looking under the hood together.

"You're still bitter about poker," Grandpa ribs his friend.

Dale only grumbles a response.

"Think I can hitch a ride with you? We're out of coffee and I got a coupon for one of those fancy frappe mocha almond creamy hot latte suckers," Grandpa says.

"Uh, I don't think that's a drink, but yeah. We can swing through the drive-thru."

"Got room for one more?" Her voice startles all of us, but I'm the only love-struck idiot who rams his head into the underside of the hood when he stands. I rub my palm over the sore spot but really, I don't feel much other than the flurry of butterflies that have released inside my chest.

"Hey, uh, hi." I trip when I step from the small stool I'm on, and I cover my clumsiness by leaning with my palm against the inside of the engine compartment. I'm not on anything solid, though, so when my thumb snags a set of wires, it pulls them loose from God knows where.

"Fucking hell," Dale says, throwing the greasy towel he's been holding at my new mess.

I grit my teeth and step back up to get a better look at what I've done, but Dale pushes me down with his hand in my chest. He shoves his keys at me with his other hand.

"No, you don't touch anything. You go shopping. And take these fools with you. I want some alone time."

I nod at Dale's order, but under the panicked façade, I'm still smiling. I couldn't erase it if I tried.

"All right, so let's hit the road," Grandpa says, already making his way toward Dale's car. It's a pretty nice ride, an actual classic Dodge Challenger, not one of those modern-day copycats. I'm a little surprised he trusts me with the keys considering his opinion of me a minute ago.

"All right, honey. You're crawling in the back because we both don't want to see me get stuck halfway." Grandpa slides the passenger seat forward and Eleanor glances at me with a coy smile before dipping her head down and working her way into the back seat.

My grandpa lets the seat fling back into place when she gets settled, but before he gets into the passenger side, he pauses to stare at me over the roof of the car while he gnaws at the inside of his cheek and squints one eye.

"What?" I ask.

I know exactly what.

"You sly dog, you, Jonah Wydner." He points his finger at me with a small waggle and coughs out one of his cocky laughs. "You sly dog."

I exhale through the heat of a blush that crawls around my neck and roll my eyes as he gets into the car. I spend a small second outside by myself before I get into the hot seat. There's no way he's stopping there.

We pull out of the driveway and get moving on the main road before he starts in.

"So when did you two kiss, huh? The tonsil tango? Lip mashing? Smooches at sunset?"

"Oh, my God," I groan, leaning my head forward until it lands on the steering wheel as we crawl to a stop at the light.

"Oh, Jonah. It's perfectly natural, kissing girls. I've done it lots of times," he continues.

"Oh, God!" I lift my head and glare out the window. My eyes dash up to the rearview mirror to check on Eleanor and see how she's handling this. Our eyes meet, and my stupid grin breaks at the sight of hers. She doesn't seem fazed in the least.

"You'd be happy to know that your grandson is a very good kisser, Mr. Wydner," she says, shifting forward so my grandpa can hear her better.

I don't know whether to soar or die. My eyes flutter with my stuttered laugh. All I can do is shake my head and focus on the road.

"It's Hank, sweetheart. You call me Hank. And he better be a good kisser. He comes from a long line of excellent kissing genes you know."

"Jesus H—" I mumble.

"Penny Solemanto!" He lifts his index finger into the air as he proclaims her name. He's going to tell the first kiss story. I've heard it. I've heard it *so many times.*

"Who's that?" Eleanor feeds into his ego.

I sigh and rest my arm on the window sill, my fist propping the side of my head as I cruise toward the center of town with one hand on the wheel.

"She was an ambassador's daughter, and she was brand

new to St. Agatha's. I was fourteen, and if I do say so myself—"

"Oh, you will!" I add my color commentary.

My grandpa turns his head to glare at me, but quickly goes on.

"I was quite the catch. You see, these legs might not look like much now, but back then? I was silk on the ice. Fastest skater on the South Side."

"Fastest skater on the South Side." I join him in his favorite line of this tale.

"That's right," he says, slapping my arm and taking the compliment. What I wouldn't give to have his ability to power through insults and turn them into positives.

"Oh, you were a figure skater, Hank?" I catch the wink Eleanor gives me in the mirror when she teases him, and I laugh out loud.

"No. No, no. I'm talking about hockey. God's gift to ice and sport. I captained our three-time state championship team. A defensive wonder, I was!" Grandpa drifts off with the memory as he talks, and I can tell he's reliving good times, so I ease up my jests.

"One look at him in his uniform, and Penny was done," I say, urging the story on.

"Oh, I bet," Eleanor adds.

"Ah, she was a beautiful girl. We were a steady thing until spring came and her family was shipped off to some other place. But my God, those lips—like honey." He chuckles at the thought, and I catch him touch his fingertips to his upper lip under his mustache.

We pull into Toby's before he has a chance to delve into more of his conquests. He never shares these kinds of stories about my grandmother, but I don't think it's because he doesn't have them. They were married for more than forty years, and from what I have gleaned, he holds her on a very precious, very high pedestal. Those intimate stories are kept close to the vest, right where I will keep mine.

"I can just run in," I say, pushing open the driver's door.

"No, I want to come," Eleanor insists, pushing my seat forward as I get out.

"I'm no third wheel. You two go on in and I'll keep the heater company," Grandpa says, unfurling his paper to read it in the car.

Eleanor takes away my insecurities about whether or not to hold her hand the second I shut the door, sliding her fingers through mine and giving me a tender squeeze. She practically skips at my side as we enter the shop, and I smile as she moves ahead of me, noting my flannel shirt tied around her waist.

Dale must have called ahead, because his coworker, an even bigger guy named Ron, flags me down before I have a chance to delve too deeply into the store. He holds up the package of clips I need as well as a few other things Dale must have discovered after I left. I pay for the parts with my poker winnings and glance around the store for Eleanor.

"Elle?" I call out, my chest fluttering with anxious nerves. For whatever reason, I immediately think of Addy, which injects my body with a rush of adrenaline that fuels my footsteps until I'm nearly running along the back aisles. I'm starting to let my mind go to a bad place when a pair of cold hands wrap around my wrist and jerk me into a small alcove between a tire display and a precarious stack of air filters.

"Shit, Elle!" I whisper-shout, smiling mostly from relief.

She giggles, and mouths *I'm sorry* against me as she lifts

up on her toes and parts her lips over mine. She tastes like maple, and her lips are smooth and soft. I breathe a quiet laugh against them while nipping at her plump bottom lip with my teeth. My hands cup both sides of her face, my right one still holding the bag of parts. The plastic smacks against her cheek, which makes both of us laugh. I run my thumb along the spot and press a soft kiss on her jawline.

"We should get back to Hank. He can't be left alone for long. He could have turned that car into a strip club by now," I joke.

She clutches my arm as I lead her back through the store and try to avoid the scowl Ron's wearing as we pass.

"Thanks for your help, Ron," Eleanor says, clearly not giving a damn.

"Uh huh," he grumbles, running a dust rag over the counter as we push through the door.

We climb into the car in a fit of laughter, which my grandpa pokes fun of all the way through the coffee shop drive-thru and back home to where Dale is impatiently pacing my driveway.

"Better not be a scratch on her," he says, practically opening the driver's side door for me.

"Just the big gash in the back end," I retort. With pursed lips, Dale holds out an open palm for his keys, which I deliver joke-free.

Eleanor joins my grandpa inside while I work with Dale to understand what I got so wrong the first time I did the wiring. He's a little nicer now that I can give him my full focus. I think he's also glad that his car is back in his sightline. We work for almost two hours and manage to get things a little further along than I thought they were yesterday.

I see Dale off and close up the garage, heading in to

rescue Eleanor from my grandfather's charms. She's curled up on the couch under one of my mom's afghans, fully engaged in the highlights from last night's games across the league. My grandpa is giving her details that only a hockey purist would care about, and she's letting him. I almost believe she's enjoying it, but I think it's less the hockey and more the company. Hank has always had a gift for making life seem normal. I think it's the biggest reason my mom welcomed him moving in with us. He brought calm and consistency to our wrecked little world.

I cough to get Eleanor's attention, staying tucked in the kitchen so I don't get drawn into the hockey world of Hank Wydner. I actually enjoy watching games with him, but all I can focus on right now is how I want to be alone with *her*.

"You all done?" She stretches her way out of the blanket, folding it on the sofa next to where she's sitting.

I nod.

"Dale get that stick out of his ass?" Grandpa yells over his shoulder.

"Not yet," I say through a smile.

"Well, some things never change," he says.

Eleanor stands and rounds the coffee table, stopping at my grandfather's side and touching his shoulder with her hand.

"Thank you for the company," she says. He pats her hand with his own and glances up with a certain fondness in his eyes. Grandpa definitely approves of my affinity for the "pretty blonde girl across the street," as he always calls her.

I glance up the stairs as she nears me and she nods with a smile. I lead her up to my room, my hands growing sweatier with each step I scale. By the time we reach my door, my heart is thumping loudly and I'm convinced if I took my shirt off she'd be able to see it.

I hold the door as she passes inside, and push it closed after her, almost stopping at a crack but going for the bold move and shutting it all the way. The air grows thin the moment the latch clicks in place.

I pulled the collection of pictures down from beside my bed on the off chance that Eleanor might come up here again. I'm thankful for my past self now that she's scooting her way to the far corner of my bed and laying on her side while her hand calls me to join her.

There is nothing relaxed about me. My muscles are all flexed and guarded, probably protecting the massive hard-on aching to break through the zipper of my jeans. Boxers are useless in situations like this, and I feel as though Eleanor is staring right at it. I push my hands into my pockets to adjust myself a little as I walk toward her, a vain attempt to hide what she does to me. I'm sure she noticed last night too. It's impossible to feel her lips with my own without biological chemistry taking over most of my reasoning skills and leaving me with an uncomfortable erection.

I sit at first, looking down where she lies. She's wearing her hair around her shoulders today. It's pretty any way she wears it, but I like seeing the various shades of gold when it's splayed out around her face like this. Her long-sleeved shirt has a daisy embroidered on the front and the word HAPPY stitched above it. It feels like a label for our moment. It's definitely an accurate assessment of me right now.

"Hi," she says, voice raspy and quiet. Seductive.

I suck in my lip and look toward my door, so quiet on the other side.

"Hi," I repeat, bringing my eyes back to her.

She giggles at my awkwardness. I can't tell her how very little experience I have with anything like this. I don't know what I'm supposed to do in these situations, but I know that sitting here literally twiddling my thumbs is a pretty lame move. I decide to take her hand in mine, and busy myself playing with her fingers, drawing invisible lines up and down the sides.

"I have to tell you something," she says. Her words still me for a second and the heart thunder takes a harsh pause in my chest.

"Okay," I say, flitting my eyes to hers then back to her hand. I continue running my thumbs along her fingers, tracing her knuckles and the few lines that have formed on her young skin. So much life left.

"I got my acceptance for college in the mail."

My heart kick starts again and I laugh out a truly nerdy smile.

"Oh, thank God. I thought—"

"You thought I was going to say I shouldn't have kissed you last night? All night? And again this morning, and about five minutes from now?"

I meet her amused eyes and shrug.

"Something like that."

She shakes her head and threads our fingers together, removing my distraction and taking charge.

"I applied for Woodsman-Still University in Texas. They have a really good cheer program, and I like their sports med school." Her eyes light up when she talks about it, and I can't help but be infected by her joy.

"Cheer, huh? So does this mean—"

"That I'm going to rip my spot back from that bitch's hands? Yeah, it does."

I cackle at her ballsy response and she pulls my hand toward her. I give in and nestle up next to her so we face one another. The view from this vantage is spectacular, and the way the sun spills into my room hits the flyaway hairs around her face, making her look like an angel.

"That was mean. She's not a bitch. She's just a sophomore and it's not her time. It's my time, and I really want this. No matter what," she says.

No matter what.

Texas.

That's why the heaviness took over her eyes.

"I'm probably going to Tech, downtown," I say.

She nods.

"I figured."

I move my finger to the tip of her nose, along the bridge, tracing around her perfectly arched brow and down the side of her face, turning my hand so the backs of my knuckles graze along her cheek. She closes her eyes and leans into my touch, and no matter how finite her truth might be, I refuse to be sad about it.

"Texas isn't that far," I say.

She laughs softly.

"It's pretty far," she says.

I look up as I pretend to calculate a fact I already know, yet one more random set of data stored in my strange mind.

"Okay, so one thousand, one hundred sixty miles, give or take," I say, meeting her eyes again.

"Give or take," she laughs out.

"Depends on what part of Austin you're in."

She holds my stare, her eyes darting from one to the other while her smile hovers on breaking wide.

"Kidding," I say, but I shake my head no, because I'm

really not. She rolls so she's laying on top of me, her palms on my chest, her chin at her thumbs as she pats her hands against me with her frustration.

"I don't get you. You're a mystery!" Her eyes widen in playful exasperation, then she tucks her chin, kissing my chest in the very center.

Her hair cuts off my view of her eyes like sets of curtains, so I reach forward and scoop both sides with my thumbs, moving her locks back to their temporary home behind her ears. She leans into my right hand again as I do, and my thumb traces the space from the corner of her eye down to the corner of her mouth.

"You really watched me come home from dates?"

I squeeze my eyes shut tight. I can't believe she's bringing this up again, and now, while we're here, lying in my bed together with nobody around. I open one eye and nod just enough to admit my guilt.

"And those guys were all bad choices?" she asks with an arched brow.

I nod slowly, sucking my lips in a hard, straight, confident line.

"And how, mathematical genius, do you know that?" She rests her head on her hands again, eyelashes batting in wait for my answer. I better make this good.

"It wasn't math," I say in a low voice.

"No?" she questions.

"Uh uh," I say, shaking my head again. She reaches up and touches my nose, tapping it a few times in a way that puts me completely under her spell. I bite at it teasingly and she recoils, tucking her hand back under her chin.

"They didn't see you. Not really," I say.

Her skeptical expression dims with her intense glare.

"And you do?" This question is the easiest one from her I've ever had to answer.

"Oh, I see you. I have always seen you, Eleanor. Always. More than anyone ever has."

I feel her chest quake against mine, cracked open by my simple honesty. Her eyes close and open a few times, almost as if they're heavy with sleep, but I know that's not it. I think maybe this is what happens when someone truly sees you for who you are. This is how it feels, both ways. It feels heavy and explosive all at once.

Pushing forward against me, she moves until her mouth is lined up with mine and dusts a feather light kiss against me as I move my hands to gently hold her face again.

"Well, okay then. If you say so," she says, eyes falling shut as her forehead meets mine. I keep mine wide open so I don't miss the minute hers do again. I don't want to miss a single flash of golden-green, a single flit of honeysuckle lashes, a single blush or curve of her smile.

"We can meet in the middle," she hums. "Wherever that is."

Arkansas.

CHAPTER Eighteen

Either Jake is getting smarter, or I am a remarkable tutor. I know what my grandpa would say, but I have to give Jake some credit for doing the work. He's managed to pull himself up from a sometimes F to a comfortable C in geometry. I am so proud of him I can't help but brag while we're working in the garage, and mostly because Gramps will overhear and have to give my friend some well-earned props.

What I don't expect is the invite to some impromptu poker later that night. I guess Gary and his wife are moving to Florida. *My mom will be so upset to see Gary go.* Even though it's not a Thursday, the gang is getting together for one more night. There're six guys coming altogether; with Gramps that makes seven.

Gary refuses to play anything greater than a five-hand table, so my grandpa needs three or four more players. I decide to let Jake feel special when my grandpa asks, instead of warning him he's been branded fresh meat by most of the guys.

He could not look more the part.

"Are you seriously wearing a green tinted visor?" I flick the underside of Jake's stupid hat while grandpa belly laughs.

Jake straightens it and scowls at our attacks.

"This hat is legit. I saw that Phil guy wear it on ESPN," Jake defends.

My grandpa rolls his eyes and leans back in his chair, cupping his mouth to pretend he's speaking only to me, though the real intent is for Jake. "Phil Hellmuth probably makes a buck off every sucker who buys one of those."

The garage booms with cigar-fueled laughter. My mom has buried herself inside with movies for the night. Her room is the farthest one from the garage, so I hope between her binge of period dramas and the house's insulation, she's able to spare herself any hint of this scenario.

"All right boys, I came ready to play. And if it's all right, I brought one more?" My heart leaps hearing Eleanor's voice, but I take a quick step back when her sister stands over her shoulder. Our eyes meet for a moment and we give each other a nod. I credit Morgan for coming around and giving her sister the boost she probably needs to truly fight for her spot on the squad.

"You got cash, honey?" Gary speaks out of one side of his mouth, his cigar precariously hanging from the other.

"I mean, I'll have yours in a minute, so does it really matter?"

The room explodes in *Ooools* at Morgan's burn. She wears the smug smile with pride after that, and I think Gary might have a rough night with this one. I get a good sense that she can walk the talk.

We divide up, Eleanor and I at a table with my grandpa and his friends Rufus and Clark. I think Grandpa wants it to be a little easy on Eleanor for her first go at the game, and Rufus and Clark aren't very big risk takers. I also think my grandpa wants to watch the showdown at the other table as Dale throws a tantrum every other hand and Morgan silently pushes them all to the brink of bankruptcy.

The play goes on for an hour without much action at our table, which is fine by me because I'm much more interested in the way Eleanor's ankle is hooked around mine between our chairs. A few people in the neighborhood walk by, all of them shouting hellos and lingering at the end of our driveway to see what fun they're missing. Some of them stop to warm themselves at the fire pit grandpa wheeled out from the shed while the rest of us cluster around the portable heater filling the garage with the acrid scent of propane. My grandpa had me help him set up the living room TV out there so we can all watch the Blackhawks game while we play. They might all be enemies at the tables, but they are united when it comes to the Chicago ice.

"They have hockey down there in Boca Raton?" Grandpa teases Gary.

"If you can call it that. You know what they do have, though? Bikinis!" Gary tips his head up from his cards and puffs out cigar smoke as he laughs.

My mom is right to avoid this place at all costs.

"What's going on in here?" There's a small break in the action in both the room and on the television that lets Mrs. Trombley's voice cut through. She's clinging to her husband's arm as if they encountered aliens and they aren't sure whether or not they're hostile.

"Mom," Eleanor says, getting up from her seat a second before Morgan does.

"We thought maybe . . . it's a good night to get out." She looks up toward her husband, his face tired but more alive than the last time I saw it.

"Yes, I mean, Morgan said she was coming over to the neighbors', and I know we don't talk much, but . . ." Mr. Trombley keeps looking to his wife for help, but she only grows more tense at his side.

Lucky for them both, Hank Wydner is in this garage, and he can set anyone at ease.

"Come on in. We were just getting ready to watch young Jacob here pull off a move I like to call Losing His Shirt."

"I mean, come on!" Jake says on cue, tossing his cards to the center of the table.

Grandpa threw my friend under the bus for a laugh, and it earns one. I get up and pull out more chairs from the far corner of the garage. I don't think we've had this many people in here since my mom tried her hand at being a scout mom. Turns out neither she nor I were made for knots, fires, and general roughing it. If I ever actually get to camp with Eleanor, I hope she knows what she's doing.

Eleanor's parents sit over our shoulders so they watch us play but also take in the game. It seems that hockey catches her father's eyes first.

"Did you see that boarding call against the Sharks last week?" Eleanor's dad could not have uttered a more welcome sentence. Within minutes, cards are abandoned and tables rearranged for better viewing of the third period against Detroit.

Morgan, Eleanor, and I slip toward the back of the garage, watching a mix of generations all come together over something meaningless in the grand scheme of things, especially amid all that's happening to the Trombleys right now.

"Gemma's on her way," Eleanor says at my side. "I'm going to wait by the curb."

"Want me to come wait with you?" I ask.

She leans forward, noting her sister watching over both of us while trying to pretend she isn't.

"No. You stay. I'll be right back," she says, rocking back on her feet. She kisses my shoulder and heads down the driveway, her body bundled in her oversized yellow sweatshirt and a pair of my sweatpants. There's something unbearably perfect about seeing her in something so casual of mine.

I tuck my hands under my arms, partly to stave off the cold, but mostly because this is the first time I've been left alone with Morgan since I boldly told her all the things she was doing wrong.

"This is nice," she says, leaning in so she doesn't have to talk very loud.

I glance at her and nod.

"Yeah, it is. My grandpa really knows how to throw a good party." We both laugh, but there's a lot of truth in my joke.

"I wanted to thank you. For the other day," she says.

"Of course," I say, giving her another tight smile.

She doesn't let me brush off her gratitude so easily, though, and reaches for my arm. My eyes jet to her hand on my forearm and I relax the hold I have on myself.

"Seriously, Jonah." I'm a little shocked to hear her use my actual name rather than an insult. I relax my arms completely and turn to square myself with her because I know what she's trying to say right now isn't easy.

"I know. But I also meant it when I said *of course.* I've

grown up watching all of you grow up," I say, glancing to the end of the driveway and not just to the Trombley home, but to the blonde gift standing on the sidewalk and waving at me. I hold up an open palm and Morgan does the same.

"Don't you dare break her, Jonah. I couldn't take losing her too."

I can't bring myself to look her in the eyes after those words, but I take them to heart. I know it wasn't a warning. It was a plea. It was the God's honest truth.

"I wouldn't dare," I utter.

The garage erupts with cheers, bringing our attention back to the warmth inside and a very rowdy group of Blackhawks fans.

"I think my dad likes your grandpa," she says, noting the high fives they exchange after a short-handed goal against the power play.

"Everybody likes my grandpa. Careful, he's single. He has no compunction about age discrepancies," I say, only partially kidding.

We step in closer to the heater and warm our hands while the remaining minutes of the period tick down, and for this little moment here in my garage, everything feels normal. It's almost like a window into lost time. These are things we could have done long ago. Rather than hiding in my own world, I could have invited the Trombleys over for spaghetti nights when my dad was alive, or to shoot off the illegal fireworks he drove down to Indiana to get. For a man I considered so preoccupied with work and numbers, he still managed to mark my life with special memories.

"Hey, Morgan?"

We both turn at the sound of Eleanor's voice. Our faces are all smiles, still caught up in the glee and joy happening inside the garage. It takes a minute to catch up to the serious expressions standing just outside. Eleanor looks uncertain, maybe even rattled. I feel as though I recognize the woman who is standing next to her, but the two men waiting back a few feet aren't familiar at all.

"She's from National Network News. They, uh, they want to do a special, on us and Addy. Maybe something she'll see, if she's . . . out . . . there." Reality hits Eleanor all at once, drowning her in its molasses-like thickness, choking off every other sensation so all she feels is the urgency and unrest that comes along with the role of being a girl with a missing family member.

A news story for the national stage.

"Oh, uh." Morgan freezes in place, her eyelids twitching while her mind switches gears. "Can we go somewhere more quiet to talk about this? I— Let me grab my parents. Really, this is up to them."

"Of course," the woman says.

Suddenly, my use of those very same words feels shallow.

I wait with Eleanor while her sister weaves through the revelry to her parents, yanking them from their brief vacation from grief. Both of their heads jerk in our direction, not to us, but to the opportunity for one more message of hope behind us. It's a ratings grab, masked as public service, but even still, how could they say no?

Eleanor's fingers brush against mine in the quiet space between our bodies, finger looping through finger until we're fully clasping hands. Her sister and parents are already headed our way, an end to a near perfect evening counting down in five, four, three . . .

"Do you want me to come with you?" I ask.

I know she doesn't. She shakes her head and whispers, "Thanks" anyhow.

I squeeze her fingers between mine before she strips them away, like grains of sand falling through the gaps. I clasp my hands behind my neck and pivot as the Trombleys guide yet one more camera crew toward their home.

Their door closes as Gemma pulls up in her car, and she walks toward me while peering over her shoulder, probably wondering what I'm looking at and what she missed. I give her the details when she reaches me, then I cash in my few remaining chips with my grandfather and make my way inside.

I can still smell Eleanor on my sheets from the day before. I've never been so happy doing nothing with another person. I think an entire hour went by without us talking. Sure, there were lots of kisses, but not every moment was filled with that. Purely feeling her warm body tucked against mine, blood running through her veins and pumping her heart in a rhythm that, when life got incredibly still, I could hear—that's what I think of now.

Too early for sleep, I pull the Bradbury book from my night table and lay back to flip through the pages. A photograph slips from the middle of the book and lands on my chin. I'm sure it's something I shoved in there at one point to mark a page.

Setting the book down at my side, I turn the picture to face me and am met with the warmest smile I've ever seen. I'm sure Eleanor took this photo of herself, her face too close to the camera lens and her eyes crossed to be silly. But it's the gleeful abandon that covers the length of the photo, from cheek to cheek, that has me turning to my side and bringing my pillow into my body to hold as if she were here in person.

I pull my phone from my pocket and send her a quick message, glad she was able to get her phone fixed.

ME: *When did you put that photo in the Bradbury book?*

I know she won't see it for a while. A quick glance out my window shows the car their media guests arrived in is still parked at the curb and the downstairs lights are still on in the house. I decide to pass my time reading my favorite parts from *Something Wicked*, and I prop the photo she left for me up against the base of my lamp so it feels as if she's not far. Maybe an hour passes before my phone vibrates with her reply.

ELEANOR: *I couldn't let you make do with that photocopy.*

I slap my own face and cover it completely with my outstretched palm. She did see how pathetic my crush was. Yet . . . she kissed me anyway.

ME: *I must look like a stalker.*

A few minutes pass before she writes back.

ELEANOR: *Pretty much.*

Great, I say to myself.

I lay on my side and look at the new photo she left for me.

ME: *It was nice of you to upgrade me to a color photo.*

ELEANOR: *A girl likes to be stalked the right way.*

I glance to my window again and wonder if she's in her room already. I set my book aside and move to my desk. She's waiting for me when I pull open my shutters.

ME: *Hi.*

She looks down to read her phone then lifts her head and holds up her hand. I sit on the edge of my desk like I did weeks ago. I was so full of questions that night yet too afraid to ask them. I couldn't even talk to her lct alone help her in the way I sensed I could.

Things are different now.

ME: *How did it go? With the news lady?*

It feels like years have passed since our street was ground zero for a media circus. In reality, though, it's only been a few weeks. That's how bad news travels—in waves. One wave comes then goes, making way for the next. Those trucks are camped out in front of someone else's worst nightmare right now.

ELEANOR: *My parents are doing the interview. Just them. They film on Monday. It airs Wednesday. It's . . .*

Almost a minute passes before she finishes that thought, messaging me again. I fight the urge to fill it in for her.

ELEANOR: *I know it's a good idea. Something like that gets seen, and if Addy really was abducted, then maybe someone will recognize her and report it or that woman.*

There's a *but* she isn't acknowledging. I know what it is because I'm thinking it, too. Morgan maybe thought it first.

But what if Addy is already gone?

Dead.

It's such a short word for the end of such a long miracle. Life has so many stages, every little development on our way to being born, our first breath, our first words. We learn emotions, we walk and talk. We experience thrills and disappointment. Love and loss. Accomplishments. Regrets. To end it all with an event so small—death.

My phone buzzes again, only this time, instead of a text, Eleanor is calling to video chat. I cradle my phone in my palm as I slide up on the screen to answer.

"Miss me already?" I don't expect her to laugh, but it's rewarding that she smiles.

"I'm too tired to type. I think the lack of sleep is finally catching up with me," she says through a yawn.

I meet her stare from across the street.

"Maybe you should try to get some sleep, then," I say, watching as she holds her palm against the glass pane of her window then lets it slip away. Her curtains fall shut and the light in her room dims.

"Would you stay on the phone with me?" she asks, yawning again.

I close my shutters and move to my bed, studying what I can see through the phone screen. Her room is a pale pink, and the little light that's on barely glows against her face.

"Yeah, I can do that. You get comfortable. I'm reading Bradbury again," I say.

She breathes out what I think is her attempt at an ominous laugh and from what I can see, she's slipped under her covers and rested her phone on its side so I can keep an eye on her for as long as she needs.

"Read to me," she says.

"Okay."

I sit with my back against the wall and the book propped up with my knees. I begin reading about boys in October and the lightning rod salesman of Bradbury's twisted imagination, and by the time I finish the first chapter, Eleanor is fast asleep. I set the book aside and turn my own lights off completely so the only light I see is coming from her. I won't hang up, and I won't fall asleep myself for quite a while. But I will make sure she finds peace.

Tonight.

Tomorrow.

Always.

CHAPTER Nineteen

Eleanor has been on edge for the last three days. The team from National Network News was warm and convincing, and by the time the crew left the Trombley home on Monday night, they'd captured an entire segment with Eleanor in Addy's room.

She showed them Addy's things. Shared the story about her sister dressing up in Eleanor's uniform because she idolized her sister so much. They got her to cry. And she hasn't really stopped.

I think everyone on our street was tuned in to the news last night. We've all lived bits and pieces of the tale, and human nature is so curious. Eleanor wanted to watch alone with her family, so I stayed home with mine. Even Grandpa Hank was subdued throughout the piece, and as Morgan and Eleanor cried on camera, so did my mom.

If Addy is out there somewhere, someone will notice her after this. I think the world is compelled to take up the cause.

Still, Eleanor insisted on coming to school today.

Nobody would have balked at her staying home the day after putting something so raw out into the world, but she's determined to keep moving forward. Tomorrow is game day, and she wants her spot back on the sidelines. She's been drowning out her anxiety with extra hours of practice, working with Gemma on the routine and making her tumbling crisp. I'm not sure what that means, but the two of them say that word a lot.

Regardless, it's good that she has this to focus on today. I only hope it helps her avoid seeing everyone else whisper behind her back . . . like they are right now.

"Dude, school lunch blows. This is why I always go out!" Jake lifts his wilting slice of pizza then drops it back down on his plate.

"There's nothing wrong with that. It came from Ango's across the street. They order dozens of large pizzas for lunch every day. It's the same. Damn. Thing," I insist, taking the slice from his plate and biting off the cheesy end. I've already finished mine.

"Yeah, well, something happens to it on the trip across the street. I don't want it." He pushes the plate closer to me and I shrug, folding the slice in half and devouring it.

"Suit yourself," I mumble with my full mouth.

Gemma and Eleanor are getting in some last-minute practice, and I didn't want to race off to lunch with Jake and miss her if she finished before lunch was up. Besides, I somehow scored two lunches for the price of one by staying.

Jake kicks his feet up on the table and leans back in his chair, pulling his phone out to scroll through social media. He shares a few stupid memes with me while I polish off his lunch and then I scoot over to watch videos with him. We're both laughing at a cat that leaps into a bucket full of water then leaps right back out, and after our third viewing, I notice a few guys nearby seem to be laughing with us.

Jake and I both look over our shoulders, and I expect to see someone close enough to see our screen. Instead, it's three dudes who spend more time smoking pot in the bathrooms than actually attending class. Maybe they're high. Still no excuse for what they're doing.

Eleanor and Gemma are weaving through the tables on their way to us, and these losers are locked onto them with their eyes, watching every sway of their hips. I never thought I was the kind of guy to get possessive, but I'm downright caveman right now.

Jake stands from his chair a hair before I do, which is good because my jealous, protective side is still new at this. I follow my friend as he pushes a few chairs out of his way and turns one around to straddle backward about a foot from the loudest of the three guys.

"Hey. I'm Jake," he says, offering his hand while brandishing a commercial-ready smile. My arms are folded over my chest as I stand behind him like some skinny body guard.

The dude closest to him gurgles out a laugh and glances to his side toward his friends.

"You believe this guy?" They all laugh the same stoned nonsense but the guy turns back to face Jake and offers him his hand.

Dumb move.

Jake's grip tightens fast and he pulls the guy toward him with enough force that he stumbles from his chair and ends up on his knees. Good thing, because I'm pretty sure he's going to need to beg his way out of this.

"You guys having a good time watching our girlfriends? Is that fun for you?" Jake's head is cocked to the side and if it weren't for the way his veins are popping out of his arms, I wouldn't think his muscles were working hard at all.

"Come on, man. You're being a dick," the guy says. I laugh out hard and run my hand over my mouth.

"He's not the one being a dick," I respond over Jake's shoulder.

My friend jerks him forward one more time and the guy's forehead hits the back of the chair Jake's straddling.

"Fuck, man!" The guy flails his other hand at Jake, slapping at him to try to break away, and a few people gather around us.

Our point is made, so I swing my hand into Jake's back to get his attention and encourage him to deescalate before we're both thrown in detention. It seems like a good plan. Only one problem—the potheads can't keep their mouths shut.

"You cry on command for that camera last night?" This shitty comment comes from the guy behind the one Jake's holding hostage, and his eyes are right on Eleanor. A darkness comes over me so fast I don't even realize what's happening until he's lying flat on his back with my knees on his chest and my fist making a third pass into his face.

"Jonah! It's all good. He gets it. Come on," Jake says, pulling at my shoulders.

Perhaps it was more than three punches to his face.

My friend drags me to my feet, and I'm snarling like a wild beast. My body is pumped with adrenaline and my eyes see the world in shades of red. I thrash against being held back, kicking at chairs while my friend pulls me off-balance and moves me to the other side of the cafeteria.

I taste metal. I shirk my arm free from his hold once I'm in a chair far from the douchebags already being circled by a few on-duty teachers. One swipe of my palm along my lip reveals a line of deep red blood and I lean to my side to spit out the taste, leaving a splatter of more on the floor. I'm still breathing hard, coming down from this strange beast mode that I didn't realize was in me, when our school resource officer bends forward to meet me at my level. I pretty much deflate on eye contact.

"We're going to have a talk in the dean's office, yeah?" Officer Mooney leans his head to the right, toward the exit, and I nod once.

I think it's our PE teacher I hear on a bullhorn telling everyone to break it up and get to class as I stand and follow behind the officer and Jake toward a set of offices I've only ever been in to receive academic awards. My chest is catching up to what I've done, and my arms and legs vibrate with nervous energy.

"I don't suppose now is a good time to tell you that you've always kinda reminded me of Mike Ditka, is it?" Humor is always my automatic defense mechanism.

Both Officer Mooney and Jake look back at me as we move down the hallway, but it's the officer's expression I zero in on. His furry brows are pulled in tight and his eyes are definitely unamused slits. He chews his gum once. One single chew that moves his mustache up and down like a wave. Then he turns forward and picks up the pace.

"You know, the old Bears coach?" I continue.

Jake's eyes widen.

"He knows who Ditka is, dude. Just, *shh*!" My friend catches up to the officer but I drag my feet so they have to wait for me when they reach the main office doors. I'm in no hurry for this next part. My mom is going to shit a brick.

Getting suspended for two days feels like a bargain. I was the last person Principal Lobeski expected to see waiting in her office when the dean sent me to await my sentencing. She actually said those words to me, in fact.

"Christ, Jonah. You're the last person I expected to see waiting in my office."

I let my shoulders bunch up a little less after that. Things got better when my mom came, too, and by the end the two of them were essentially ready to present me with a certificate of honor for defending Eleanor.

I guess my version of how the fight went wasn't quite accurate. In my head, I was dominating, but judging by the massive black eye I'm sporting, it seems Stoner Face Douchebag was able to land more than a few good punches of his own.

I was sent home for today, and I'll spend tomorrow here too. I'm ahead on my homework so really, it's a high school student's dream. Only, I'm not able to sit on campus and wait for Eleanor now, to see how she did at cheer practice. And I won't be able to see her at the assembly tomorrow either, which is really the only thing I have enjoyed about assemblies for the last four years.

The Bronco, on the other hand, is coming together. Grandpa let Dale know about my sentencing so he plans to spend his day off tomorrow helping me piece together some last details with the electrical. There's a chance that this son-of-a-bitch might actually make it to a gas station soon.

I've spent most of the day in the Bronco's driver's seat with my dad's notebook. Jake keeps saying I should change out the seats because the fabric is pretty worn and faded, but I don't know. There's something about the idea that my dad sat in this exact same seat I am now. I flip down the visor to check out the mirror on the back. That might need updating. Even rubbing it with the sleeve of my sweatshirt doesn't do much to clear the reflection.

I lean forward and breathe on the glass to fog it up and give it one more attempt, but it's no use so I flip the visor back up. My eyes scan the window lackadaisically, and I don't realize I'm looking at Eleanor for the first few seconds. I jump in my seat when it dawns on me and I fumble my way out of the truck, hitting my head on the roof on my way out.

Hand rubbing the new knot on my head, I squint one eye closed as I slide my feet closer to her waiting arms.

"Hey, how'd it go?" I ask. She already has her hands on my face, inspecting my injuries.

We texted a few times today after I got sent home. She feels guilty about my suspension, but I don't want her to. Anyone who makes fun of her pain has a whole lot more coming.

"Oh, you know," she sighs out, tilting my head slightly as if to get a better view of the nice purple tone on my cheekbone. Her eyes shift a hair, meeting my gaze, and she breaks into a huge smile.

"You did it? You got your spot back?" My hands automatically move to her face.

She nods, her elation undeniable.

"I knew it! I knew you could do this," I say, pulling her mouth to mine and kissing her through both of our smiles.

I wrap her up in my arms and rock us side-to-side as she shivers. She's still wearing her uniform and her arms are covered in tiny bumps from the chill. I lift up on my toes as she tucks her chin and I kiss the top of her head.

"I gotta change. Wanna come over for a bit? Or are you,

like, grounded or something?" She arches a brow as she pulls back, our hands linked by a couple of fingers.

"I'm eighteen so I don't think I can technically *be* grounded," I say, scrunching my face.

"Good point," she says through soft laughter.

"My grandpa actually gave me twenty bucks and a pat on the back. Mom said I get my fighting skills from my father," I say, pointing to my colorful face.

Our hands drop their connection as she takes a few more steps out of the garage while still facing me. Her bag looks heavy at her side, so I reach toward it, insisting on carrying it for her. The sky is a greenish-type of gray. The sun is about to set completely, so the glow must be coming from a full moon buried underneath. It's supposed to rain again through the night, but it's cold enough to form ice so who knows what we're getting. It makes the air feel humid, though, and every breath I exhale forms a cloud.

The heat in Eleanor's house is a welcome reprieve, and I drop her bag inside the door and rub my arms to work the chill away. She pauses near the stairs as I move toward the sitting room sofa.

"You're not coming up?" she asks.

"Oh, I . . . your privacy and all that stuff," I say, the chill completely melted now. My body temperature jetted up to a thousand at the mere thought of going up to her room.

"I want you to see my room. You know, not through video chat or when you're carrying me to bed drunk off my ass?" She laughs, blushing at the memory.

"See your room," I repeat her offer, as if I have to consider anything in this decision. I push my hands into my back pockets and glance up the stairs before taking a step toward her. "Sure, yeah. Let's see what photocopy pictures of me are taped on your wall."

"Ha!" Her laugh is bold and loud as she climbs the stairs.

"Wow, it wasn't *that* funny. I mean, you *could* have a picture of me up there," I say, my pulse picking up speed with every step.

"I could. That is true," she says, leading me toward her room. She pushes the door open and the first thing I see is a half-naked man flexing his abs in a poster on her wall. He's the lead singer from some band I don't recognize, but his image is massive.

I point to it and squeeze the back of my neck with my other hand. "That's not my best picture. I can't believe they even decided to use that one for promos. Let me get you a better one," I joke.

She spins on her heels as she walks backward toward the center of her room. If I have won Eleanor's heart in some way, I'm convinced it must be the way I make her laugh. It's my best gift, and nobody makes a sound quite like her when she does.

I lean against the edge of her door while she toes off her shoes and kicks them to the side. She lifts one leg and tugs her sock off, throwing it by the abandoned shoes, and as she pulls off the other, she glances up at me with a look that has me realizing we are home alone.

"Where's, um, Morgan," I say, swallowing down a thousand-pound rock made of teenaged boy hormones.

"My grandparents drove back today. They're up north, near Woodstock. My parents and Morgan went with them. They knew I had cheer, though, so . . ."

"So, it's just you." My voice cracks in the middle of this short sentence. It makes Eleanor smile on one side.

"Well, I mean, *you're* here," she says, tossing the second sock off to the side.

I lick my lips because, honestly, I think I might be drooling.

"And that guy. He's here," I say, pointing to the poster man. My self-deprecating humor earns me another raspy laugh. I'm literally clawing at the denim of my back pockets while I try to meld against the wood of the door.

Eleanor's eyes flit to the open floor between us, then flutter their way up my body until our gazes lock. She tugs her hair free of the tie that's been holding it up and shakes her head enough to let the waves cascade down her arms. Her flexibility is a wonder in and of itself as she reaches behind her back and tugs her uniform zipper down her spine slowly until both sides fall open and she's left hugging the blue and gold material against her chest.

"Jonah?"

"Uh huh?" My mouth doesn't move with the words; it just hangs open in awe.

"Think you could close that?" She points to the door I'm attempting to fold in half with my weight.

"Uhm." I swallow again. Those knots form fast. "Sure," I say, turning to push the door closed behind me. I turn back as she lets her shirt fall to the floor, leaving her in a sports bra and a very short skirt.

Her eyes bore into mine, but I can't not follow the trail her right hand makes down the front of her body to the side of her skirt where a single zipper holds it on her hips. She pinches the zipper between her thumb and index finger and pulls it down the length of her hip until the fabric falls down her thighs, her knees, her ankles.

"Elle," I say, trying to keep my head on straight in the face of pure temptation. I keep telling myself this is no different than seeing her in a swim suit, which I have before, several times. But I'm a liar because this . . . *this is different.*

"I didn't fight that guy just so you would . . ." I say my fear out loud, laying bare my reservation for giving in. I never want to be the guy who takes advantage of her.

She steps close enough to touch her hand to my cheek and my eyes lift to meet hers.

"Jonah, it wasn't much of a fight," she says, winking to take the edge off her joke. My shoulders shake with my uncomfortable laugh, but I do feel better about whatever is to come.

"It was bigger than most. I heard he was in the UFC," I mumble.

"*Shh.*" She cuts me off, lifting up on her toes and pressing her lips to mine.

One touch of her mouth strips away the rest of my reservations. My hands slide up her shoulders and neck, into her hair as I shift her head to the side so I can kiss her deeper. Her hands gather up the bottom of my sweatshirt and T-shirt underneath, and I lift my arms to help her pull them up and over my head. She trails her fingertips down my bare chest, a light scratch that she carries down to the button of my jeans. She undoes it easily and drags the zipper down just as I've backed her up to the edge of her bed, all fluffy and pink with pillows and blankets everywhere. She falls into the softness on her back while I push my jeans down my hips and awkwardly kick them off while trying to do the same thing with my shoes.

"Damn it!" I say as her head falls back in laughter. I pull one leg up at a time to untangle my mess then move to crawl my way above her as she scoots back enough to make room for both of us.

She lies back, caged between my arms as I nip at her

neck and kiss my way down to the center of her chest, where the cotton hides her breasts. Arching her back with each kiss I leave behind, she drives me to keep going until my mouth breathes against her belly button and my thumbs flirt with the lace trim of her panties.

"I want you, Jonah," she says.

My eyes shut and my hard-on flexes. I have no idea what I'm doing.

"Are you sure?" I ask, glancing up at her, male hormones screaming at me to shut up.

She bites her lip and nods.

I keep my eyes on her and let my fingertips dive under the lace of her underwear, slowly pulling them down the curve of her hips as she lifts herself from the bed. Every new thing revealed ratchets my pulse to the point I think I might pass out. She's completely naked on her bottom half as I sit back on my knees and brace myself for what comes next.

"I have a . . . in my wallet. I mean, just so I'm always prepared. Not that it's old. It's new, I mean. Not that I bought it today."

Her teeth clamp down on her bottom lip as her laughing smile stretches the width of her face.

"Get the condom, Jonah," she finally says.

I freeze for a beat and hold her stare, partly to make sure this is real, and also to help myself slow down.

"Right." I nod. I rush to my abandoned pants and dig out my wallet and the condom, tearing the packet open with my teeth while Eleanor sits up and pulls off her sports bra. I step out of my boxers and slip the condom on as she lies back again and raises her knees, my eyes glued to her exposed breasts.

I slide up between her legs as they fall open to make

room for me, and hold myself above her to stare into her wide-open, pools-of-green eyes. Her fingers stroke along my swollen cheekbone then move up the side of my face, into my hair. I lower myself enough to dust her lips with a timid kiss.

"I've never . . ." I close my lips tight and pull in my brow, a little embarrassed to be admitting this.

"It's okay. Me, neither," she says.

I nod, shaking my head in tiny, staccato, scared-as-hell movements.

"I trust you, Jonah. I want to do this with you," she says.

"Me, too," I say, not giving a damn how weak it might make me seem. Nobody matters right now besides me and Eleanor. This is about us.

"Are you ready?" I ask, shifting to align myself with her.

She nods and then shuts her eyes as I push inside her a little. Her mouth falls open with a gasp, and her face looks pained. I shift back, but she clutches my sides.

"No, don't stop. I'm okay. I'm okay," she says, eyes opening to meet mine.

I study them intently as I move back into her, watching for any sign that this needs to stop—that *I* need to stop. I ease into her further as she exhales, and when I don't think I can go any farther, I pull back. The sensation of sliding in and out of her once is enough to knock my breath out completely.

I pause before rocking my hips again, and this time Eleanor moves with me, her fingers clawing along my back to hold me close. I collapse against her, holding our bodies close while her mouth searches for mine, her teeth leaving small marks up the length of my neck until she grabs hold of my lip with her mouth.

With every push into her, she exhales against my

mouth, her pants turning to tiny cries that begin to exalt pleasure, building my confidence until I move in and out of her at a faster pace. The rush comes fast, and I think it's too soon, but Eleanor's thighs squeeze at my sides, her body bucking up to meet mine with each pulse until her head falls back, exposing the nape of her neck as she lets out a stuttered cry. I muffle my own moan against her bare neck, sucking enough to leave a tiny pink mark in my wake.

I roll us to our side after we finish, my body exhausted and hers covered in a slight sheen of sweat. Rain pelts against her window, and all is right in the world.

I should have gotten in a fight a long time ago.

CHAPTER Twenty

This is definitely a record number of football games for me. I wouldn't have missed tonight's game for the world, though. Actually, I couldn't give a shit about the game; I'm here for half time.

I'm here . . . *for her.*

"So you and Elle, a serious thing now for real, huh?" Jake's been good about not prying too much. I know it's less about him respecting my privacy and more about respecting Eleanor.

I lean forward before answering to check and make sure his friends aren't listening to our conversation. They're busy trading someone's phone around to watch some guy light his pants on fire while passing gas. Right now I'm grateful for dumb videos like that.

"We are, yeah. We're pretty serious." My stupid grin betrays me, and I'm sure Jake has read all he needs from my expression. He laughs a proud kind of chuckle and slaps the back of his hand against my leg.

"You dog! Look at you!"

I tighten my mouth and look up, practically under my eyelids. Heat from his attention to this topic creeps around my neck and down my back, squeezing my chest and stomach.

"It's not just that. It's . . . it's more than that," I say, leveling him with a warning glare that there will be no more details.

"You love her," he says, and it takes me a few seconds to read how serious he is.

I nod and look out to the track, to the girls lined up and reviewing their moves for the upcoming routine. Eleanor's face is painted with concentration, her mouth counting out every move, her arms motioning what she'll do.

"Yeah, Jake. I love her," I admit.

I glance back to my right and meet what I can only categorize as a proud stare. I think maybe there's a part of him that's in love, too, but that's a conversation for another time. It's too loud out here to get into miracles, and Jake being completely owned by a girl, that's a miracle. I think maybe Gemma is the only one capable.

"You ask her to prom yet?" Jake can't help but gloat over the fact that he won our bet. I was tempted to hide it from him, but I was too excited when Dale and I fired up the Bronco for real and took it for a spin. We spent another hour making sure everything was solid so I could drive us to the game.

"Not yet. I think she'll actually be kinda bummed you're not streaking," I joke.

"Oh, I don't need a bet to do that. Maybe that can be my gift to you two," he says, standing at the announcement that the Badger Pride Cheer Squad was taking the field.

I look up at him for a few seconds before joining him. I

don't think he's kidding about running through the gym naked.

Any questions I have get put on hold the minute the speakers crackle with the loud boom of cheer music. I'm half-tempted to force everyone to pay attention, but I'm quickly mesmerized by Eleanor and the genuine and confident red smile that stretches the expanse of her being.

Kacey, the girl who was supposed to replace her is still in the routine, which I know was a big deal for Eleanor. She struggled with taking something away from the girl when she learned how hard she worked to learn the entire routine. Coach worked it out so Kacey has a part for the competition, and Eleanor said her tumbling is really strong so having her on the mat—whatever that means—will earn them more points.

For two and a half minutes straight, these sixteen girls fly at each other while flipping, somehow never running into one another or dropping bodies on the ground as they toss them into the air. Eleanor is the star, though. She soars through the air, twisting while somehow holding her body completely straight, only to turn around and balance her weight on her heels which are held on either side by teammates as she moves into a perfect split. They come together to push her into a standing position and she leaps, tucking for a flip before her feet plant perfectly still in the grass. Jake and I both cup our mouths and shout as the music ends, his friends looking at us as if we're love-struck tools. But I don't give a rip.

I'm not a single bit shy about my affection. I have no doubts about how Eleanor feels in return, either. I rush down the bleacher steps and hop over the edge, a drop that was a little farther than I thought, which causes me to trip over my feet when I land. None of that slows me, though, and I step up to the fence by the track with my fists up in the sky as Eleanor marches across the lanes to get to me.

"Was that good?" *She knows it is.*

"Fucking epic, Elle," I answer, bringing my hands down as she holds herself up, gripping the top of the fence. I cup her face and kiss her in front of everyone who gives a damn to see. And she kisses me.

"I have to finish the game," she says as we part.

I shrug.

"But do you? Really?" Our team is being shut out, forty-one to zero so far. I can't imagine two more quarters of this.

Eleanor pats my cheek before walking backward to join Gemma and the others.

"I do. Really," she says. "But maybe I can get a ride home after the game? I hear you drove something special."

I nod, mentally putting us in my parents' place from all those years ago.

Unlike last week's game, Eleanor does not bolt from the locker room in an attempt to break away and avoid people. Quite the opposite, she seems to be giving out autographs and talking to anyone who wants to praise her.

Eleanor finally doles out her last hug and turns to face me from the other side of the parking lot. I'm leaning against my Bronco, doing my best Jake Ryan impression. It's the one lesson my mom gave me about romance—when in doubt, go with Jake Ryan. I must have seen Sixteen Candles a dozen times with her over the last four years. I don't get it; the guy seems like a bit of a dick to me, but

Mom swears by him. And so I stand here, ankles crossed, hands in my pockets until I can't take it anymore and have to meet Eleanor half way.

"Sorry I took so long," she says, bunching up her shoulders with guilt as we get closer.

"So many fans," I say, prompting her to roll her eyes.

I came prepared today, and though I don't own a Badger sweatshirt, Eleanor will look very nice in my Harvard Math Club hoodie. I hold it open at the bottom for her to crawl inside, and she slips her head and arms in quickly after dropping her gym bag to the ground. I pick that up to carry for her and grasp her hand at my side on our way back to the Bronco.

Every bit of her and me feels right. She belongs at my side; her hand fits perfectly. It's as though our arms are made to work in sync, the lengths lining up to meet at their ends, her fingers the perfect width for the spaces between mine. None of that can be a coincidence. It may sound corny to believe two people are made for each other, and I'm not normally naïve enough to believe in anything beyond the moment I'm in, but Eleanor makes me stretch the boundaries of what I think is possible. She makes taking risks feel wise.

"I'm in love with you," I blurt out before the feeling passes.

Her body pauses, dragging a step behind me as her hand tightens in mine. I still know this isn't a mistake to say right now. Now is the *perfect* time to say these words. I turn to face her, her eyes wide but her mouth not bent in regret. I think there is a smile hiding in there.

"I just had to say it. I, boy, *oof*." I adjust the weight of her bag over my shoulder and run that hand through my hair, feeling the tension. I glance to the side for a beat and blow out a heavy breath before coming back to meet her perfect green eyes. That hint of a smile has grown.

"I love you, to put it more clearly. I love you, Elle." I'm too far gone to stop now.

She inches closer to me, bringing my hand up to her mouth and kissing the back of my palm before rising on her toes and kissing my mouth.

"I love you, too," she whispers. My heart cracks open, releasing hundreds, maybe thousands of butterflies that bounce off the walls of my body and set my skin ablaze.

"Yeah?" I laugh through a broad smile that pushes my cheeks up into my eyes.

She nods, but I ask again. I think I have to convince myself I'm not dreaming. By the third time I decide that this is all real and that I am very much awake. I also decide that a cheap college sweatshirt is probably not enough to keep a girl in a super short cheer skirt warm, so I urge Eleanor to follow me back to the Bronco so we can fire it up and get the heat working as well as possible.

"Did you catch my Jake Ryan? The car lean?" I ask when we get buckled up inside.

Eleanor holds her hands out in front of the vents, then rubs them together to generate more heat.

"Uh, sure. Who's Jake Ryan?" She gives me a sideways look that I can't read at first, but after a few seconds, I gather she's serious. *My mom is full of crap.*

"He's nobody." I smile, shaking my head. "Never mind."

Almost everyone at the game tonight is headed in the other direction, toward the Molinas' house. It's rare for them to have two parties in the same month, given how much work they have to do to clean up after each one, but it's near the end of the year, so their parents are traveling even more than normal.

I asked Elle a dozen times to confirm she didn't want to go, and I ask again as I pull up to the last light between the highway and our street. I point to the on-ramp and she shakes her head, taking my hand and pointing my finger toward home.

"Thank God," I breathe out, turning to the right instead.

Eleanor sinks back into her seat but keeps my hand in hers, shaking it to the rhythm of the song playing on the radio. I actually know this one; it's a hit. I fake my way through most of the lyrics, but Eleanor sings them all, even hitting the high notes that I don't even attempt. We roll down our street, blissfully ignorant and lost in our own high school clichés, neither of us noticing the pile of cars and media vans camped out in front of both of our houses until it's way too late to flip the truck around and dart away.

"Jonah," she breathes out my name, letting go of my hand and covering her mouth with cupped hands.

Lead weighs in my belly and fire burns through my chest. It's been a month, almost to the day. It's as if our lives are on rewind, forced to relive something absolutely awful. Only, this is nothing like the first time.

No. This . . . it has to be worse.

Eleanor opens the door before I come to a complete stop, jerking her arm free from her seat belt as she sprints through the neighbor's yard toward her sister and her parents. I watch, pinned to my seat, as Morgan backs her away from their crying parents and delivers news that cripples the girl who owns my heart and drops her to her knees.

Breathing becomes hard, and I lean forward, hugging my steering wheel as I pull the key from the ignition and flip off the lights, removing a spotlight that the Trombleys desperately don't need right now.

My eyes scan the scene, the same but different. I've come to know the players, the reporters the same ones who have been with Eleanor and her family all along. They are the bridge between the brokenhearted and the aloof. Me? I'm purgatory. I have no idea what to do, where to go, how to help. I get out of the Bronco because I have to, but from there, I shuffle forward, almost aimlessly, until I hear my grandfather call my name.

I find him in the driveway, standing next to Mom's car.

"Where's Mom?" I ask, as if that's the information I need. I don't want to know the other part. It's inevitable, but it doesn't mean I can't postpone it.

"She went over to help. She's trying to give them space. Damn media showed up a minute after they found out," he says. His eyes drift from the chaos to me, and they are filled with apology.

I suck in a hard breath when the tears hit my eyes, a burning sting forcing them down my cheeks without warning. I wipe them away only to make room for new ones.

"They found her body." It isn't a question, and he confirms the statement with a nod.

"I have to go . . . go help or something," I stammer, moving away from him on newly unsteady legs.

I amble across the street, ignoring prompts from reporters begging for answers and a peek behind the curtain. I act as though they're ghosts, passing right through them on my way to the Trombley front door. I work the handle, expecting it to be locked, but when it isn't I step inside and lock it behind me.

Morgan rushes from the living room, ready to fight an

intruder, but when she sees it's me, she throws her arms around my neck and bawls into my shoulder, wailing muffled cries as I hold her up and keep her from dropping to the floor.

"I knew this was coming," she says. She whispers these same words over and over as we stand by the front door for what feels like an hour. I don't make it inside to see Eleanor until all of the reporters have gone and I've helped Morgan appease them with some sort of statement, not that there is anything one can say when they find out that their youngest, most fragile family member was found buried in a heap of snow in a deep ravine next to the body of the deranged woman who stole her.

They'd been there for at least a week. Police found the car first and figured they must have gotten out to walk so they expanded their search. Their bodies were down a ravine a mile away from the woman's crashed car at the side of the road. It's not clear whether they fell first and then snow covered them, or if it was snowing all along when it happened. But it was the impact from the severe fall, not the cold, that ended their lives.

My mom is working in their kitchen as Morgan and I lock up for the final time, and she hands us a cup of coffee. We both refuse, and I point up the stairs where I assume Eleanor is hiding.

"They all went up a few minutes ago. The police sent an advocate to help with the process. Shit," my mom hisses, setting both coffee mugs back on the counter and letting go of the tears she's clearly been holding back.

"Thank you," Morgan says, stepping into my mom and embracing her.

I leave them with each other and hesitantly climb the stairs. I don't know if I'll make things better, but I can't fathom leaving Eleanor alone. Not after this. Her day was an enormous wave, the ride joyous and heartrending all within the span of hours. This will change her, more than she already has been. It can't be helped. I would know, yet I can't possibly know.

"Hey." I speak quietly along with a gentle knock on her barely open door.

She is drained of life, her body flat on her bed, one leg hanging off, and her wet, red face contorted where it lays along the back of her hand.

I look down at the line of her threshold. Wood floors from the hallway become carpet in her room, and I don't know whether I should cross that border.

"Stay," she croaks out. It's barely audible, but when I look up to find her outstretched hand reaching for me —*needing me*—I have my answer.

"Of course," I say, stepping inside her world and closing the door to keep the rest out.

CHAPTER Twenty-one

Addy's services are today. It's been more than a week since the Trombleys got the worst and only closure they're probably going to get.

I don't own the right kind of clothes for something like this, so Jake brought over a few of his things and I've been trying on combinations that fit and don't make me look like a boy playing dress-up. The best I've got so far is the black dress pants, gray shirt and one of my grandfather's ties. I don't know how to tie one, though, so I'm thinking of abandoning that part.

I turn at the knock on my door and meet my grandpa's soothing face as I drop the ends of his tie in frustration.

"Come here. I got it," he says, curling his fingers to call me close.

We square our shoulders with one another as he tugs free the mess I made and re-tucks the tie under the collar of my shirt.

"The trick is to make the short side shorter than you think you should."

His glasses are balanced on the tip of his nose while he concentrates on his work. I've been thinking a lot lately about how lucky I am to have him. I guess I've also been thinking about how old he is, and death.

Loss.

In a few quick motions, he forms a perfect knot that he slides up to the base of my throat. A few tugs and pulls on either side evens it out and he spins me around, giving me a little push toward my mirror. I touch it with my hand but there's no adjusting needed.

"Thanks," I say.

"Of course." His reply lifts my mouth into a short smile. It's funny the little things that get passed down the line. I don't remember it, but I have a feeling my dad said that to people a lot too. We're a lineage of men who try to do the right things. I'm honored to inherit that.

"You see her today?" He's talking about Elle. Last night was the first one I didn't go over to her house at midnight to coax her to sleep.

"Not yet. I said I'd meet her there, so she can ride with Morgan."

Grandpa nods and steps forward, resting his hand flat over my heart. He pats twice and meets my eyes before heading back downstairs.

Eleanor missed another week of school. I don't know if she's coming back. I don't know if she's eating. She barely talks. It's as though she and Morgan traded places. Her sister spent the last few weeks mentally preparing for this moment. Eleanor spent those days living her life. Then the switch flipped; it flipped everything.

Deciding I look appropriate enough to do right by Addy, I leave my room and head downstairs to meet my mom and Grandpa Hank. I stand up straight so my mom can inspect me, and her face falls.

"It doesn't seem right to say you look nice," she says.

"You should have seen the tie before Grandpa helped," I add.

"Well then, that'll do," she replies, stepping close to straighten the knot to her liking.

"I think I'm going to drive myself." Both of them nod in agreement, understanding my desire to be alone, and my hope that maybe Eleanor will let me drive her home later.

We all head out together, and we're at the service hall within minutes. It's only a block away from Toby's, and I can't help but glance at the sign as I pass and think about the laughs shared with Eleanor inside that store. What I wouldn't give to hear her laugh like that again.

I park next to my mom at the far end of the parking lot, leaving most of the spaces open for family and those who knew Addy best. We huddle together on our way into the hall, and I find Morgan once I'm inside. My mom and grandpa take a seat near the back while I slip out to talk with her. She texted me early this morning asking if I could talk to her before the service.

We make polite smiles to a few people who arrive as we step outside. Morgan hands me an envelope as soon as they pass and I stare at it, not sure I want to know what's inside.

"I need your help, Jonah. It's Elle," she says, and my heart squeezes.

"Okay," I agree. Elle is an automatic for me. I study the packed manila envelope in my hand, though I don't dare unfasten the flap. I'm afraid everything will spill to the ground.

"She's going to quit. She's going to skip the showcase competition and turn down Woodsman-Still in Texas."

My head lifts at that.

"Why would she do that?" The question is rhetorical. I know why. Guilt. Loss. Grief. Self-blame. Punishment she thinks she deserves. A lack of passion.

"She can't, Jonah. I feel like it's my fault, maybe. I was so hard on her, and now—" Morgan breaks down a little but dashes away the threat of tears and draws in a breath for strength. "She can't quit, Jonah. She's too good at what she does. And it makes her so happy. Addy, she would want her sister doing her thing for everyone to see."

A soft smile breaks through her devastated face and I find I'm smiling at that thought, too. She taps on the envelope in my hands.

"You're a smart kid. I thought maybe you could figure out how to do something with this stuff, like a video or something. There're pictures and there's a memory card in there with a bunch of videos of Elle and Addy together. She just needs to see how happy she made her sister. A push back in the direction of trying again."

The weight in my hands suddenly feels a lot heavier than a bunch of paper and a microchip. I don't know that I can deliver all that she wants, or all that Eleanor needs. But I will try. I will try so fucking hard.

"Okay." I nod, giving her the temporary relief that comes with hope.

She hugs me once more then slips inside, making her way to the front where her family is one member smaller than it should be. I hover outside, peering through the doors for as long as I can before joining my family that carries along a ghost of its own.

One at a time, people stand and share stories that are meant to offer healing. Every word seems to open a wound, though. It's Thanksgiving next week. There is nothing in this space that feels worthy of thanks.

Zoning out on the words from the pulpit, I turn my attention to the envelope, slipping it open carefully to get a sense of what's inside. It catches my mom's attention when I do, so she unfolds her hands from her lap to help me sort through the contents one item at a time. There are photos of Addy as a baby being rocked to sleep in Eleanor's arms. Addy getting hearts painted on her cheeks like her sister. A tea party with nothing but Barbie, a stuffed teddy bear and Eleanor as guests. I hold on to the image of the youngest Trombley dressed up in her big sister's cheer uniform for a long while, my heart soothed by the story that goes along with it.

I think maybe I *can* do this. If the video is anything like the photos Morgan compiled for me, there's potential. More than that, there's comfort and peace.

It's late evening by the time we get home from services. Eleanor wanted to ride with her sister, which I completely understand. I still wanted her with me, though. I want to fix things somehow, to make it all hurt a little less. But I don't know how to do that. I feel as if I'm back at the very beginning with her, unsure of my words and my actions. I don't know exactly who I'm supposed to be around her, or rather, what version of me she needs most. I don't think I actually have versions.

I've been sitting in the Bronco in the garage for the last hour sorting through these pictures, trying to find a way to weave them into a story. Not only Addy's story, but Eleanor's too. And I need to give that story a happy ending.

"You thinking of moving into that thing now that you've got it running?" My mom stands with one foot in the house and the other in the garage.

"It's not really a *live-in* kinda comfortable," I say.

She chuckles and moves toward the passenger side, letting the door to the house fall shut behind her.

"Oh, I know. Your dad took me camping in that thing a few times. We basically lived in it for weekends at a time. And it was . . . tight." She arches her back to one side, cracking it.

"Wanna join me?" I glance down at the empty passenger seat.

"I thought you'd never ask." Mom pulls the handle and lifts herself up into the seat. She slams the door shut at her side and breathes out a heavy sigh as she leans back then forward to touch the familiar dashboard.

"My God, the memories in this thing," she says through a fond smile. Her eyes trace the windshield's surface then travel down to the console. She reaches forward to push a few buttons, ejecting a cassette tape from the dated stereo deck.

"What the hell is that?" I tease. I know what cassettes are. Grandpa has a box full in his closet, though when his current player quits working, I'm not sure he'll have a way to play them.

She slaps my arm then hands the cassette to me for a better look. It reads KARA'S FAVORITE SONGS.

"Dad made you a mix tape?" I quirk a brow as she takes it back from me, eyeing it fondly.

"He sure did. There are a lot of great songs on this thing. Lots of mod stuff, like The Cure." I swear she's traveling back to her teenage years before my eyes.

"You want me to turn the key and we can give it a listen?" I offer.

"Oh, no. I'm pretty sure that thing will just eat it. You can't sit in a storage lot for twenty years without wear and tear, and I'm pretty sure Kara's Favorite Songs are not meant to be played on a cassette anymore."

"You mean because you're old?" I joke.

She smacks my arm again, playfully, because she knows I'm teasing.

"What are you going to do with that?" She glances down to the photos I've pulled out to rest on my thighs for inspiration. I look down at them and we both take in the faces and memories that aren't ours but that we deeply understand.

"I'm going to build Eleanor some courage with them . . . I guess." I lift my gaze and look to my mom, expecting her to be as baffled by how as I am. Instead, she nods with an assuredness I haven't seen in her eyes in quite a while.

"You'll figure it out," she says, pulling the handle at her side and slipping out of the Bronco. She shuts the door and leans in through the window.

"I hope so," I answer. I look back down at the photos as she walks to the front of the garage. A few seconds pass before she reaches in again, this time dropping my dad's notebook in her empty seat. "Here's another guy who built someone some courage, ya know."

I blink from the book to her face and she winks before turning and heading back inside. I pull the book into my lap and prop it open on a random page against the steering wheel. If ever the universe was talking to me—*my dad is talking to me*—it's right now. Right there in the middle of a step-by-step instruction on how to replace the weird-ass vintage headlights is a line from KARA'S FAVORITE SONGS mixtape. I can almost guarantee it's The Cure. He wrote "Friday I'm in Love."

"Yeah, Dad. I really, really am," I say, feeling in my soul that somewhere, he is listening.

Chapter Twenty-two

It took me two full days to make something I felt was up to the challenge. There was a bit of a learning curve with the software, and I had to borrow a lot of things from school, along with some help from the digital media teacher, who I'm pretty sure did not like me when I took his class my freshman year.

The good news is Mr. Luvello loves Eleanor. Basically, everyone loves Eleanor. And that love has been the key to creating this miracle that amounts to two minutes and forty-seven seconds of video. Now, I just need to persuade Elle to watch it.

I ring the Trombley bell and ready myself for her dad to appear at the door. He's usually the one who answers when I come over. He's handling the closure and the loss a little easier than his wife, but neither of them come out much. I think this video might be good for all of them. Either that or it's going to be terrible. I'm sort of prepared for things to go either way.

"Jonah, hey. Come on in," Mr. Trombley says, opening their front door wide for me to step inside.

"She's still upstairs. Hasn't been down much today, but she did eat," he says, picking up a plate with a half-eaten sandwich that she must have left at the entry table. He's been helping me encourage both Eleanor and her mom to get out and eat a little more.

He looks down at the laptop tucked under my arm, so I hold it up and move toward the stairs.

"Actually, do you think your wife could maybe join us in Eleanor's room? I have something I think you all might want to see. Something I made, with Morgan's help." I glance over his shoulder to the den where Morgan has been hovering.

"It's done?" She's picking at the end of her sweater, clearly eager to see the finished product.

"It is. Want to see the grand premier?" I lean my head toward the stairs as she smiles.

"Wouldn't miss it," she says, nodding to her dad to reassure him that he's not getting in over his head. I really hope she's right.

We gather at the top of the steps and the hallway is already a tight fit. It gets even more crowded when Mrs. Trombley comes out of her room to join us, and I worry Eleanor is going to think this is an intervention when we all convene on her at once. I suppose, in a way, it is.

"Let me set this up with her first, if that's okay?" I say, stopping right outside Eleanor's door.

Morgan nods and I leave her parents with her as I slip inside Eleanor's room. She's sitting up and watching something on her phone with her headphones on. It's good to see her engaging with something, and there's a touch of color to her face. She's wrapped herself in my flannel shirt, which is flattering. She's worn it for about five days straight, though, so it might be time for me to swap it out with something different.

To keep from startling her, I crouch down to catch her eyes. She still jumps a little, but pulls her headphones off and sets her phone to the side.

"Sorry, I was watching some home improvement competition. They're turning storage containers into beach houses." She's more animated than she has been in days. This is promising.

"Sounds . . . sandy," I reply, moving to sit next to her on her bed.

Her attention drifts to my laptop and she curls her legs in, hugging them to her body, already guarded. I open my mouth, ready with the talking points I practiced, but I suddenly realize I'm better off the cuff. I can't be polished and rehearsed with this girl. I have to be honest and heartfelt. It's all I've ever really been, and it's taken me—*us*—far.

I pull in a deep breath that I sense makes her nervous.

"It's nothing bad. I promise," I say to set her at ease.

"O-kay," she hums, shifting her gaze to me then back to the laptop. She lets go of one of her legs and loosens the grip on her knees. Baby steps.

"You know how you made me that music playlist, for my birthday?" I refuse to admit I'm starting to enjoy country music, but I've listened to those songs every day for the last month. I have most of them memorized, even the super sappy ones.

"Did you make me a . . . *playlist?"* She lifts a brow, clearly not sure where any of this is going.

"Right, no. Not exactly. But I did use one of your songs. Not the Bronco one, but that song that you were singing in the car the first time you went to Toby's with me."

Her mouth softens, almost a smile.

"Used it for what?" she asks.

I exhale, a little relieved that this is working. She's taken the bait, so to speak.

"It's sort of a multimedia project. And I got a little help, so I wondered if you would mind if—"

"If?" she interjects.

"If, maybe I invited your entire family into your bedroom to watch something with us?" I grin through gritted teeth to show her how guilty I feel. She also usually can't resist me when I play up being pathetic.

"Are they right out there?" She laughs, but shuts her mouth when she gleans from the face I'm making that *yes, in fact, they are.*

"Guys?" My head sinks into my shoulders with guilt as Morgan unlatches the door and slowly exposes everyone gathered in the tight hallway space.

"Oh, my God, you guys are ridiculous!" Eleanor says. I'm just glad she finds this amusing. So far.

I sit on the floor with the laptop in front of me while her mom and sister nestle in next to her, and Mr. Trombley stands to the side, behind me. I feel as though this requires a set-up, at least, so I flip my computer open but not fully so I can block the screen. The first thing they will see is Addy's face, and I don't want them—Eleanor—shutting down before I even start.

"Elle, I know you're thinking about calling your cheer coach and asking them to put Kacey in for the competition this weekend. And, don't be mad at your sister, but she also told me you're thinking about passing on Texas."

Eleanor's mom gasps behind me, but before she can turn this moment into something it's not, both Morgan and I hold up our hands.

"Give him a minute, Mom," Morgan says.

My gaze slides back to Eleanor, and she's holding her thumbnail tightly between her teeth, fear spiraling behind her eyes.

"Before you change up your entire path . . ." I'm careful not to use the word *derail*. If I learned one thing from my mom's months of therapy sessions, it's that people do not like to be accused of derailing anything. It's the one word my mom would hold on to after every appointment, and repeat it like it was a weapon. I honestly believe that word is the reason she quit going to that doctor.

"Take a look at these memories you built, you *all* built, with Addy. And if you erase those things that you do, that she was such a huge part of, you might end up erasing a part of her." My dad's book flashes through my mind as I say this. All I thought I was missing was the guy who left early and came home late from work. But I missed so much more. I wish I had an ounce of the shared experiences Eleanor has with her little sister.

"Okay," I say, steeling myself before flipping my screen back for everyone to see. I turn the volume up and click play, then hold my breath for two minutes and forty-seven seconds.

The room is silent for the first part, which is mostly a slideshow of Addy in their lives. When it gets to her and Eleanor playing together, learning cheer routines and high-fiving at Badger games, I can literally feel the air move and lightness fill the room. Mr. Trombley chuckles as the video shows his youngest daughter attempting a cartwheel, but his hand grips at his heart when the next scene is his middle daughter physically holding his youngest through an entire flip just to prove to her that she can do it.

There are slow dances together, Addy standing on top of Eleanor's feet, and then there's a scene where both Morgan and Eleanor hide in a box to surprise their parents because Addy told them to. Her voice can be heard between the lyrics of Eleanor's favorite song, and it's as if Addy is singing along with it, her cadence made for song. It's her essence, simply the way her words come out. She breathes life and music, and from a quick survey of the people around me, she makes it impossible not to smile.

God, I wish I'd known her better.

The video fades to a single photo at the end, from this year. It's Addy sitting on Eleanor's knee while she poses with both arms up, ready to cheer, and she's wearing her sister's away uniform while Eleanor is in her home blues. It's about three sizes too big on Addy, and if she stood, it would probably slip right off. But this is the moment Eleanor was telling me about. It's the last sliver of hope to keep her from making rash decisions in her time of grief that will only fill her with regret later.

"She loved to watch you cheer," Eleanor's mom says, sniffling with emotion behind me.

I close my computer and turn to face them all, my eyes catching Morgan's first. She nods through teary eyes and gives me a thumbs-up that she keeps close to her chest. I hope she's right and this did the job it was meant to do. Their parents thank me for putting something so special together, and I hand over the laptop when Mr. Trombley asks if he can play it again so he can pause on a few of the pictures.

It's Eleanor I'm the most interested in, though. Her chin rests on her knee, bouncing as she gnaws at her thumb, eyes transfixed on the empty space between me and her. I wave my hand, slicing through the air, and she doesn't react. My shoulders deflate, but I try again, waving longer this time. Her eyes shift to mine eventually, and they are full of fear.

"I don't know if I can do any of this without her," she says, her voice bleeding with ache and sorrow, barely audible but enough that it stops everyone in the room.

Her parents pause the video and set my computer down so they can tend to their daughter, and Morgan slides an arm around Eleanor in an attempt to move her rigid body into an embrace. Eleanor shakes her head, slow at first but her movements grow more fitful and unnerved with every beat of her heart.

"I can't do any of it without her," she repeats.

"You won't be," I say. That's really the message of all of this. None of them have to go on without her. They carry her inside.

Tears rush to fill her eyes, spilling over to her cheeks until they drip from her jaw.

"Honey," her mom says, wiping them away with her palm.

"She's not here," Eleanor says, her eyes still locked on mine, lips quivering.

I know what she means, but I also know that in some ways, she's wrong. Swallowing hard, I dig deep for the right thing to say, something that will give her faith. She needs something to believe in, a way to talk to Addy. That will give her strength.

"Addy *is*. She always will be."

In six words, I manage to break down the last of the dam as tears pour out of Eleanor, along with all the pain she has been too afraid to walk through on her own. I get to my knees and wrap my arms around her, bringing her to the floor where she falls into my body and sobs in my lap.

Morgan moves next to her and rubs her back while her parents look on. Every single one of us is crying. We mourn the young spirit who's missing but left behind so much good.

But after an hour of tears and sharing stories and laughter, and even long minutes with no words at all as those thoughts and feelings sink in, I believe Addy gets her way.

She is. And she always will be.

"For the record, I don't think any of this is a good idea."

I'm not wrong. Jake knew that at some point today Eleanor would need a spark. I kinda thought maybe a poster with her name on it, or T-shirts we all could wear. Jake had other ideas.

I've already lost the bet, so what he has planned is one hundred percent straight from the heart, if you can call a six-foot-three bare-assed naked guy sprinting across a cheer mat heartfelt.

Jake swears you can.

"Dude, these sweatpants are really riding up my crotch." He squats as he stands along the balcony railing next to me and I move over a few feet because . . . *gross.*

"I don't know why you took off your boxers," I mutter, shaking my head.

"Are you kidding me? I'm going to need to be quick. And speaking of quick, after I do this, you have to come pick me up because once I start running I'm not stopping until I get to the park bathrooms on Apricot and Third."

I gawk at my friend. He's really put a lot of thought into something incredibly dumb. If he put half this much effort into geometry, I wouldn't have to tutor him. If I didn't think this scheme would at least distract Eleanor from the pull of sadness, I would have forbidden it. I think it will make her laugh, though. The good kind of laugh. The kind we all miss hearing.

"Promise me you'll pick me up," he says.

"Promise me you'll put pants on before you sit in my Bronco."

He grimaces as if my request is weird.

"Fine, yeah. I'll pick you up." I'm not rushing out behind him, though. No way in hell do I want anyone thinking I'm a part of . . . *that.*

Our conversation gets cut off by the announcement calling Oak Forest High to the mats. The lights dim, but I can tell, even in the darkness, which one is Eleanor as everyone on the squad spreads out to their positions. I'm nervous for her. Not for the tumbling and stuff. She could do that in her sleep. It's the other stuff, the things inside that are still very much trying to take her down. Her support system is behind her, though. All of us. Her parents, grandparents and sister are all sitting at the side of the stage. My mom took today off from her second job to be here. I left Mom and Grandpa in the chairs by the floor. I want to be able to film everything on my phone so Eleanor can relive it when she's ready, and the view up here is perfect.

When the lights go out completely, I steady my phone between my hands and begin to record. The spotlights come on as the familiar—and by this point fairly obnoxious—music kicks in.

The first few passes of tumbling look good and from what I can tell, nobody's out of place. Bodies shift and move like clockwork, girls being tossed and caught in sync with sound effects. Seeing this routine go down in a place like this makes it all seem so much more intense. Maybe it's acoustics, or maybe it's the fact that inside, you can tell exactly how high those girls are being thrown.

I recognize sections and brace myself when Eleanor's first solo tumble is coming up. I take a deep breath, imagining myself in sync with her, and hold my breath as she backs herself into the far corner of the mat, nodding when she's ready. Her feet thunder toward the open middle, and she dives with her hands forward, punching the mat with enough force to spring her body around completely, feet over her head, head over feet, until she stops hard in the very center as if a magnet drew her feet to the perfect spot.

I don't let my breath out until I hear the crowd cheer, but within a beat I'm holding it again. Pass after pass goes by without a single error that I can see. They're getting close to the part when Eleanor finishes with the splits, so I focus on the view through my phone, taking special care not to miss any of the big tricks, and to make sure I don't jiggle the focus.

"Damn!" Jake muses next to me just as Eleanor holds her body weight up in a position that would give both of us nightmares.

The end of the music is approaching. It's sad that I actually know this compilation by heart. There's one trick left, the one with Eleanor's twist. All eyes follow her, and I count to myself while her teammates pump their arms, priming them to send her soaring up to the rafters. On three, she goes up, and her body makes its full rotation. As she comes down, though, her leg slips loose right before she's caught, sending her along with two of her teammates tumbling to the ground.

"Shit," Jake says, and I stop recording because I don't think she's going to want to see this part, or hear our friend's commentary.

"She's okay, right? Is she okay?" I ask Jake as if he can see something I can't. I'm bouncing on my toes, wavering and unsure whether I should rush down there or wait this out. The music has stopped and all of the lights are back on. Her coach is crouching next to her, stretching and flexing her leg while the training team climbs up on the mat. Her team is huddled around her, all of them kneeling while she grabs at her ankle. She's definitely crying.

"I should go," I say, but Jake holds his arm across my chest before I turn, stopping me. He motions to the floor.

Eleanor is attempting to get to her feet. Her coach on one side, Gemma on the other, she steadies herself as they brace her under her elbows. Eleanor keeps shaking her head, and I can't tell if those are winces of determination or excruciating pain. Finally, after a full minute of testing her weight on her ankle with the help of her team, she sets out to try it on her own. Everyone backs away to give her room, and she hobbles to the far corner then tumbles her way to the center. It's obvious that she isn't one-hundred percent. Her right foot never fully lands on the mat, but what's even more impressive is the way she holds it a half-inch from the ground to make it look like her landing is clean. The strength of that left leg and foot is epic.

Hopping toward the front of the mat, Eleanor leans forward to say something to the judges.

"Come on, guys. Give her a break. Come on." I'm not sure what request she's making, but I silently demand them to grant it, no matter how unreasonable or unfair or against whatever rules her ask might be.

After a few minutes of the judges conversing through whispers, the woman who seems to be the lead nods toward the coach. Eleanor puts her hands together and bends forward to say thanks before hobbling back to the middle of the mat. Someone near the floor whistles, and I swear it's my grandfather. The crowd begins to clap in rhythm, so I bring my phone back up to my chest and steady it to record. I begin right before Eleanor's team regroups, all of them back in their places to pick up where they were right before things went wrong.

"Are you getting this?"

"Yes. *Shh*," I hush Jake.

Just like the time I lifted her to the sky in the middle of our street, I count down for her final moment.

Three, two . . . one.

Her body sails through the air, as tight as the first time, the rotation just as crisp. This time, as she lands, every arm is intact, every hold solid, and with one final swing, Eleanor's team sends her back up in the air for her to flip with one knee out and the other tucked against her chest.

With sheer will and precision, and with Gemma's hands gripping her leg like hell, Eleanor balances above her team and holds the position for a full three seconds before tucking and landing safely in her team's cradled arms.

The gym erupts in celebration. There's no way we're placing first, not with the mistake. But it doesn't matter. That one bobble is not what anyone is going to remember about today, especially not Eleanor. She's going to remember facing adversity, and then overcoming it like mad.

I record all the way through the team's exit from the

mat, wanting to be sure I capture every whistle and the standing ovation that follow the Badgers' exit. When we hear the team roar with their own cheer behind the stage, Jake and I head down to join them.

Morgan is waiting off to the side, Eleanor's things bundled in a bag at her feet. I step up beside her to wait while Eleanor hugs her parents and grandparents and celebrates with her friends. She and her mom cry as they embrace, and I know they feel Addy's presence. That finish —that was her doing. I'm sure of it.

"If they don't get a trophy, I'm stealing one," Morgan mutters next to me.

I shake with a laugh and tell her to get prepared because I may know a distraction is coming. She smiles, not getting my joke. But she will, soon enough.

"They don't judge these things based on heart," I add.

"Well, that's too damn bad," she responds.

Indeed, it is.

The drama from the Badgers' performance caused quite a stir, and the judges are being kind, giving everyone a brief break so the other squads can come congratulate Eleanor too. She's practically glowing, and I know she's proud of herself. I'm not sure how many people in this building know her full story, but I am sure many do. There's a reason this entire gym full of people clapped and cheered to encourage our team.

The crowd begins to break up and teams head back to their seats. I'm finally able to catch Eleanor's attention, and I shove my phone in my back pocket to ready myself for the collision of her body into mine as she rushes toward me. I lift her up when we meet, but quickly let her slide into my hold, nuzzling my nose against hers. I can't believe I get to be her boyfriend.

"How'd that feel?" I ask, whisking away the mix of tears falling along her cheeks.

"It felt—" She lifts a shoulder and smiles with a short stuttered cry. She's happy, but she is also overwhelmed. For her, this is like the moment when I played the Bronco song and really listened. It's a collision of feelings, a place where happiness and grief collide and work to soothe each other.

"She would have loved it," I say, feeling Morgan squeeze in at my side. I step back so they can embrace as they agree with my sentiment. It's a truly beautiful moment, and from the corner of my eye, I catch a glimpse of something that is about to dramatically shift the atmosphere.

I probably should have warned them, but in my defense, I didn't think Jake would do it so soon after our school finished their routine. There are still something like six schools left to compete. But that doesn't matter now. The judges finally settled the chaos, and it's about to explode once again.

It starts with a single screech from the old woman at the side of the stage. I'm sure she's a volunteer, but she did not sign up for this. Her squeal is what gets most people to turn and look. Eleanor pushes up on her toes to see what the fuss is about, but I cover my face with my palm then glance to the side of the stage to locate the pants I'm going to need to pick up in a few seconds.

"Is that—?" Morgan begins to ask. There's no need for me to answer as my best friend rushes across the mat, completing his version of a cartwheel as he crosses the center, exposing everyone to *way* more than his pale-ass butt cheeks along the way.

Morgan is laughing so hard she can hardly breathe, meeting my deadpan stare when she realizes what I meant about a distraction. Putting it all together only makes her laugh harder.

Eleanor turns to face me, hands resting on her cheeks and mouth ajar. She looks positively stunned. I don't really think she needed this extra boost Jake planned, but apparently he was hell bent on delivering it. Who knows? Maybe he was so amped up after Eleanor's amazing stunt, he just had to top it with one of his own.

"I cannot believe he did that," Eleanor says, her shoulders shaking with building laughter. Or maybe shuddering in revolt. Her teammates are all gathering around Gemma, who I am sure is mortified. If she stays with him after this, I'm stealing that trophy for her.

"He didn't even lose the bet," Eleanor says.

"Nope. He did not," I add, glancing to his lonely pile of clothes off to the side of the stage. I turn my attention back to Eleanor and ask if she needs to see the trainer. I can tell, even standing, that her foot is swollen. I'm sure if we took her shoe off, we'd see colors.

"It's just a sprain, but yeah. I'll get it wrapped and get some ice," she says.

The doors near the back of the gym smash open and light spills in from outside. I know without looking that it was Jake exiting. It took him a while to lose security, I'm guessing. He's heading toward Apricot and Third now.

"Let me grab that idiot's pants, then I'll help you get to the trainer," I say.

"Shouldn't you, I don't know, get his pants *to him?*"

I purse my lips with pretend care and thought as I glance down then back up to her.

"He'll be all right."

She laughs, but doesn't argue with me. Through the

chaos, I slip toward the stage and snag the track suit that Jake was wearing while commando. I shove it under my arm so I can support Eleanor on my other side, and together, we hobble our way toward the trainer's area. He gives me one of the bags he uses for ice when I let him in on the secret that I'm carrying the streaker's clothes. I drop them between my feet while I wait for Eleanor to get checked out and taped up for her ride home.

I'm tempted to wait through the awards ceremony too, but sitting through six more routines feels cruel. Besides, he has no way to call for help.

I have his phone, in the pocket of his pants. In a bag between my feet.

Eleanor is quiet. I think she's anxious, or maybe coming down from the high of the competition. She's been this way since I got back from dropping Jake off at home. I came back to see the last few teams compete and to watch our Badgers take home third. Eleanor seemed excited to hold the trophy, but her smile was always temporary, falling after every picture someone took.

Maybe this has all been too much.

"Do you want to play some music?" I offer her my phone so she can play something other than the four stations I can tune in on the Bronco. She shakes it off though with another temporary smile. She hasn't even watched the video I filmed.

The sinking pit in my stomach lowers.

It's probably all in my head, but everything about the sudden mood shift feels like . . . like a breakup. Only, I know it's not. I reach toward her to take her hand and she gives it to me willingly, no attempt to let go. As I pull her hand up to kiss the inside of her wrist while we wait at the stoplight leading to our street, she slides closer to the center so she can hug my bicep when I'm done. She rests her head on me, and I don't even scold her for abandoning the shoulder strap of her seat belt.

"Hey, you okay?" I ask. I kiss the top of her head as she gazes up at me through her lashes.

The pregnant pause before she answers is a warning.

"Yeah, just . . . tired probably," she says. Again, the smile is temporary.

I'm sure she really is tired, so I can't fairly accuse her of lying. But there is something else weighing on her mind, and I'm not sure whether I should pry harder or be glad she's protecting me from whatever it is.

Turns out, I don't get much of a choice in the matter. As we turn down our street and approach home, the reason for her gloom becomes quite clear in the form of a white post nailed at the edge of her lawn with a bright and glaring goodbye message hanging from it.

FOR SALE

I stop abruptly in the middle of the road, and it jerks Eleanor forward. Her hands slap the dashboard but she doesn't complain. She freezes in that position and stares at the truth ahead. This is what she couldn't say.

A car slows to a crawl behind me, honking and snapping me out of my daze, so I roll down my window and wave an apology then pull to the side of the road, right next to the offending sign in Eleanor's yard.

"I thought maybe if I just reversed out of here I could pretend I didn't see it." It's a dumb joke, and neither of us laugh.

There's not much to say. I can't be mad at her. It's not her choice, and I know that. But it sucks. It really fucking sucks.

"Too many memories for my parents," she finally utters.

"I get it," I answer quickly. I don't want her to think there is any blame. There's not. There's just . . . hurt. I hurt. *This* hurts!

"When I'm gone, it will only be the two of them, so . . ."

"Yeah." I nod slowly. I can't seem to peel my eyes off that sign. It's more than just what it is. It's the added fact that there's a sticker across it that reads SALE PENDING.

"Why even put up the sign?" Again, I joke. I manage a short, forced laugh. Eleanor remains silent. "If it's already sold, I mean. Seems like a real waste of resources. Some guy had to come out here today and pound in that pole, and then there's probably a sticker guy."

"I think it's the same guy," she interjects. "Not one for poles and one for stickers."

Our heads swivel and our gazes meet in the middle, a hint of humor in our eyes and on our lips. Even like this we can make each other laugh.

"Where will you go?"

I know the answer, which is why I can't be upset at her.

"Texas. If they buy there, I can get residency, and in-state tuition," she says.

"Makes sense." Both of our stares drift back to the sign.

I hate that sign.

"It went up fast." I blink at it. As much as I don't blame her for anything, I can't help but feel she's known about this a little longer than since she exited the mat at the competition.

"I wanted to tell you." She stifles a cry and I feel terrible because it's my fault. I can't seem to get myself to say it's okay. I do reach for her hand and cup it between both of mine. We sit in the quiet of the Bronco, the motor gurgling through gallons of gas. I'm not moving, though. Not as long as she wants to sit here with me. If I have to push this thing back into the garage, I will.

"They signed to list it the day of the service. Someone made a cash offer that night. I guess the company likes to get backups though, so that's why they went ahead with the sign," she says.

I nod and look back at our house. For all the reasons the Trombleys want to leave, my mom is fighting to stay and keep making the mortgage payments. She likes the memories in our house. I do, too. At least, I did. I don't know that I'll be able to look out my window ever again.

"When do you move?" More questions I don't want the answers to, but I need to know.

"Last day of the semester. We'll be set up in Texas by Christmas."

I break down a little at that thought. That's in two weeks. I'm going to miss Christmas with her. I had so many grand ideas.

"But we can visit! And I'll call and write," she says, shifting in her seat to face me as she grabs on to my arm. She's forcing the upbeat tone, and shame on me for killing it. I just can't help it.

"Sure." That's the only response I give. Pathetic. Cruel.

She sinks back into her seat, and after a few more minutes she gathers her things at her feet and pushes on the handle of the door.

"I love you, Jonah. That's still true."

I roll my head to the side and force my mouth up as high as I can on the corners. It isn't very far.

"I love you, too."

She slips out of the cab and pushes the door shut, not even gratifying me with a slam so I can ease the pain and guilt. Gentle, loving and perfect, all the way to the bittersweet end. And that's what this is—a really bittersweet end.

Moving day came fast. I think maybe because the last two weeks have been filled with packing and making donation runs to the thrift store in town. The Trombleys are leaving the scene of their nightmare, but they aren't leaving Addy. Of the dozens of boxes I helped them take to the donation center, I think only one was filled with Addy's things. They'll have to work through this slowly, a process that will probably take years. My dad's shirts still hang in my Mom's closet. I think if she boxed them up and asked me to take them to town, I'd lie and hang them in mine just to keep them longer.

The Trombleys hit the road at five in the morning tomorrow. Elle and her mom will ride together in the big moving truck, and her dad is following behind with the family car. The Volkswagen was one of the first things to go in the donation binge. Apparently they made more off it as a write-off than what it was worth for sale. I regret not buying it.

I have literal hours left with Eleanor, but I can't seem to

get myself to sit with her in her emptying house. Besides, Gemma deserves a little time with her, too. I'm half-tempted to throw a wrench in the Bronco engine to give me something to work on again. It would beat sitting at the kitchen table picking at the crust on the peanut butter sandwich as I've been doing for the last hour and a half. I'm pretty sure it's no longer edible.

Grandpa tosses the Sunday paper down in front of me to wake me up, and I sit back in my chair to feign looking alive.

"Hey, you bum. Why aren't you over there squeezing out every last second of time with your girl?" He takes his regular seat and divvies up the sections of the paper. He slept in today, a rarity for him. I think perhaps the cigar stench in the garage and the empty case of Pabst has something to do with that. The boys were over late last night.

"I'm giving her space. That's all," I say.

"Horseshit. You're sulking," Grandpa says.

I shrug and take the insult because he's probably right.

I pick through some of the sections of the paper, sliding the sports section to Gramps when I notice the Blackhawks photo on the front. He mumbles something about the coach getting sacked, but I'm not really listening. I spend about twenty minutes on a section of the paper that I don't read. I just let my eyes lose their focus and try to form pictures with the words. It gives me a headache after a while, so I get up to track down some aspirin right as Jake pulls up in front of the house.

"What's that idiot doing here?" Grandpa says, glaring out the front door from over his paper. I guess Grandpa Hank got an eyeful of Jake's stunt at the cheer competition.

"He's probably here for Gemma and to say his goodbyes," I say, searching through the medicine cabinet for something to dull my everything.

"Then why's he coming in the house? Hey! Pants required in this joint, numb nut!"

I shut the cabinet door to verify my grandpa's observations. He's right. I nod to my friend as I toss two aspirin into my mouth and tilt my head back, swallowing them dry. When I right my head again, Jake is glaring at me with disgust.

"How can you do that?" he asks.

"Uh, how can you run four blocks naked?" I throw back at him.

He twists his lips and appears to be mulling over a comeback, but comes up short.

"Fair point," he says, poking me with his index finger.

"Why are you here?" I move to sit back down for more non-reading, but Jake swoops his hand under my arm and lifts me back up, proceeding to drag me out the front door.

"Bye, Mr. Wydner!" he shouts over his shoulder.

"Dumbass," Grandpa mumbles.

The door bangs closed behind us and my feet grow heavy in an effort to slow us down as we near his car.

"Jake, I'm not in the mood," I gripe.

"A bet's a bet." He stops short of his car and turns me to face him, folding his arms over his chest as though he's some superhero ready to stop me from destroying the world. What a shitty villain I would make. I don't even feel like destroying the world.

"I'm not streaking through the neighborhood," I say.

"Har har," he mocks.

It's an irritating habit he's picked up from some of his bros on the basketball team.

"That wasn't our bet. Our bet was that the Bronco runs

by Thanksgiving and you get your ass to prom." He stares me down as if everything should be clear now. It's not.

"I remember the bet. It's December, Jake. Prom is not until April. Plus, I really don't want to go alone and stand by the punch bowl like a legit loser."

"Which is why," he says before I can continue, "you are going to come with me right now and pick up a tux. I happen to know that your date is across the street, and she is being pampered by my very capable and talented girlfriend, so you know she is going to be *hawt!* You cannot show up for your prom wearing— What are you wearing?"

He gestures up and down the length of my body, enjoying this power trip.

"They're pajama pants," I say through a grimace.

"Right, and this math club sweatshirt, very chic. But still, not the right aesthetic." He's playing this up as if we're really going through with it. I back up a step and wave my hands.

"Wait, wait. Where are we supposed to have a prom, Jake? She leaves in hours." My pulse is starting to race with this inflamed sense of urgency he's triggered.

"Again, the *where* is in my girlfriend's very capable hands. My only task is to get you a suit and make you look presentable. So, how about you give me a break and get your ass in the car?" He marches to the passenger side and holds the door open wide while wearing the sternest expression I've ever seen him make.

"Is that . . . is that your game face?" I ask, pointing to him but relenting and heading toward the open door.

"Yes. Yes, it is. Look at what you did. You made me go game face. Are you happy?" He starts snapping, urging me to pick up my pace, so I do. I'm playing along with his game, and while part of me tells myself I'm doing it just to mess around with my friend, a part of me is also a little excited by the whole idea. The romantic that I thought died in my soul is taking a breath and waking up a little.

For the next three hours, I basically become Jake's personal Cinderella, and he's my barely functioning hairy godfather.

December is a big month for suit rentals. The selection is slim, and the prices insane. Apparently, though, my mom has been in on this little plot too, so she hooked Jake up with some spare cash to make this happen.

"You really think I can pull off powder blue?" The suit is vintage. It was one of three in the price range, and the other two really felt like funeral attire. I could not show up in anything somber. Though in a strange way, I think I might be rocking this look.

"For sure. It makes your wild hair make sense, too. Like cosplay," he says.

I pause from straightening my collar in the mirror and stare at his reflection. He finally meets my gaze and gives me his usual palms-out, "What?"

"Just what every girl dreams of when going to prom. Oh, I hope my date shows up looking like a cartoon." I roll my eyes and get back to work on my tie, trying to emulate what I learned from my grandfather.

"I didn't say cartoon. I said cosplay. Very different."

I laugh at his reasoning. *Is it, really?*

With my third tie attempt complete, I turn to face my friend and he brushes his hands down my sleeves to straighten the fabric. Grandpa pokes his head in and cuts

Jake off, undoing my work and giving me an actual Windsor knot.

"You'll get it. It takes time," he assures me, pulling it a little too tight against my neck. I cough and loosen it when he turns.

My mom came home early. I heard her milling around downstairs, and Jake has been in constant communication with Gemma across the street. I'm actually sweating from nerves, and if I hover in my bedroom much longer, I'm going to sweat this powder blue suit right into navy. I give Jake a nod and he leads the way out of my room and down the stairs. My mom is waiting at the bottom, and the minute I step into view, she starts snapping photos with her phone. She is maybe the only person on the planet who I will not give grief to for keeping the fake camera sound installed.

"You look—"

"Beautiful?" I finish.

She gives me a sideways glance and steps closer.

"Handsome, I was going to say." She does the mom thing, pulling on my collar that does not need her touch, but I let her have her way. She hands me a small box with a pink flower inside.

"Corsage," she explains.

"Ah, right," I say. "It goes well with the baby blue. At this point, I look like a gender reveal party."

My mom lightly slaps the top of my hand.

"The flower is for her, Jonah. You get this handkerchief," she says, tucking a silk square into my pocket. I catch the dark blue initials stitched on the corner and move my gaze to her eyes, waiting for her to finish making the fold perfect. She nods to my unvoiced question, and I touch the tips of my fingers to the embossed R and W stitched on the silk. This was my dad's.

The doorbell rings and a new wave of adrenaline spills down my spine. Nothing about this thrown-together gala is traditional. For example, if this were four months from now and Eleanor were not leaving for Texas, I would be backing out of my driveway and pulling into hers to pick her up for steak or lobster followed by some really bad dancing with an overpriced DJ in our high school gym.

But that's not the prom I'm getting. And neither is she.

I ball my fists at my sides while Grandpa goes to open the door, welcoming Gemma inside. She's still wearing her jeans and sweatshirt, which means Jake wasn't kidding when he said this special night is solely for me and Elle.

What felt weird a second ago stops the instant Eleanor Trombley steps through my door. Her black gown drapes to the floor and fits every curve of her body as if it were tailor-made for her. A slit cuts up the side, making it more than just possible for her to walk—it also shows off her long muscular leg every other step. Silver shoes with crystals shine on her feet and lift her a good four inches, making her exactly my height. Even though in terms of attractiveness in this room, she blows me out of the water, she still blushes and looks down while biting her lip when my eyes adore every inch of her face.

"Holy wow," I utter, fumbling my way through holding out her corsage and stretching the band for her wrist.

My mom is serenading us with her fake camera sounds, capturing every embarrassing and wonderful moment, and I already intend to use my newfound video skills to compile it all for the first email to Eleanor when she leaves.

Tomorrow.

She leaves . . . tomorrow.

I shake off the sadness and focus on the now. Eleanor lifts her wrist and smells the flower, touching the soft petals to her nose.

"My mom helped with that part. I don't really know what I'm doing," I stammer. Even if everyone weren't staring at us, I'm pretty sure I would be babbling like an idiot. I'm wearing a seventies leisure suit and I'm being paired with a supermodel.

"I love it. Thank you," she says to me, then looks over her shoulder to my mom, who the words are really meant for.

I take advantage of the twist in her neck to admire the way her hair is pinned up on top of her head, thin curls falling around her face and along her back. This must be the magic Jake spoke of in terms of Gemma's talent. She catches me admiring her when she turns back and our eyes meet.

"Do I look okay?" she asks.

I guffaw because damn, if that's not fishing.

"Uh, yeah. You—" I straighten my shoulders and clear my throat, glancing down to gain more composure before meeting her eyes again. "Elle, you look beautiful."

"Beautiful," she repeats that last word, lips closing in a deep red, satisfied smile.

I hold out my arm for her to take as everyone parts, giving us room to walk back out the door. "Shall we?" I ask. "I'm sure your parents want photos, too."

"They do," she confirms.

For the next several minutes, life goes slow. It's like a little gift for the two of us as her mom fusses over how cute we are, and her dad gets misty-eyed over his little girl. We take care to pose for a few shots with Addy's picture, too. Her spirit is everywhere and in everything, always. A new house won't change that, but the feel of her with us isn't what they're running from. They're just bringing the good parts along for the ride.

Somehow, in the middle of all this chaos with moving boxes and the business of getting two people ready for a formal dance just for them, Gemma managed to transform my garage into something damn near enchanted. Grandpa raises the door while Eleanor and I cross the street, and the space is filled with silver balloons and lights and a punch bowl that I'm pretty sure they put there for me.

Eleanor giggles nervously at my side, burying her face against my shoulder as our family and friends all look on while we step into our own private milestone backdrop. "I can't believe you guys did all of this," she says.

I spin her to face me and lift her chin with my fingertips. I hold her gaze for a long, quiet moment, enjoying the tension. "They did it all for you. Because you deserve the most amazing prom ever, even in December," I say.

My mom takes the thin silk wrap that Eleanor has been wearing over her shoulders, and I hold up one hand and rest the other on her hip, electricity popping with every brush and touch of skin to skin. The music fills the garage and I begin to sway her around the room with everyone still watching. It's her favorite song, which I hoped it would be. Behind her, flurries dance in the night sky, landing on the driveway and sticking long enough to coat everything in a glaze of crystal and white. Grandpa's heater roars inside, keeping the chill at bay just enough, but I would dance on ice if that's what I had to do to live this moment with this girl.

My eyes meet Jake's as everyone backs away to give us privacy.

"Thank you," I mouth to my friend. He offers a quick

wink and puts his arm around Gemma, leading her to his car.

It's strange to be in here with Elle alone all of a sudden, but I don't let it change a single thing about our path. We dance through a dozen songs without stopping. All of them slow, and when the fast ones come, we treat them like slow ones too. I memorize her scent, and draw a million lines with my lips along the curve of her neck.

"I love you, Jonah Wydner," she says.

And I know she means it.

I spin her around, her feet leaving the ground just long enough to pull the world's best laughter from her chest, and under the spell of joy, I make the same promise to her.

"I love you, too, Eleanor Trombley."

EPILOGUE

Eleanor Trombley

I'm sure leaving my childhood home forever would have left a mark no matter when the time came, but the circumstances I ended up with were devastatingly spectacular. I never expected to fall in love so completely. I never expected to lose my sister. More than that, though, I never expected to be so strong.

I danced with Jonah until the sun was close to coming up. At some point, we ran out of music. It didn't matter. That garage—his garage—was our tiny little bubble where time stood still. Neither of us were going to do a thing to burst that precious capsule until life forced us to.

Maybe we were both all cried out. Or maybe we both knew it would be okay. Whatever the reason, I didn't shed a single tear when we left. And neither did Jonah. At least, he *says* he didn't.

I left with hope.

I left with a letter.

The same one I've read a thousand times over the last five and half months. Gemma keeps begging me to read it to her, but I refuse. Jonah's note, written in the most perfect handwriting I've ever seen, was only meant for me.

That letter contains instructions for goal number one. That goal comes due today. To get here, we both had to commit to actual face-to-face video chats once a week. We had to write something—even if it was only a joke—to the other person once a day. We had to listen when the other person needed understanding ears. And we had to believe that when this day came, we would both show up at the same time ready to set a new goal, and another one after that, all the way until we've strung together a future where we're finally together in the same place, maybe even with the same last name.

But life is short and precious and unpredictable. So his letter, it only asks for us to both have faith for things one at a time. I do, and so does he.

I've read this note so much the paper has wrinkled. I had to retrace the map he drew for me with an ink pen to make sure I wouldn't get lost. It's taken me this far though. A blue line drawn from a star for Austin, Texas to this spot —Little Rock, Arkansas. It's not quite halfway. My trip was shorter, and his was longer. He gave himself more to do, as Jonah would.

"Of course I'll drive more," he said.

Of course he would.

Even through keeping our promises, there's still a giddy sense of uncertainty sending tingles all over my body. I haven't seen him in person in months. People are different when you can touch them, kiss them.

I intend to do both.

I see the Bronco turn from the highway in the distance along the flat horizon. I parked right under the FREE CUP OF COFFEE sign for Olga's Diner, like he said to do. It's not my old Volkswagen I'm in, but I probably wouldn't have made it in that thing anyhow. Dad insisted I have a good, reliable form of transportation to get to and from college in the fall. He expects me to visit home often. I think he also knows there will be many trips to Arkansas.

The Bronco tires kick up clouds of dust as Jonah pulls into the parking lot, and my heart skips two beats when he comes to a stop right in front of me. I feel deliciously faint, and I can hardly feel my hands or feet. I force them to work, though, and open my door and step out of my car as he does the same. I wore the yellow sweatshirt just like he asked, and he's wearing his gray button-down, this time no long-sleeved shirt underneath. It's a little warmer than I expected, so I push my sleeves up as I step closer to him, my palms shaking while I hold on to my own arms.

"Hi, Eleanor," he says, his voice like velvet home.

I bite my lip and grin in relief. Sometimes, life carries on as you want it to.

"Hi, Jonah," I say, holding out for a single second before leaping into his ready arms and remembering what his kiss feels like.

Two weeks exploring Arkansas, and then we'll make a new plan and pick a new date. And I believe we will always pull through.

Because Jonah and I *are.* And we always will be.

ACKNOWLEDGMENTS

Holy moly, this book was a joy. Don't get me wrong, it wrung out my soul a little, but wow! It felt good. I have so many people to thank for this story, and it starts with my heart and home—my boys, Tim and Carter. The family theme is strong in Candy Colored Sky, and I owe that to them. We are this strong, perfect little triangle, a pod of 3 in a world full of family four-packs, and I wouldn't have it any other way.

I have many more to thank for helping me along the way through this Candy Colored journey. First, Tracey Breeden, I don't know what I did to deserve a truly inspiring friend like you, but I'm glad I got you. You never even flinch at my often strange research questions. Thank you for schooling me! Dylan Allen—THANK YOU for your trust and guidance (and for inspiring me so damn much with your own words). Mariah Dietz, I don't know that Candy would have made it to the finish line without your encouragement. Thank you! Enormous gratitude goes to my patient and awesome betas, Jen, Shelley and

TeriLyn. For once, I gave you something rather finished. Please don't expect this often LOL! And Aly Stiles, best CP in the world, you push me to be better and I can see myself growing because of you.

Brenda Letendre, you are my polish and shine. Without you, as Jonah would say, I would be *derivativeless*. And Tina Scott, aka mom, thank you for always helping me send these babies out into the world knowing I did my best.

If you have discovered my words, it's likely because of the incredibly hard work of Autumn and Wordsmith Publicity (unless I just wore you down on my own). I got a soul sister when I got you, and the faith you have in me gives me life.

If you liked this book, please don't be shy about it. I wanna hear. More than that, I would be so grateful if you would tell others. Reviews are life for us authors, but so are things like recommendations in person or on websites, posts on social media and those ever-adorable stars on Goodreads. I am so grateful for your help in sharing my words with others. My readers amaze me on the daily, and the fact that through all my awkward weirdness so many of you have stuck around is just mind-boggling. I promise to write my heart out for you, always. But first, I have to go catch a sunset.

The Hard Count by Ginger Scott

Nico Medina's world is eleven miles away from mine. During the day, it's a place where doors are open—where homes are lived in, and neighbors love. But when the sun sets, it becomes a place where young boys are afraid, where eyes watch from idling cars that hide in the shadows and wicked smoke flows from pipes.

West End is the kind of place that people survive. It buries them—one at a time, one way or another. And when Nico was a little boy, his mom always told him to run.

I'm Reagan Prescott—coach's daughter, sister to the prodigal son, daughter in the perfect family.

Life on top.

Lies.

My world is the ugly one. Private school politics and one of the best high school football programs in the country can break even the toughest souls. Our darkness plays out in whispers and rumors, and money and status trump all. I would know—I've watched it kill my family slowly, strangling us for years.

In our twisted world, a boy from West End is the only shining light.

Quarterback.

Hero.

Heart.

Good.

I hated him before I needed him.

I fell for him fast.

I loved him when it was almost too late.

When two ugly worlds collide, even the strongest fall. But my world...it hasn't met the boy from West End.

For More Info:

https://books2read.com/TheHardCount

The Varsity Series

Varsity Heartbreaker

Varsity Tiebreaker

Varsity Rulebreaker

The Waiting Series

Waiting on the Sidelines

Going Long

The Hail Mary

Like Us Duet

A Boy Like You

A Girl Like Me

The Falling Series

This Is Falling

You And Everything After

The Girl I Was Before

In Your Dreams

The Harper Boys

Wild Reckless

Wicked Restless

Standalone Reads

Candy Colored Sky

Cowboy Villain Damsel Duel

Drummer Girl

BRED

Cry Baby

The Hard Count

Memphis

Hold My Breath

Blindness

How We Deal With Gravity

Ginger Scott is an Amazon-bestselling and Goodreads Choice and Rita Award-nominated author from Peoria, Arizona. She is the author of several young and new adult romances, including bestsellers Cry Baby, The Hard Count, A Boy Like You, This Is Falling and Wild Reckless.

A sucker for a good romance, Ginger's other passion is sports, and she often blends the two in her stories. When she's not writing, the odds are high that she's somewhere near a baseball diamond, either watching her son swing for the fences or cheering on her favorite baseball team, the Arizona Diamondbacks. Ginger lives in Arizona and is married to her college sweetheart whom she met at ASU (fork 'em, Devils).

FIND GINGER ONLINE: www.littlemisswrite.com

SIGN UP FOR GINGER'S NEWSLETTER:
www.littlemisswrite.com/newsletter

facebook.com/GingerScottAuthor
twitter.com/TheGingerScott
instagram.com/authorgingerscott

Made in the USA
Middletown, DE
02 June 2023

31631760R00177